Don't
Tempt Me

Also by Sylvia Day

Don't Tempt Me

SYLVIA DAY

KENSINGTON PUBLISHING CORP.
http://www.kensingtonbooks.com

KENSINGTON BOOKS are published by

Kensington Publishing Corp.
119 West 40th Street
New York, NY 10018

All Kensington Titles, Imprints, and Distributed Lines are available at special quantity discounts for bulk purchases for sales promotions, premiums, fund-raising, and educational or institutional use. Special book excerpts or customized printings can also be created to fit specific needs. For details, write or phone the office of the Kensington special sales manager: Kensington Publishing Corp., 119 West 40th Street, New York, NY 10018, attn: Special Sales Department; phone 1-800-221-2647.

KENSINGTON and the K logo are Reg. U.S. Pat. & TM Off.

ISBN-13: 978-0-7582-1764-6
ISBN-10: 0-7582-1764-1
First Kensington Trade Edition: April 2008
First Kensington Mass Market Edition: August 2016

eISBN-13: 978-0-7582-9064-9
eISBN-10: 0-7582-9064-0

10 9 8 7 6 5 4 3 2

Printed in the United States of America

Acknowledgments

To my critique partner, Annette McCleave
(www.AnnetteMcCleave.com),
for her encouragement and support. I'm grateful.

Prologue 1

With her fingers curled desperately around the edge of the table before her, Marguerite Piccard writhed in the grip of unalloyed arousal. Gooseflesh spread up her arms and she bit her lower lip to stem the moan of pleasure that longed to escape.

"Do not restrain your cries," her lover urged hoarsely. "It makes me wild to hear them."

Her blue eyes, heavy-lidded with passion, lifted within the mirrored reflection before her and met the gaze of the man who moved at her back. The vanity in her boudoir rocked with the thrusts of his hips, his breathing rough as he made love to her where they stood.

The Marquis de Saint-Martin's infamously sensual lips curved with masculine satisfaction at the sight of her flushed dishevelment. His hands cupped her swaying breasts, urging her body to move in tandem with his.

They strained together, their skin coated with

sweat, their chests heaving from their exertions. Her blood thrummed in her veins, the experience of her lover's passion such that she had forsaken everything—family, friends, and esteemed future— to be with him. She knew he loved her similarly. He proved it with every touch, every glance.

"How beautiful you are," he gasped, watching her through the mirror.

When she had suggested the location of their tryst with timid eagerness, he'd laughed with delight.

"I am at your service," he purred, shrugging out of his garments as he stalked her into the boudoir. There was a sultriness to his stride and a predatory gleam in his dark eyes that caused her to shiver in heated awareness. Sex was innate to him. He exuded it from every pore, enunciated it with every syllable, displayed it with every movement. And he excelled at it.

From the moment she first saw him at the Fontinescu ball nearly a year ago, she had been smitten with his golden handsomeness. His attire of ruby red silk had attracted every eye without effort, but Marguerite had attended the event with the express aim of seeing him in the flesh. Her older sisters had whispered scandalous tales of his liaisons, occasions when he had been caught in flagrant displays of seduction. He was wed; yet discarded lovers pined for him openly, weeping outside his home for a brief moment of his attention. Her curiosity about what sort of shell would encase such wickedness was too powerful to be denied.

Saint-Martin did not disappoint her. In the simplest of terms, she did not expect him to be so . . . *male*. Those who were given to the pursuit of vice and excess were rarely virile, as he most definitely was.

Never had she met a man more devastating to a woman's equanimity. The marquis was magnificent, his physical form impressive and his aloofness an irresistible lure. Golden-haired and skinned, as she was, he was desired by every woman in France for good reason. There was an air about him that promised pleasure unparalleled. The decadence and forbidden delights intimated within his slumberous gaze lured one to forget themselves. The marquis had lived twice Marguerite's eight and ten years, and he possessed a wife as lovely as he was comely. Neither fact mitigated Marguerite's immediate, intense attraction to him. Or his returning attraction to her.

"Your beauty has enslaved me," he whispered that first night. He stood near to where she waited on the edge of the dance floor, his lanky frame propped against the opposite side of a large column. "I must follow you or ache from the distance between us."

Marguerite kept her gaze straight ahead, but every nerve ending tingled from his boldness. Her breath was short, her skin hot. Although she could not see him, she felt the weight of his regard and it affected her to an alarming degree. "You know of women more beautiful than I," she retorted.

"No." His husky, lowered voice stilled her heartbeat. Then, made it race. "I do not."

There was sincerity in his tone. Against better sense she believed in it, a faith she held close to her heart when summoned to her mother's parlor the next morning.

"Do not entertain girlish notions regarding Saint-

Martin," the baroness ordered. "I was witness to the
way he looked at you, and how you admired him in
return."

"All the women present were admiring him,
even you."

Her mother rested her arm along the back of
the chaise she occupied. Despite the relative earli-
ness of the hour, her face and wig were already
liberally powdered, and her cheeks and lips were
rouged a lush pink. In the soft silver and white
décor of her private sitting room, the baroness's
pale beauty was showcased to advantage, which
was by design.

"You, my youngest daughter, are to be a wife.
Since the marquis already enjoys the wedded state
with another, you must set your aim elsewhere."

"How can you be certain Saint-Martin enjoys it?
Their marriage was arranged."

"As yours will be if you do not heed me," the
baroness continued with a note of steel in her voice.
"Your sisters made fine matches, which frees me to
give you more license. Use it wisely, or I will choose
your spouse without consulting you. Perhaps the Vicomte de Grenier? He is rumored to be similarly
randy, if that is your attraction, but he is younger
and therefore more malleable."

"*Maman!*"

"You are not equipped to manage a man of
Saint-Martin's ilk. He sweetens his tea with naïve
girls such as you and then gorges on less refined
tarts."

Marguerite had held her tongue, aware that she
knew nothing of the man but rumor and innu-
endo.

"Stay away from him, *ma petite*. A breath of scandal will ruin you."

Knowing it was true, Marguerite acquiesced and firmly intended to keep her word. "I am certain he has forgotten me already."

"Naturellement." The baroness offered a sympathetic smile. Marguerite was her favorite, and the daughter most like her in both looks and temperament. "The point of this discussion is to ensure that you follow suit."

But Saint-Martin proved to be more determined than they had anticipated. Over the next few weeks, Marguerite found him everywhere, a circumstance effective in preventing her from forgetting him. Speculation abounded as to why he was suddenly less interested in his more jaded pursuits, which seduced her with the possibility that he was seeking her out deliberately. Unable to bear the suspense and distracted from her pursuit of a suitable husband, she resolved to confront him directly.

Ducking behind a large potted plant, Marguerite waited for him to pass her location in his pursuit of her. She attempted to regulate her breathing to facilitate a calm exterior, but the effort made her dizzy. As had happened from the first, the nearer his proximity, the more disconcerted she felt. She could not see him, yet she sensed his every footstep. *Closer . . . closer . . .*

When Saint-Martin came into sight, she blurted out, "What do you want?"

The marquis drew to a halt and his wigged head turned to find her. "You."

Her breath caught.

He pivoted to face her directly and approached

with animalistic grace, his narrowed gaze assessing her from head to toe. As his dark eyes roamed, they heated, and when they paused boldly on her chest, Marguerite felt her breasts swell in response.

"Stop." She snapped her fan open as a barrier between them. Within the confines of her corset, her nipples hardened such as they did when she was cold. "You will cause a scene."

His jaw tightened. "And ruin you for the marriage you seek?"

"Yes."

"That is not a deterrent."

She blinked.

"The thought of you wed to another," he growled, "compels me to insanity."

Marguerite's hand rose to her throat. "Say no more," she begged in a whisper, her mind reeling. "I lack the sophistication required to banter in this manner."

His prowling stride did not falter. "I speak the truth to you, Marguerite." Her eyes widened at his use of her given name. "We lack the time for meaningless discourse."

"It is not possible for us to have more."

The marquis's pursuit forced her to retreat until her back hit the wall. Only the delicate barrier of leaves shielded them from view. They had a moment alone, at most.

He tugged off his glove and cupped her cheek. The touch of his skin to hers made her burn, his spicy scent made her ache in unmentionable places. "You feel it, too."

She shook her head.

"You cannot deny the affinity between us," he

scoffed. "Your body's response to mine is irrefutable."

"Perhaps I am frightened."

"Perhaps you are aroused. If any man would know the difference, it is I."

"Of course," she said bitterly, hating the possessive jealousy she felt.

"I have wondered," he murmured, his gaze on her parted lips, "how it would be to make love to a woman such as you—beautiful and sensual beyond compare, but too innocent to wield it as a weapon."

"As you wield your beauty as a weapon?"

A smile tugged at the corner of his sculpted mouth. It stopped her heart to see the way it banished the lines of cynicism that rimmed his eyes. "It pleases me to know that you find me attractive."

"Is there any woman who does not?"

The marquis shrugged elegantly. "I care only for your opinion."

"You do not know me. Perhaps my opinion is worthless."

"I should like to know you. I *need* to know you. From the moment I first saw you, I have been unable to think of anything else."

"There is no way."

"If I found the means, would you indulge me?"

She swallowed hard, knowing what her answer should be but unable to say it. "Your lust will pass," she managed.

Saint-Martin released her and backed away, his jaw taut. "This is not lust."

"What is it, then?"

"An obsession."

Marguerite watched the deliberation with which

he pulled his glove back on, one finger at a time, as if he needed the delay to reclaim his control. Could she believe that he was as affected by the attraction between them as she was?

"I will find a way to have you," he rasped, then he bowed and left her.

She watched him move away, shaken and yearning.

Over the next few months he chipped away at her resistance in that intense, focused manner. Seeking out whatever stray moments he could. Asking a question or two about her life, tidbits that told her he followed her activities with avid interest.

Until her mother grew impatient and followed through with her threat to select the Vicomte de Grenier as Marguerite's husband-to-be. A few months earlier, Marguerite might have been pleased. The vicomte was young, handsome, and wealthy. Her sisters and friends exclaimed over her good fortune. But in her heart, she pined for Saint-Martin.

"Do you want de Grenier?" the marquis asked gruffly after following her to a retiring room.

"You should not ask me such questions."

He stood behind her in the mirror, his face hard and austere. "He is not for you, Marguerite. I know him well. We have spent more than one evening in the same questionable establishments."

"You seek to counsel me against a man who resembles you?" She sighed when he growled. "You know I have no choice."

"Belong to me instead."

Marguerite covered her mouth to stem a cry and he pulled her close.

"You ask too much," she whispered, studying his

features for some hint of deception. "And you have nothing to offer in return."

"I have my heart," he said softly, stroking across her bottom lip with the pad of his thumb. "It may not be worth much. Still, it is yours and yours alone."

"Liar," she spat, striking out in self-defense, painfully wounded by the flare of fruitless hope his words evoked. "You are a consummate seducer and I have resisted you. Now an acquaintance of yours is about to best you. That is the driving force of your interest."

"You do not believe that."

"I do." Wrenching away, she fled the room.

For several nights after, Marguerite took great pains to avoid him, a vain and belated attempt to kill her growing fascination with a man who could never be hers. She claimed illness for as long as possible, but eventually, she could remain hidden no longer.

When next they met, she was shocked by his appearance. His handsome features were drawn, his mouth tight, his skin pale. Her heart ached at the sight of him. He stared at her a long taut moment, then jerked his gaze away.

Worried, she deliberately stood in an intimate corner and waited for him to approach her.

"Belong to me," he said hoarsely, coming up behind her. "Do not make me beg."

"Would you?" The question came out as no more than a whisper, her throat too constricted to allow volume. His nearness caused tingles to sweep over her skin in a prickling wave, creating a sharp contrast to the numbness she had felt the last week.

That their miniscule interactions had come to mean so much was frightening. But the thought of not having them at all was even more terrifying.

"Yes. Come with me."

"When?"

"Now."

Abandoning everything she knew, Marguerite left with him. He took her to the residence he presently occupied, a small house in a respectable neighborhood.

"How many women have you brought here?" she asked, admiring the elegant simplicity of the ivory and walnut palette.

"You are the first." He kissed the bared nape of her neck. "And the last."

"You were so certain of my capitulation?"

He laughed softly, a warm and sensual sound. "Until a sennight ago, this place served a far less pleasurable purpose."

"Oh?"

"A tale for another night," he promised, his deep voice raspy with desire.

The house had been her home ever since, her refuge from the censure of Society for forsaking their approval to become his mistress.

"Je t'adore," Saint-Martin groaned, his thrusts increasing in speed and power.

Inside her, his thick cock swelled further, inundating her with delight. She whimpered and his embrace tightened, pushing her forward so that he could pump deeper. His lean, powerfully built body mantled hers, and his mouth touched her ear.

"Come for me, *mon coeur*," he whispered.

His hand slid between her legs, his knowledgeable fingers rubbing her distended, swollen clitoris with precision. His carnal expertise and the long, rhythmic strokes of his cock made the impetus to climax irresistible. Crying out, she orgasmed, her hands reaching behind her to cup his flexing buttocks. She tightened around him in rippling waves and he groaned, jerking with his own release, filling her with the rich creamy wash of his ejaculate.

As he always did in the aftermath of their passion, Philippe clung to her, his parted lips pressing openmouthed kisses along her throat and cheek.

"Je t'aime," she gasped, nuzzling her damp cheek against his.

He withdrew from her and bent to lift her into his arms. The thick, golden strands of his hair clung to his damp neck and temples, accentuating the flush of his skin and the satiated gleam in his dark eyes. He carried her to the bed with the ease of a man accustomed to physical labor, a proclivity which led to his magnificent form. Marguerite could never have imagined that he was so beautiful beneath his garments, but then he kept a great deal hidden under his dissolute façade.

A knock came to the outer bedchamber door just as Philippe began to crawl over her reclining body.

He cursed and called out, "What is it?"

"You have a visitor, my lord," came the muffled reply of the butler.

Marguerite looked at the clock on the mantel and noted the hour. It was nearly two in the morning.

He cupped her cheek and kissed the tip of her nose. "A moment, no more."

She smiled, knowing it was a lie but indulging

him regardless. When he had first confided his activities as an agent in something he called the *secret du roi*—a group of agents whose purpose was to further the king's hidden diplomacy—she had been stunned and unable to reconcile this new image of him with the one he cultivated in Society. How could a man known as a voluptuary who lived only for his own pleasure be in truth someone who risked life and limb in service to his king?

But as love grew from their lust and their daily interactions progressed to a true joining of the minds, Marguerite realized how layered her lover was and how brilliant was his disguise. The proliferation of mistresses had not been entirely an affectation, of course, but he was not heartless. To this day he felt remorse for luring her to her "downfall."

When she had professed a similar regret for leading him away from his wife, he'd held her and revealed a surprising truth: Marchioness Saint-Martin—so pitied in private discourse for her husband's excesses—maintained her own lovers. Theirs was a marriage of duty. It was not unpleasant and they were both content to proceed with separate agendas.

Marguerite watched him shrug into his robe of black silk, then walk to the door. "I will miss you," she said. "If you are gone too long, I might cry out in the streets for you."

He paused on the threshold and arched a brow. "*Mon Dieu*, do not believe that nonsense. It was one woman and her brain was afflicted."

"Poor thing. However, I doubt it was her brain you were attracted to."

Philippe growled. "Wait up for me."

"Perhaps . . ."

He blew her a kiss and made his egress.

As he shut the bedchamber door behind him, Philippe's smile faded. He belted his robe more securely and descended the stairs to the lower floor. Good news was rarely delivered at this hour, so he approached the coming discussion with grimness. With the scent of sex and Marguerite still clinging to his skin, he was more aware than usual of how vital her presence was in his life. She kept him connected with his humanity, something he feared had been lost by years of pretending to be someone he was not.

The door to the parlor was open and he entered without slowing his stride, his bare feet crossing onto the rug from the cool marble of the foyer.

"Thierry," he greeted, startled by the identity of his visitor. "You were to report to Desjardins this evening."

"I did," the young man replied, his cheeks still flushed from his ride. "That is why I am here."

Philippe gestured for the courier to take a seat on the settee while he sank into a nearby chair.

Travel-stained and disheveled, Thierry sat gingerly upon the edge. Philippe smiled at the care displayed to protect the new burgundy velvet. When the home had served as a bastion for *secret du roi* agents, the furnishings had been abused without thought. But the house had been abandoned after a time, an oft-used tactic to avoid suspicion, and he had removed all traces of the house's former use and refilled it with luxuries suitable for the love of his life.

"I apologize for disturbing you," Thierry said wearily, "but I have been ordered to depart again in the morning and I could not chance missing you."

"What news is so urgent?"

"It regards Mademoiselle Piccard."

Straightening from his semireclined state, Philippe studied the courier alertly. "Yes?"

"When I arrived at Desjardins', he had a visitor and I was asked to wait outside his study. I do not think he realized how clearly his words travel."

Philippe nodded grimly, having always found it noteworthy that such a slightly built man would have such a booming voice. He did not, however, find it interesting that the man would be discussing Marguerite. It was alarming because, quite simply, his very sanity rested with her well-being and proximity. Comte Desjardins was young, ambitious, and hungry for the king's regard. Those qualities made him dangerous to those who stood in his way.

"I heard the name *Piccard*," Thierry said softly, as if he might be overheard, "and though I attempted to turn my thoughts elsewhere, I could not help but listen more closely."

"Understandable. You cannot be faulted for hearing conversations spoken within earshot."

"Yes. Exactly." The courier offered a grateful smile.

"About Mademoiselle Piccard . . . ?"

"Desjardins was discussing how preoccupied you seem of late and how best to manage it. It was suggested that Mademoiselle Piccard was to blame for your decreasing participation."

Philippe tapped his fingertips atop his knee. "Do you know who this visitor was?"

"No, I am sorry. He departed through a different door than the one I waited outside of."

As he blew out his breath, Philippe's gaze moved to the banked fire in the grate. This parlor was considerably smaller and less appointed than the one he shared with his wife, yet this residence was home to him. Because of Marguerite.

Who could have foreseen how a reluctantly accepted invitation from the Fontinescus would become the turning point of his life?

Thoughts of Marguerite filled his mind, and he smiled inwardly. He had been unaware of how the many diverse and competing aspects of his life had been affecting him negatively until she'd brought his attention to it.

"You are so tense," she noted one night, her slender fingers kneading into the sore muscles of his neck and shoulders. "How can I help?"

For a brief moment, he had considered forgetting his troubles with a few hours of passionate sex, but instead he found himself telling her things he told no one else. She had listened, then engaged in a discourse with him that brought to light alternate solutions.

"How clever you are," he'd said, laughing.

"Smart enough to choose you," she replied with a mischievous smile.

There was no doubt that even had he known how meeting her would affect him, he would change nothing. Her beauty was astonishing and a source of endless delight, but it was her pure heart and innocence that won his deeper regard. His love for her filled him with contentment, an emotion he had come to think was not meant for a man such as himself. His joy was nearly complete; his only regret was his inability to offer her the security of his name and title.

Philippe inhaled deeply and looked again at Thierry. "Is there more?"

"No. That is all."

"You have my gratitude." Philippe rose and moved to the escritoire in the corner. He opened it and withdrew a small purse. Thierry accepted the proffered coin with a grateful smile, then departed immediately. Philippe exited the parlor after him and sent the butler back to bed.

A few moments later he rejoined Marguerite. She lay curled on her side, her lustrous blond curls scattered atop a pillow, her sapphire blue eyes blinking sleepily. In the light of a single bedside taper, her pale skin glowed with the luminescence of ivory. She extended her hand to him and his chest ached at the sight of her, so soft and warm and filled with welcome. Other women had told him they loved him, but never with the fervency that Marguerite expressed. The depth of her affection was priceless. Nothing and no one would ever take her from him.

He shrugged out of his robe and rounded the bed to slip between the sheets behind her. He draped an arm over her waist and her fingers linked with his.

"What is it?" she asked.

"Nothing for you to be concerned with."

"Yet you are concerned, I can feel it." Marguerite turned in his arms. "I have ways to make you tell me," she purred.

"Minx." Philippe kissed her nose and groaned at the feel of her warm, silken limbs tangling with his. He related the conversation with Thierry and stroked the length of her spine when she tensed. "Do not be alarmed. This is a minor irritant, nothing more."

"What do you intend to do?"

"Desjardins has high aspirations. He needs to feel as if every man working with him is as committed. I am not, which was proven when I began rejecting any mission that would send me to Poland."

"Because of me."

"You are far more charming than the Polish, *mon amour.*" He kissed her forehead. "There are others who will give him the level of dedication he requires."

Marguerite pushed up on one elbow and gazed down at him. "And he will allow you to simply walk away?"

"What can he do? Besides, if he feels that my effectiveness is so diminished that he must concern himself with my private life, then my withdrawal should be a relief to him."

Her hand slid over his chest. "Be careful. Promise me that much."

Philippe caught her hand and lifted it to his lips. "I promise."

Then he tugged her down and took her mouth, soothing her fears with the heat of his passion.

The gathering of close friends and political acquaintances in Comte Desjardins's dining room was loud and boisterous. The comte himself was laughing and enjoying himself immensely when a movement in the doorway leading to the foyer caught his eye.

He excused himself and stood, moving to the discreetly gesturing servant with calculated insouciance.

Stepping out to the marble-lined hallway, he shut

out the noise of his guests with a click of the latch and arched a brow at the courier who waited in the shadows.

"I did as you directed," Thierry said.

"Excellent." The comte smiled.

Thierry extended his hand and in it was an unaddressed missive bearing a black wax seal. Embedded within that seal was a ruby, perfectly round and glimmering in the light of the foyer chandelier. "I was also intercepted a short distance up the street and given this."

Desjardins stilled. "Did you see him?"

"No. The carriage was unmarked and the curtains drawn. He was gloved. I saw nothing more."

The same as always. The first letter had arrived a few months past, always delivered through a passing courier, which led Desjardins to the conclusion that the man had to be a member of the *secret du roi*. If only he could determine who, and what grievance the man had with Saint-Martin.

Nodding, the comte accepted the note and dismissed Thierry. He moved away from the dining room, heading toward the kitchen, then through it, taking the stairs down to the cellar where he kept his wine. The missive went into his pocket. There would be nothing written within it. After a dozen such communiqués he knew that for a certainty.

There would be only a stamp, carved to prevent recognition of handwriting, imprinting one word: *L'Esprit.* The ruby was a gift for his cooperation, as were the occasional delivered purses of more loose gems. A clever payment, because Desjardins's wife loved jewelry and unset stones were untraceable.

The volume from the bustling kitchen faded to a dull roar as Desjardins closed the cellar door behind him. He rounded the corner of one floor-to-ceiling rack and saw the smaller, rougher wooden planked door that led to the catacombs. It was slightly ajar.

"Stop there." The low, raspy voice was reminiscent of crushed glass rubbed together, grating and ominous.

Desjardins stopped.

"Is it done?"

"The seeds have been planted," the comte said.

"Good. Saint-Martin will cling to her more tenaciously now that he feels threatened."

"I thought he would weary of the same bedsport months ago," Desjardins muttered.

"I warned you Marguerite Piccard was different. Fortunately for you, as it has led to our profitable association." There was a weighted pause, then, "De Grenier covets her. He is young and handsome. It would be a thorn to Saint-Martin to lose her to him."

"Then I shall see that de Grenier has her."

"Yes." The finality in *L'Esprit*'s tone made Desjardins grateful to be this man's associate and not his enemy. "Saint-Martin cannot be allowed even a modicum of happiness."

Prologue 2

"The Vicomte de Grenier has come to call."

Marguerite lowered the book she was enjoying and stared at her butler. It was the middle of the day, not a time when Philippe was known to be visiting with her. Regardless, only those privy to the *secret du roi* felt such urgency that they would seek him out at his mistress's home.

"The marquis is not here," she said, more to herself than to the servant who knew that already.

"He asks for you, mademoiselle."

She frowned. "Why?"

The butler said nothing, as was to be expected.

Frowning, she snapped her book closed and rose. "Please send for Marie," she said, desiring her maid's company so that she would not be alone with the vicomte.

When the maid arrived, Marguerite descended to the lower floor and entered the parlor. De Grenier rose upon her arrival and bowed elegantly.

"Mademoiselle Piccard," he greeted with a gentle smile. "You steal my breath."

"*Merci.* You also look well."

They sat opposite one another and she waited for him to reveal why he would seek her out. She should have, perhaps, refused him. She was another man's mistress. In addition, she would be de Grenier's wife now, if she had followed her mother's wishes. From the slight flush along de Grenier's cheekbones, that uncomfortable realization did not elude him either.

The vicomte was a young man, only a few years older than she was. Tall and slender, he bore handsome features and kind eyes. He was dressed for riding and the deep brown color of his garments created an attractive contrast against the pale blue décor of her parlor. The smile she offered him was genuine, if slightly bemused.

"Mademoiselle," he began, before clearing his throat. He shifted nervously. "Please forgive the importunateness of my visit and the information I am about to share with you. I could conceive of no other way."

Marguerite hesitated a moment, uncertain of how to proceed. She glanced at Marie, who sat in the corner with head bent over a bit of darning. "I have recently gained a new appreciation for bluntness," she said finally.

His mouth curved and she was reminded that she'd always liked him. The vicomte was charming, making it easy to feel comfortable around him.

Then his smile faded.

"There are matters of some delicacy that Saint-Martin oversees," he murmured. "I am aware of them."

Her breath caught as she realized what he was

attempting to tell her. How extensive was the *secret du roi?*

"Is something amiss?" she asked, her fingers linking tightly in her lap.

"I fear for your safety."

"*My* safety?"

De Grenier bent forward and set his forearms atop his knees. "Saint-Martin has proven to be very valuable to the king. In addition, he is well respected, and when it comes to traversing certain . . . *intimate* channels, he is unsurpassed. And missed."

Marguerite's stomach knotted with jealousy. Of course the women who had known Philippe intimately would want him back. But would that be enough to jeopardize either of them? "What are you saying?"

"He has withdrawn from service and assists with matters only when they do not take him from your side. This has led to some unrest."

The vicomte steepled his fingers together and lowered his voice to barely a whisper, forcing her to bend forward to hear his words. "The king has begun to pressure Desjardins to bring Saint-Martin back into the fold. So far, his efforts have met with failure, leading Desjardins to a state of frustration and aggravation that concerns me. I overheard him mention your name in a discussion with one of his associates. I suspect he has some plan to remove you. He sees you as an obstruction, yet the more he urges Saint-Martin to set you aside, the more contrary the marquis becomes."

Her gaze moved to Marie, then rose to the portrait of herself above the empty grate. Saint-Martin had commissioned it soon after their affair had begun. In the swirls of colorful paints she was forever arrested in her youth and innocence, her blue eyes dreamy with love and desire.

"What can I do?" she asked.

"Leave him."

Snorting softly, she said, "You might ask me to rip out my heart with my bare hands, it would be easier."

"You love him."

"Of course." Her gaze returned to his. "I have been ostracized. I could not have survived it if not bolstered by love."

"I would still have you."

Stunned, Marguerite froze. She stared at him, confused. "Beg your pardon?"

The vicomte's mouth lifted into a rueful curve. "I want you. I would take you in."

She pushed to her feet. "You must go."

De Grenier rose and rounded the small table that acted as a barrier between them. She retreated and he halted. "I mean you no harm."

"Saint-Martin will not be pleased that you were here." Her voice shook slightly, forcing her to lift her chin with bravado.

"Very true." The vicomte's eyes narrowed. "There has always been some rivalry between us. He knows the danger, yet he does not act because he suspects how I feel about you."

"What danger?"

"The king's agenda is of tremendous importance and secrecy. If Desjardins feels it is necessary to remove you, he will do so. If Saint-Martin cared as much for you as you do for him, he would end your affair to protect you."

"I do not care." Her hand lifted to cover her roiling stomach. Her protests would mean nothing when pitted against the will of the king. "I would be miserable without him. Better to stay and enjoy what I can, while I can, than to leave and have nothing."

"I can give you all that you have lost." He stepped closer.

"I have gained more."

"Have you?" His jaw tightened. "You have lost your family, friends, and social standing. You have no life beyond these walls, waiting to serve the pleasure of a man to whom you are a peripheral indulgence. I have seen what happens to the women he discards; I could not bear to witness a similar end for you."

"You offer the same," she snapped.

"No, I offer my name."

Marguerite felt the room spin and reached out to grip the carved wooden edge of the settee. "Go. Now."

"I would wed you," he said, his voice low and earnest. "I am being sent to Poland for a time. You would come with me. There is safety there and the opportunity to begin your life anew."

She shook her head, wincing as it throbbed with painful pressure. "Please leave."

De Grenier's fists clenched at his sides, then he bowed in a fluidly graceful motion. "I leave in a sennight. Should your feelings on the matter change between now and then, come to me." His shoulders went back, drawing her attention to the breadth of them. "In the interim, ask Saint-Martin to reveal the gravity of the situation you both face. If you know him as well as you believe, you should see the truth of what I have told you."

He left the room with a hard, determined stride

and Marguerite sank weakly into the seat. A moment later a glass filled with red liquid was held out to her and she accepted it from her maid with a grateful smile.

All the servants in her household had been carefully selected for their discretion. How Philippe knew whom he could trust or not was beyond her comprehension. But then everything he did with regards to the *secret du roi* was a mystery to her.

"Mon coeur."

Dazed, she glanced up and saw Philippe enter the room in a rush. He still wore hat and gloves, and the air around him was redolent of horses and tobacco.

"What transpired?" he asked, sinking to his haunches before her.

Her gaze drifted over his shoulder to the window and she saw how the shadows cast by the sun had moved across the floor.

Time had lapsed and she'd been unaware, lost as she was in her confusion and disquiet.

"Marguerite? Why was de Grenier here? What did he say to you?"

She looked at her lover, the fingers of her right hand releasing their hold on her glass so that she could touch his cheek. He nuzzled into the contact, his blue eyes darkened by concern.

"He says Desjardins is determined to separate us," she related grimly, "and that I am not safe from harm. He did not say whether it was physical harm or emotional, and I did not think to ask until a moment ago."

Philippe's jaw tautened. "This is madness."

"What?" Marguerite reached around him and set her glass on the gilded side table. "What is happening? He intimated that you were hiding something from me. If you are, I want you to tell me what it is."

"I do not know." Growling, he stood and began tearing off his outer garments. Hat, gloves, coat. All tossed on to the settee with obvious frustration. "I cannot make sense of it. You have nothing to do with anything."

She knew it was foolish to be hurt by the careless statement, but for the first time since she met him, she felt as if she were unimportant. A diversion. A peccadillo.

"Of course not," she whispered, rising to her feet. Her cream-colored skirts with their bloodred flowers hung heavily around her shaky legs. Her toes tingled with the rush of returning blood.

How long had she been sitting there, picturing life without Philippe in it? For the last year, she had lived under the illusion that they would always be together. This afternoon was the first time she had ever contemplated otherwise.

"You misunderstand," he murmured, catching her close. "You are everything to *me*, but nothing to them. There is no cause for them to focus on you. That would suggest there is something else they want. Something they believe you have."

"You?"

Philippe shook his head. "I offered myself to Desjardins. Told him I would go wherever he required for up to three months at a time, just as I did before, although in truth I do not know how I would survive even three days without you when three hours' length is torture."

He pressed his cheek to her temple, the roughness of his afternoon stubble a familiar, welcome sensation. "My only request was that you be kept safe and comfortable here. But he refused. He claims my attention is diminished and he prefers me unencumbered."

"I do not understand why he cannot replace you," she complained, searching his face for clues to his thoughts. "Despite how accomplished you are, surely there are other men who can perform the services you provide."

Lips whitening from the force with which he pursed them, Philippe took a moment to reply. "Would you believe de Grenier over me?"

"I am to choose between his words and your silence?"

"Yes."

For a moment, she was angered by his arrogance, then she laughed softly. "How do you do it?" she asked, shaking her head.

He caught a swaying powdered curl between thumb and forefinger, and rubbed it tenderly. His voice, when it came, was low and intimate. "Do what?"

"Make yourself indispensable. All afternoon I chastised myself for placing myself in this precarious position. I have nothing in this world but your favor and no certainty that I can hold on to that. Now others are exerting their weighty influence to part us and there is nothing I can do to prevent or deter them." She set her hands on his chest, her fingertips touching the edges of his skewed jabot. He was dashing clothed, semiclothed, unclothed. "Yet here you stand, mulishly determined to hoard your secrets and I want you regardless."

"I have no secrets. I tell you everything." Philippe caught her hand and linked their fingers. He turned toward the door and pulled her along after him.

"You did not tell me that they continue to urge you to set me aside."

"Because they do not signify."

As they entered their private sitting room, he released her. He moved to the window and pushed aside the sheer panel to look outside. It was dusk, soon to be night. A year ago, the setting sun would have been a cue to begin initial preparations for an evening of social engagements. Now they had only supper and a quiet evening alone to occupy them. For her, it was enough. Was it for him?

"I can hear your doubts from here," he said, pivoting to face her. "What did he offer you?"

Marguerite had learned many things about taming a man in the year she had been Philippe's mistress. One powerful bit of knowledge was the understanding that he could deny her nothing when she was naked.

She presented her back to him, then glanced over her shoulder to watch him approach with heated eyes. "The better question would be: What did he not offer?"

Philippe set his fingers to work on the cloth-covered buttons that trailed her spine. "As you wish. What did he not offer you?"

"His heart."

His movements stilled. She heard him exhale. "I could contract you, Marguerite. I could reduce our . . . *arrangement* . . . to terms of goods exchanged. You might feel safer then."

"Or I might feel like a whore."

"Which is exactly why I have not suggested such a

thing until now." His hands settled atop her shoulders, then exerted pressure to turn her around. He stared down into her upturned face. His was agonized, his dark eyes roiling with emotions she could not name.

"What can I do?" she asked in a whisper. "How can I fight, when I do not know what I am fighting against?"

"Can you not leave this to me?" He pressed his lips to her forehead. "I do not believe, even partly, that this matter has anything to do with our relationship. Not so long ago, de Grenier was suggesting that I step aside completely and Desjardins was very close to agreeing with that sentiment. Their sudden change of heart does not sit well. There is an ulterior motive at work here and I will learn what it is."

"*Je t'aime,*" she breathed, hating the fear that dampened her palms.

Her lower lip quivered with her distress and he licked across the curve, then deepened the contact into a melding kiss. He stole her breath with his expertise, leaving her panting and clinging to his hard body.

"As I love you. I will not lose you," he vowed, pulling her tight against him.

This time, it was Marguerite who led the way. With his hand in hers, she tugged him toward the bedchamber, where they could forget their troubles for at least a few hours.

The Comte Desjardins entered his cellar and stopped in the same spot he was ordered to occupy every time *L'Esprit* called upon him.

"I do not believe de Grenier was successful in luring Mademoiselle Piccard away." *L'Esprit*'s grating voice scraped down Desjardins's spine and made him shiver.

"It is too soon to tell."

"No. I watched him leave. He appeared dejected, not hopeful. She has forsaken everything for her affair. She has only one thing left to lose."

"Saint-Martin."

"Exactly." There was a smile in *L'Esprit*'s rasp. "She will not leave him for *her* benefit, but I believe she will leave him for *his*."

Desjardins shook his head. He had no notion of what Saint-Martin had done to anger *L'Esprit*, but he pitied the man. Desjardins suspected *L'Esprit* would not rest until everything Saint-Martin held dear was stripped from him. "What would you have me do?"

"I will see to this task myself," *L'Esprit* said. "I do not want him dead. That would be too kind."

"As you wish."

"You will hear from me if I have further need of you."

Turning away, Desjardins opened the cellar door and climbed back up to the kitchen. He jumped as he heard the slamming of the portal *L'Esprit* used as a shield.

It was fitting that the man came from the bowels of hell.

There was fury in *L'Esprit* and madness. The comte deeply regretted ever being lured into associating with him.

A pretty bauble for his wife, no matter how costly, was not worth his soul.

* * *

With his thoughts firmly directed toward Marguerite, Philippe was too distracted to admire the beauty of the Parisian afternoon. He was lost in his private musings, unaware of anything but the sense that he was missing the obvious. His horse cantered toward Marguerite's home without direction, the steady clopping of hooves lulling its rider into a thoughtful trance.

Around him pedestrians milled, creating a feeling of safety in numbers.

But he was not safe. Had he considered, for even a moment, that he would be used against Marguerite rather than the reverse, he would have been more circumspect. As it was, he turned the corner and took the devastating blow to the chest without any attempt at self-defense.

Thrust backward while his mount moved forward, Philippe was unseated and tumbled to the ground on his back. The air was knocked from his chest, leaving him dazed and unable to move.

The sky above him darkened as men swarmed around him. A booted foot connected to his side. As Philippe's rib broke under the assault, a grotesque cracking sound rent the air. More kicks. Shouting. Laughing. Pain.

Agony.

Philippe prayed for the strength to roll to his side and curl, but his body would not heed his command. The violence escalated. His vision dimmed.

Then mercifully went black.

* * *

"The afternoon's post, mademoiselle."

Marguerite looked up from the dining table, where she was perusing the week's meal plan, and found the butler standing in the doorway. She gestured him in and pushed the menus to the side.

"Thank you," she murmured, reaching for the topmost envelope on the silver salver as it was placed before her.

She went through the marginal task with only partial attention, her mind on Philippe and how withdrawn he had appeared over the last few days. She was a veritable prisoner in her own home, barred from even the swiftest of trips into town. Additional servants had been retained to protect her. The sparse amount of correspondence she received was the only contact she had with anyone beyond the walls of her house.

Her focus sharpened when she came to the missive sealed with thick black wax.

Very few people corresponded with her. Her mother and father had disowned her. Her sisters wrote only sporadically and briefly. Yet it was *her* name on the exterior of the envelope, not Philippe's.

Prying it open carefully, she read the bold scrawl with mounting confusion.

> *Saint-Martin has two choices. Choose you or choose his life. I know how he will decide. The question is, how will you?*
> *L'Esprit*

Marguerite frowned, then called out for the butler. When the servant appeared, she asked, "Who delivered this?"

"A groomsman brought it in. I will ask."

She nodded and waited, rereading the cryptic words and examining the odd seal.

Several moments later, he returned. "He does not recall."

"Hmm . . ."

"A courier is at the door, mademoiselle, requesting to see you."

An apprehensive shiver coursed down Marguerite's spine. She carefully refolded the note before leaving it atop the polished wooden tabletop. As a footman pulled her chair back, she stood and ran her hands carefully down her muslin skirts. Hesitating. She had been on edge for days. The odd happenings of this day only worsened her unease.

Rounding the table, she exited out to the hallway and moved toward the visitors' foyer.

Every step weighed heavier and heavier. The hairs on her nape stood at attention. She was being threatened directly now. As disquieting as that was for her, she knew it would be more so for Philippe. If only they could ascertain what the root of the problem was . . .

"Mademoiselle Piccard."

She tilted her head in acknowledgment of the courier's greeting and drew to a halt by the main staircase, which was several feet away from him. "Good afternoon."

"Comte Desjardins sent me."

Her stomach knotted. "Yes?"

The man's shoulders went back. That telltale sign of nervousness stiffened her spine. There were other concerning indicators, as well—the damaged and dirty state of his clothing, spatters of some dark liquid on his tan breeches, his disheveled hair.

"The Marquis de Saint-Martin was attacked just hours ago," he said grimly.

"No . . ." She stumbled as her knees weakened under the weight of her greatest fear. Reaching out, she caught herself by gripping the baluster.

"He was gravely injured. He has since been moved to his home, where he is being attended, but his situation appears dire. Comte Desjardins wanted you to be made aware."

The room spun and Marguerite gasped for air, fighting a tightening in her chest that threatened to rob her of consciousness.

"Made aware," she repeated, her thoughts on the letter sitting on her dining table.

Every instinct screamed at her to go to Philippe, to be with him, hold him, nurse him back to health.

Which was not possible. His wife would care for him, as was her right.

Dear God . . .

Marguerite sank to the marble floor in a puddle of yellow skirts, her vision distorted by hot flowing tears. The butler hurried toward her, but she halted him with an upraised hand. "Is your cousin still employed at the Saint-Martin residence?"

"Yes, mademoiselle." Understanding lit the servant's pale blue eyes. "I will send someone to learn what they can from him."

"Urge them to haste."

As the courier backed away as if to leave, her attention returned to him. Fury gave her the strength to rise to her feet.

"As for you," she said coldly, stepping toward

him with fists clenched. "Return to Comte Desjardins and give him a message for me."

"Mademoiselle?" He shifted uncomfortably.

"Tell him that if the marquis does not survive, neither will he."

He bowed and departed, leaving Marguerite with a life in shambles. For the space of several heartbeats she stood in place, hardly breathing.

How would she survive without Philippe?

A hand touched her arm tentatively. Marguerite turned to find Celie standing beside her.

"What can I do?" the maid asked.

"What can anyone do?" Marguerite replied in a hoarse voice. "Everything is in the hands of God now."

"Perhaps the Vicomte de Grenier can be of assistance?"

Marguerite frowned, startled by the suggestion. She had no one to whom she could turn for help. Her sisters, perhaps, but they had nothing to offer and would most likely believe that such was the fate of fallen women.

"Why would he help me?" she asked.

Celie shrugged and winced.

"Send someone," Marguerite ordered, thinking he would already know about the day's events, regardless.

The maid curtsied and scurried off.

It was a few hours later before de Grenier arrived. He entered the parlor behind the butler looking windblown and handsome, despite the tightness of his mouth and the grimness in his eyes.

Marguerite rose from her seat, expending great effort to ignore how the knot in her stomach tightened upon seeing him. "My lord."

"I came as swiftly as possible," he said, striding up to her and collecting her hands in his.

"I am grateful."

"I went to Desjardins first, to see what he knew."

She gestured for him to sit and he did, choosing to share the small settee with her.

"Was he forthcoming?" she asked.

"He was startled by my involvement, then wary. I believe it was only desperation that led him to speak openly."

Her fingers tangled together in her lap and her breath caught. "Desperation?"

De Grenier exhaled and the sound conveyed such finality, she felt ill. "I have always thought of Desjardins as immovable as a mountain, despite his youth. There are very few people who I would believe above any form of coercion and he is one of them."

"Coercion?" she repeated, the word sticking to the roof of her dry mouth.

"Yes." He paused. "Marguerite . . ."

"Just tell me, damn you!"

"There is some speculation that a cache of missing and important documents is being held by Saint-Martin in this house."

"Where?"

"I do not know. Desjardins is not even certain the tale is true. He only knows that he has been receiving threats the last three months, all promising harm to Saint-Martin *and* you, if what the fiend desires is not returned."

Confused, her gaze moved around the room as if she could find the needed papers. "We have been so wrong."

"Beg your pardon?"

"Saint-Martin believed that I was distracting him from his duties to the *secret du roi* and that is what the grievance was. Neither of us understood how a mistress could signify, but we were unable to conceive of what else it could be."

"*You* were unable to conceive of it," the vicomte said gently. "Saint-Martin was aware that he had possession of something valuable; he simply did not share the information with you."

Marguerite heard the note of smugness in de Grenier's words and knew he hoped to incite a rift. Such machinations were wasted on her, however. She was a practical woman. She did not find it odd or secretive for Philippe to withhold information about his covert activities from her. There was nothing she could do with such knowledge besides worry unduly about things she had no power over.

"So what can I do?" she asked. "Who is this person who needs these documents and what hold does he have over Desjardins?"

"I do not know." The vicomte leaned forward. "I only know that you cannot remain here, Marguerite."

"Of course not. If they want something in this house, they must have it. We cannot risk Saint-Martin's life."

"They also want you."

She blinked. "Why?"

"Whoever this individual is, they carry great enmity toward Saint-Martin. They want him to lose everything he holds dear, including you. Desjardins is deeply disturbed by the brutality of the attack today. He fears that the next step will be the loss of Saint-Martin's life, despite having been told that death would be too merciful an end."

Pushing to her feet, Marguerite wept openly. "Did

he share any of this information with Philippe? Or did Desjardins allow him to remain ignorant of these threats?"

De Grenier rose. "I do not know, nor do I care. My concern is only for you. You are innocent in this, yet your life has been compromised by association."

"My life is with Philippe."

"And when he is dead?" the vicomte spat out, his large frame tense with frustration. "What then?"

"Are you suggesting that my removal from Philippe's life will spare him?"

"It might. Desjardins believes that he can use your departure to soothe this man he called *L'Esprit*. It will give him an opportunity to locate the papers and perhaps end this."

"*L'Esprit* . . . " Turning, Marguerite rushed from the parlor and crossed to the dining room, where the note from earlier waited. She reread the cryptic words and felt ill. Her hand fell to her side, the paper crinkling within her tense grip.

Large hands settled atop her shoulders and squeezed gently. "Allow me to help you."

"You already have and I thank you." She faced him. "I cannot afford to be any further in your debt."

His handsome features softened and he cupped her cheek. "You do not have the means to extricate yourself on your own."

"I have some jewelry . . . "

"*Mon Dieu!*" he scoffed. "You cannot survive indefinitely on so little."

"No," she agreed, "but there is enough to sustain me until Saint-Martin is well and the documents are dealt with."

"If he survives the night, it will be only because of the grace of God."

She felt the blood drain from her face, leaving her dizzy and weary. She clung to the back of the chair, but de Grenier caught her arm and forced her to sit.

"You are not well," he said.

"I must rest. Certainly you can imagine how taxing this afternoon has been."

The vicomte appeared prepared to argue, then he bowed. "My previous offer still stands."

He moved to take a seat beside her. He caught up her hand, which lay motionless on the table surface. She looked into his eyes and saw compassion.

"I cannot discuss this now." It made her sick to think of it. Life without Philippe? Life spent with another man? The thought was inconceivable to her.

And then her day, already unbearably agonizing, worsened.

An urgent knocking came to the open door. Marguerite turned in her chair to see Celie ringing her hands in her apron. "Mademoiselle, a word, please."

Marguerite stepped out to the hallway and found the servants scrambling. Fear froze the blood in her veins, making her shiver. "What is it? What has happened?"

Celie's pale eyes were reddened, as was her upturned nose. "Cook made stew for the servants from the scraps. I was late—"

With her nerves stretched to the limit, Marguerite had no patience for nonsense. She grabbed Celie by the arms and shook her. "What happened? Has he passed?"

"They all passed!" the maid screamed. "Cook . . . the footmen . . . They're all *dead!* All of them . . ."

De Grenier burst from the dining room in a full run, skidding momentarily across the marble floor before finding purchase and heading toward the rear of the house. Marguerite followed despite Celie's pleas, her heart racing so violently she feared it might burst. The vicomte entered the kitchen a few strides ahead of her. He cursed, then spun around quickly, catching her in his arms and dragging her back.

"Poison," he said grimly with his lips to her ear.

The ground fell away beneath her feet and she was swallowed by the inky darkness of unconsciousness.

Chapter 1

Paris, France—1780

He was the sort of man who could enslave a woman with a single glance.

A glance such as the one he was presently giving to her.

Lynette Baillon watched the notorious Simon Quinn with similar shamelessness, admiring the raven blackness of his hair and the brilliant blue of his eyes.

Quinn lounged against a fluted column in the Baroness Orlinda's ballroom, his arms crossing his broad chest and one ankle hooked carelessly over the other. He looked both leisurely and alert, a dichotomy she had noted the first time she saw him riding through the moonlit Parisian streets. Tonight he was dressed in somber shades of dark blue and gray, a combination that created an understated elegance she found extremely appealing. Amid the flagrantly sensual theme of the intimate gathering—candles scented of exotic spices, chaises cleverly hidden by a faux forest, and servants dressed in revealing costume—he was austerely attractive. His quiet intensity was far more alluring than the deportment of those who cavorted in blatant rut.

For her part, she was dressed in white for effect, her skirts accented with rich cream-colored bows and silver thread. Combined with her pale skin and hair and the dark ruby red of her half-mask, the ensemble drew all eyes toward her.

Drew his eyes toward her.

They had never been introduced. She'd learned his name by eavesdropping on surrounding conversations, listening with avid interest to whispered tales of his wickedness and common origins. He stood on the fringes, alone. Coveted by the women and shunned by the men for the exact same reasons—he had only his reputed expertise as a lover to recommend him and no title, property, or moral compass to redeem him. The widowed baroness enjoyed shocking Society, which explained his presence. He was a novelty and appeared to be comfortable in that role, but Lynette felt a strong pull to join him, to stand beside him, to enter the solitary enclosure he occupied.

Quinn was a tall man, and a big one. His jaw was strong, his nose a blade. Boldly winged brows gave him a hint of arrogance, while long, thick lashes added a touch of softness. To her mind, however, the most alluring part of his rugged handsomeness was his mouth. The lips were perfect, neither too full nor too thin, and when they curved in a smile—as they were doing now—they were irresistible. She wanted to lick them, nibble on them, feel them move across her bare skin.

"Between you and your sister," her mother had

once said, "you are most like me. Your passions run high, your blood hot. Pray you do not succumb to it."

Her blood felt hot now. Her chest rose and fell rapidly in response to his stare. Her heart raced. That a stranger could incite such a response in her despite the crowd that surrounded them and the distance separating them only exacerbated her reaction.

Then he straightened abruptly and approached with a predator's easy, yet determined gait. His long legs ate up the space between them, his pathway direct and unconcerned with those who were forced to move out of his way. She inhaled sharply, her palms dampening within her gloves.

When he reached her, her head tilted back to allow her to gaze upon his face and fully appreciate its savage beauty. She breathed him in, becoming intoxicated by the combination of tobacco and musk. The primitive scent was delicious and she fought the insane urge to rise to her tiptoes and press her nose into his throat.

"Mademoiselle."

She shivered as the sensual inflection with which he spoke wrapped around her like a lover's embrace.

"Mr. Quinn," she greeted, her voice husky and inviting.

Quinn's gaze narrowed into an examining perusal. Without warning, he caught her elbow and pulled her away from the wall. She was so startled by his action that she was unable to voice a protest.

At least that was what she told herself. She wasn't yet prepared to admit that she wanted to be claimed by a man such as him. A man whose polished exterior encased raw masculinity.

He led her through the crowd and down a hallway, opening a closed door and pushing her ahead of him into the room. The interior was dark, and for a moment, she was blinded by the dearth of illumination after the blaze of the massive ballroom chandeliers.

Her eyes slowly adjusted to the softer moonlight spilling in through the windows. When she could see, she stepped farther into the large, liberally furnished library. The smell of leather and parchment teased her nostrils, reinforcing the sensation of being primitively claimed.

The door latch clicked into place and she jumped, her nerves stretched too thin. The sounds of laughter and music faded from her perception, leaving her aware only of Quinn and the fact that they were alone together.

"What game are you playing?" he asked gruffly.

"I was staring," she admitted, turning to face him. She appreciated having the light behind her, which shielded her features in shadow while revealing the whole of his. "But then, every woman here was doing the same."

"But you are not just any woman, are you?" he growled, coming toward her.

So . . . he knew who she was. That surprised her. Her mother had insisted they hide their identities. They stayed with a friend instead of at their own property and were using an assumed surname. Her mother said it would prevent her father from becoming angry with them for deviating from their stated destination—Spain. She would have agreed to anything in order to come to Paris. In all of her life, her family had never visited here.

But then . . . If Quinn knew her true identity,

why would he pull her away from the festivities in such a public manner?

"*You* approached *me*," she pointed out. "You could have kept your distance."

"I am here because of you." He caught her elbows and jerked her roughly into him. "If you had stayed out of mischief for a few days longer, I would have been far from France now."

She frowned. What was he talking about? She would have asked if he had not placed his hands on her. No man had ever been so bold as to accost the daughter of the Vicomte de Grenier. She could hardly believe Quinn had done it, but she could not jerk away because the sensations elicited by his proximity stunned her. He was so hard, like stone. She could not have expected that.

As her breathing quickened, she felt herself sway into him, her chest pressing into his. It was madness. He was a stranger and he seemed to be angry.

But she felt safe with him, regardless.

For a long, taut moment Quinn did not move. Then he yanked her toward the window, impatiently pushing the sheer curtain aside so that moonlight touched her face. With a tug of his fingers, he untied the ribbons of her mask and it fell away, leaving her exposed. She suddenly felt naked, but not nearly naked enough. She felt a reckless, goading need to strip off every article of clothing while he watched. It was heady to be the focus of such heated, avid interest from so handsome a man.

He loomed over her, scowling, his mouth set in a grim line. "Why are you looking at me like that?" he snapped.

She swallowed hard. "Like what?"

Quinn made an aggravated noise, dropped the curtain, and caught her about the waist. "As if you want me in your bed."

Mon Dieu, what did one say to that?

"You are . . . very attractive, Mr. Quinn."

" 'Mr. Quinn,' is it?" he purred, his large hands cupping her spine, making her feel tiny and delicate. Conquered. "I always knew you were mad."

Her tongue darted out to wet her dry lips and he froze, his gaze burning.

"What game are you playing?" he asked again. This time, she heard something else in his tone. Something darker. Undeniably arousing.

"I—I think we are both c-confused," she said.

He moved, cupping the back of her neck and the side of her hip, mantling her body with his. "I'm bloody well confused, curse you." He tugged, forcing her spine to arch, leaning over her so that she had no leverage to move.

Every inhale was his exhale. Every movement was an enticement, their bodies sliding against each other in a wanton dance. She felt a fever in her blood, a conflagration that had started with that first smoldering glance in the ballroom.

"Do you want to be fucked?" he purred, his head lowering so that his lips touched her jaw. The caress was divine and wicked at once, making her shiver with delighted apprehension. "Because you are begging for it, witch, and I am insane enough in this moment to indulge you."

"I—I . . ."

Quinn turned his head and kissed her, hard, his lips mashing against hers. There was no finesse, no tenderness. Her mouth was bruised by his volatility and ardor. She should have been frightened. He seemed barely leashed, his emotions swaying from irritation to consuming desire.

She whimpered, her hands fisting in his jacket to keep him close. Enamored with the taste of him, she licked his lips and he groaned, his hips grinding restlessly into her. She surrendered weakly and he gentled his approach, seemingly soothed by her capitulation.

"Tell me what you are involved in," he murmured, his teeth nipping at the corner of her mouth.

"You," she breathed, tilting her head to deepen the contact. She felt drunk. The room spun behind her closed eyelids and she suspected she would crumble if he weren't holding her so tightly.

Quinn turned slightly and sat in a nearby slipper chair. The change in position stole her balance and she settled between his spread legs nearly prone.

"Why now?" he asked, nibbling his way to her ear.

She wrapped her arms around his shoulders and bared her throat. His hot, open mouth suckled the tender skin and she writhed in mindless pleasure. "Mr. Quinn . . ."

He chuckled, surprising her with the warmth of the sound. "Who knew you burned so hotly beneath all that ice?"

"Kiss me again," she begged, more infatuated with his mouth now that she had experienced its skill.

"We must leave, before I lift your skirts and take you here."

"No—"

Quinn suckled her lower lip and her body softened further, becoming hot and damp and aching.

"Then let us retire to a more private venue, Lysette. Before lust rules my better sense."

Lysette.

She stilled, the beat of her heart arrested by the sound of the name that was not her own.

The sudden understanding of all his questions horrified her. Simon Quinn knew her sister. Her twin. Her dearest friend and most agonizing loss.

For Lysette was dead, her body entombed in a beautifully sculpted crypt in Poland.

How, then, did Quinn know her and believe her to be alive?

Chapter 2

The coast of France, three days earlier . . .

Lysette Rousseau, an accomplished assassin, inhaled the sea air through the cabin window and wondered why her rapidly approaching demise did not frighten her. Her livelihood had shown her many faces of death. Most had been terror-stricken and accompanied by desperate pleas for mercy. She attempted to dredge up similar attachment to her own life and felt nothing. Death would be a reprieve; she could think of it no other way.

The ship she was prisoner upon would dock on the coast of France by morning. What awaited her there was unknown. She had been sent on a mission to recover information in England and was instead captured. Two more French agents had been held behind as leverage. Another was dead by her hand. It was quite possible, given the disastrous results, that this night would be her last. Yet the knowledge had such little impact, she scarcely felt it.

She was not a woman to ruminate over her emotions, but she did ponder how her lack of memory had become a lack of *joie de vivre*. Her past prior to two years ago was a mystery to her. Without roots to ground her and give her an anchor, Lysette was adrift. Aimless. Perhaps some would find it strange that an existence fueled by the power of others would be so exhausting, but for her it was.

The lock turned in the door behind her and her keeper entered.

"I have brought you supper," Simon Quinn said in a voice designed to lead women to ruin. The sensuality of the low, deep tone was not an affectation; it was inherent to the man.

Lysette turned to face him, noting how his simple attire of shirtsleeves and breeches together with his dark, unbound hair gave him the appearance of a pirate. In truth he was a mercenary who had spent the last several years in service to the Crown of England. That made him her opponent in a fashion, yet she felt safer with him than with any other man. He felt no sexual attraction to her, a state proven by the last few months of near constant proximity to each other. She had even offered sex to him once, and he had declined. Due to his lack of interest, she almost liked him. *Almost.*

"I am not hungry," she said, watching as he set a plate of salted meat and hard biscuits on the round table in the corner.

A black brow lifted and brilliant blue eyes assessed her from head to toe. Simon was Irish, his breeding evident in both his coloring and the inflection that tinged his every word. He was stunningly attractive and dangerously charming. He could offer a woman the world with a single smile . . . with the caveat that it was only a temporary gift. Simon was not a man to become a permanent fixture in anyone's life. That sense of transience was a potent lure. She'd watched women fall into his lap without any effort on his part.

"You need to eat," he said.

"The rolling of the ship does not sit well with my stomach."

He ran a hand through his inky locks, the gesture rife with frustration. The movement of his arm was graceful, the large biceps flexing powerfully. Simon bore the form of a common laborer, which attracted more women than it repelled. Lysette admired it with the same offhand attention with which she contemplated death.

"Does our arrival tomorrow . . . disturb you?" he asked grudgingly.

"Would it plague your conscience if it did?"

The glare he shot her made her laugh.

She knew he regarded her with wary confusion. He sensed the division in her caused by her lack of memory, but he had yet to learn the reason for it. Lysette viewed her missing past as a vulnerability, and she had learned—in the most heinous fashion—that she could not afford any further liabilities beyond her gender.

"You do not even attempt to be likable," he complained.

"No," she agreed, moving to occupy the only chair in the room, a walnut spindle-back with a contoured seat. They shared a fairly comfortable cabin and yet the first days had been some of the tensest in her short recollection. She was not accustomed to keeping such close quarters with men, especially over a length of time. "You will be free of me tomorrow."

"Ha!" Simon sat on the edge of her bed to remove his boots. A hammock slung across the far corner served as his sleeping place. It swung gently as the ship rolled, a sight that often lulled her into daydreams of a brighter future. "I would have been free of you in England, if you had not been lying, deceiving, and making mischief the entire length of our association."

"That is my livelihood, *mon amour.*"

"Soon to be inflicted on some other unfortunate soul."

"Your hypocrisy is impressive."

He glared. "I resigned my commission before leaving England. I am returning you to France only because of my men. If not for them, I would be elsewhere. Far from you."

"Ah."

While she wore a mocking smile on the outside, on the inside she admired his loyalty and sense of responsibility. His underlings—a dozen men who had worked covertly on his behalf—were now being held against their will as insurance for her return. His resignation freed him from any obligation for their safety, yet he pressed on, regardless.

"As to whether or not I will be free of you tomorrow, I doubt it. This will not be a swift exchange," he said, surprising her. "I will see all of my men first. Should one of them be injured, we will wait for his full recovery before proceeding. In addition, we must negotiate the terms for Jacques and Cartland. Much will depend on how cooperative Comte Desjardins is."

"And if you do not regain all of them?"

Simon glanced at her. "Then, your people will not regain you."

"Perhaps you will never be rid of me."

He growled. "That would not be pleasant for you."

"Oh, I might beg to disagree. You are pleasing to the eye and you maintain a surly sort of charm."

When other men would have made her life a misery, Simon had seen to her comfort and care, albeit grudgingly. His tarnished honor fascinated her. Lysette had spent their time together attempting to discern what fueled him. If she could discover that, the knowledge would be to her advantage.

"Witch," Simon muttered in response to her taunting.

She placed her slippered feet atop a roughly hewn wooden footstool with a silent sigh. Did she have a family or anyone to care for her and miss her? Did someone pine for her and wonder at her disappearance from their lives? She had no notion of what motivated a man like Simon, what roads in life had led him to hire himself out for money, but she knew what motivated her—the desire to regain the knowledge of her identity. She required funds and resources for such an undertaking, and the skill to kill anyone who impeded her quest.

When she had set out for England with Simon, she'd planned to return under far different circumstances. The Comte Desjardins had promised her freedom in return for the identity of the mastermind behind Simon's spying in France. Instead, she returned a prisoner.

"Eat," Simon ordered, gesturing to the table.

Lysette considered demurring again, then decided she did not want to spend her last night arguing with the only person in the world she liked at all.

So she obeyed, pushing thoughts of the morrow far from her mind.

Chapter 3

The knock came to the door of Simon Quinn's Parisian home at exactly eleven o'clock in the evening.

The longcase clock chimed the hour and hid a secret door from view, one of many escape routes Simon had commissioned when he purchased the residence three years ago.

He listened to the exchange between his expected visitor and his butler, then rose as the voices approached the study, where he waited. Since disembarking from the ship that morning, he had spent the day making arrangements for this assignation, eager to conclude this last mission and begin his life anew. He'd sent a missive to Desjardins immediately upon arrival and requested a visit with his men to ascertain their condition. If they were well, he would schedule the exchange for the morrow.

He was dressed for riding and his greatcoat was slung over a leather wingback near the door. A dagger was strapped to his thigh and a small sword hung comfortably around his hips, not with any expectation of use but for appearances and to act as a distraction. Simon's greatest weapons were his fists, the only defense an impoverished lad could depend upon.

He was prepared in all ways and confident. He'd left the ship and returned to his home with a cloak-shrouded figure beside him. An hour later, a disguised Lysette was taken to another location to ensure the failure of any attempt to wrest her away without a fair exchange.

"Mr. Quinn."

Simon studied the person who filled his door-way. Lean and sinewy, the man bore the coarse appearance of one who lived by his teeth every day. Few would believe that so blunt an individual would associate with the suave and lauded Comte Desjardins, but it was true. The lackey would not be here if he did not.

Desjardins's man was conspicuous within the studied sophistication of Simon's residence. Although Simon had grown into manhood on the mean streets of Dublin and London, fighting for every meal and a place to sleep, his comeliness had eventually led to him spending a handful of years as the kept paramour of the beautiful and wealthy Lady Winter. Maria had taught him many things, including the value of appearances. Because of her, he dressed with understated elegance, knowing that a man of his breeding could not carry flamboyance. He conveyed this sensibility to everything he owned, from horseflesh and car-riages to his homes. His wealth could not be ques-tioned, neither could his taste.

"Shall we?" the lackey asked in a nasally rendition of a gentleman's discourse.

"I am ready," Simon said, striding forward and collecting his coat along the way.

They exited Simon's townhouse and mounted their horses. There were two more lackeys nearby, but Simon was confident in his ability to dispatch the lot of them, if necessary. Besides, if Lysette's value was such that she was worth a dozen men, he had little to fear alone.

Which created an entirely new dilemma.

The comte was willing to release all twelve men immediately for only Lysette, which would leave the *Illuminés*—the group of individuals with whom Desjardins worked—with no leverage to demand the return of Jacques and Cartland, the two men still imprisoned by Lord Eddington—Simon's former superior—in England. Something was amiss.

However, it was no longer Simon's purview to find out what that might be, and while his natural curiosity prodded at him, he ignored it. He was eager to leave this covert life behind. His recent visit to England and a brief, nonromantic reunion with the now-married Maria reminded him of times when he had been content with his lot. It contrasted sharply with the last few years of restlessness and told him it was time for drastic change. Good or ill, he needed his life to be altered. Continuing his employment was not an option.

The horses' hooves clopped along the road in an easy canter and the night breeze blew in gentle caressing gusts across Simon's cheek. Around them, an infrequent carriage passed and pedestrians walked along the street edge at a brisk pace. He noted everything and everyone around him by habit, his existence so dependent on his awareness of his surroundings that it was second nature.

For years he had believed his livelihood took no toll, but now he contemplated a future lacking the ever-present concern that he would be ambushed at any moment, and he smiled.

"Here we are."

Following the example of the riders with him, Simon urged his mount down an alley and drew to a halt beside a hitching post. Once all the horses were secure, he was directed through an iron gateway and found himself in a cemetery.

"I'll have to cover your eyes," a lackey said.

"No." Simon withdrew his blade.

"Just 'til we go under," the man assured him, smiling in a way that chilled.

"I have a terrible memory," Simon drawled. "You needn't worry that I will join the dead in haunting you."

"You either wear it, or we'll have to turn about," the man insisted.

Simon hesitated, trying to gauge their intent. He even feigned departure and headed back to where his horse waited. They followed alongside him, which reinforced their claim that they would not relent.

Shoving his blade back into its sheath, he conceded. "A few moments, no more. And my hands remain unbound."

"Mais oui."

He was blindfolded and pulled forward by two men, one at each elbow. They crossed damp grass, then descended stone steps. The air grew musty and Simon stumbled over uneven ground. He cursed and was laughed at.

"Arrête," one of them said a moment later.

Simon stopped and pushed the blindfold off. He blinked and found his suspicions confirmed—he was in a catacomb beneath the city. Torches lined the walls at regular intervals, telling him this pathway was frequently traveled. He grabbed one, both for illumination and as a weapon. When his companions stared at him warily, he arched a brow in challenge. The leader shrugged and led the way without protest.

They walked some distance, venturing deeper via the many twisting pathways. Eventually they arrived, entering a cavernous room that had been modified into a dungeon of sorts. Simon found his men restrained in three cages, four in each, with some lying on the floor and others sitting with their backs against the bars. Several guards watched over them, though all were presently engaged in a card game.

"How fare you?" he asked, addressing the group with a sweeping glance. They were filthy and malodorous, their appearances haggard and unkempt, but they stood in a concentrated rush and seemed to be uninjured. They grabbed the bars with fisted hands and stared at him with hope-filled eyes.

"In need of a bath," one replied.

"And ale," said another.

"A woman?" Simon queried with a smile.

"Aye!"

"You will be freed tomorrow," he explained, stepping closer. "I wish it could be now, but I wanted to be certain you all were in good health before I relinquish what I have that they desire."

A man named Richard Becking extended a

grimy hand through the cage and Simon took it without hesitation.

"Thank you, Quinn," Richard said hoarsely.

"Thank you, my friend," Simon returned, tightening his grip and thereby hiding the passing of a tiny rolled note.

Richard's eyes narrowed almost imperceptibly, a silent assurance that he would keep the missive's existence a secret. It detailed Simon's plans for the exchange and the way he wished to be told of their safe release before turning over Lysette.

With that, Simon bade them farewell and returned to the surface the same way he had left it: partly with sight and partly blindfolded. He parted ways with Desjardins's men when they reached their mounts and directed his horse to return home.

The streets were less populated now and only one carriage crossed his path on the journey home. He studied it in passing, noting the obviously female gloved hand curled over the window ledge and the noble coat of arms emblazoned on the door. Both attributes made the equipage and its occupants innocuous and easily forgotten.

The man on horseback was so comely, he stole her wits.

Lynette Baillon straightened from her reclined position on the carriage squab and leaned forward, twisting to watch the rider through the window until he was out of sight.

He rode tall in the saddle, his grip on the reins one-handed and loose. His other hand rested casually atop the hilt of his small sword, but she was not fooled. He was aware of everything around him. His eyes followed her equipage as it passed, his breathtaking features revealed by his lack of a hat.

"What is it?" her mother asked from her position opposite.

"I was admiring a handsome man," she explained, settling back into her seat.

"Shameless," the vicomtess admonished. "What if he had seen you craning your neck in that manner?"

"It is too dark," Lynette argued, "since you will not allow us to turn up the lamps."

"There is danger everywhere." Her mother sighed and rubbed at her temples. "You do not understand."

"Because you refuse to tell me."

"Lynette . . ."

The weariness in the beloved voice made Lynette abandon the subject, just as she had done for years. Now that her sister was gone, she felt compelled to be a comfort to her mother. It was a role that did not suit her well. Lysette had been the gentle one, the quiet one. Lynette was the outrageous one, the flamboyant one, the one forever concocting schemes that landed them in trouble.

"Forgive me, *Maman*."

"No need. It has been a long journey."

The vicomtess had the appearance of a delicate beauty with her pale golden hair and finely wrought features, widely lauded attributes that she'd passed on to her children. Age had not diminished her appeal; she remained as ethereally lovely as always. Regardless, the impression of fragility was a false one.

Marguerite Baillon, Vicomtess de Grenier, was a re-markably strong woman. When she set her mind to something, she could not be swayed.

Unless it was a request from one of her daughters.

She had never been able to deny them anything, and after the loss of one, she was even more likely to indulge the other. It was why they were in Paris now. Lynette had always wanted to visit the famed city, so when the vicomtess suggested a trip to Spain in an effort to cheer them both, Lynette had begged for a short detour. Although Marguerite disliked Paris and had rarely returned to France over the past two decades, she had conceded reluctantly to her daughter's wish.

The vicomtess yawned. "I wish for a hot bath and two days in bed."

"But you allow us only a sennight to visit!" Lynette protested. "You cannot sleep two of those seven days."

"I am jesting, *ma petite*. However, your father is due in town for business then," her mother reminded her. "Neither of us wants a scolding for deviating from our stated plans."

Her father was as cautious as her mother. He insisted on knowing their whereabouts at all times. "No, of course not."

Lynette's gaze moved back to the window and the view of the city beyond it. Her joy in the trip was tempered by the ever-present longing for Lysette to be with her. They had been inseparable from the moment of conception, and despite the two years since Lysette's passing, Lynette still suffered the agony of loneliness that only a twin would know. It felt as if a part of her was missing and she was ever cognizant of that lack.

I will enjoy this adventure for the both of us, Lysette, she thought, her hand rising to her aching heart. *I will see all of the places we talked about, even the ones I said I had no desire to see. I will pretend that you are with me, showing me the world through your eyes.*

"I miss her," Lynette whispered through a throat clenched tight with sorrow and guilt. "Dreadfully."

"We will live for her," the vicomtess murmured. "Every day."

"Yes, *Maman.*" She slouched against the squab and closed her eyes.

Oddly, the man on horseback entered her mind again. He had been so vital, so alive even from a distance. She would have spoken with Lysette about him, if she had been here.

Have you ever seen a man more handsome? Lynette would have asked.

Men such as him are trouble, her sister would say. *Better to find a quiet companion who shares similar interests and will be steadfast. Wild men do not marry. Hence the reason they are wild.*

Her impulsiveness had always been tempered by Lysette's unshakable reason. Her sister had been her anchor, and without her, she felt adrift.

Lynette would give everything and do anything to have her sister back. But death had stolen Lysette away. Now, she would have to learn how to go on alone.

The Comte Desjardins was in his cellar searching for a particular burgundy vintage when a scraping sound heralded the opening of a door. He stiffened, his blood running cold.

"My lord."

Desjardins exhaled with relief at the sound of a normal albeit coarsely accented voice, the knots of tension in his shoulders diminishing only slightly. At this point, even that was a blessing. One could never be relaxed when he danced to the tune of another.

He turned and faced the waiting lackey, his gaze briefly lifting over the man's shoulder to the rock-hewn stairs that led to the catacombs below. Searching for the devil, even though *L'Esprit* had ceased to communicate directly with him years ago.

Missives were all he received anymore.

His brows rose and the man nodded. No words needed to be said. The exchange with Quinn would take place on the morrow, and the lovely Lysette, arguably his greatest assest, would be returned to him.

He still had difficulty believing that she had been taken prisoner. In the two years she'd worked for him, there had never been an instance of failure. Perhaps she had been compromised? He prayed that was not the case, because he required the assistance of a beautiful woman now. One who could lie and kill without a qualm. Sadly those were few and far between.

The man slipped back into the tunnel and Desjardins ascended the stairs to the kitchen, passing the many industrious servants who prepared supper for his family and their guests. He left the bottle of wine on a counter and returned to the formal parlor.

It was his least favorite room in the house. His wife had decorated the space in a mixture of white and a blue so pale it was nearly white. All the metal accents in the room were silver, creating the impression—for him—of a snow cave of some sort. The only spot of color in the room was provided by the portrait of Benjamin Franklin that graced the wall.

He liked and felt a deep respect for Mr. Franklin. The man was charming, brilliant, and the Grand Master of the *Lodge Les Neuf Sœurs.*

He was also the latest target of *L'Esprit.*

Desjardins had received another damnable missive just a sennight past. Rejecting monetary compensation had not been sufficient to sever that tie. Now he received nothing for his efforts beyond the promise that his family would not be harmed.

Because of this, he was grateful that Lysette had failed in her mission. He had hoped to discover the identity of the mastermind behind Simon Quinn's activities in France, hoping to use the information to lure *L'Esprit* out in the open. However, this recent focus on Franklin made her continued cooperation a necessity. *L'Esprit* wanted reports of Franklin's meetings, conversations, and correspondence. In-depth accounts, not merely generalizations such as one would find through gossip.

"I found it," Desjardins said as he drew to a halt beside the man who had become a pivotal part of his plan.

Edward James turned his gaze away from the portrait of Franklin and tilted his head in acknowledgment. The comte had yet to see the man smile. "I appreciate the effort expended and look forward to sampling the wine you speak so highly of, my lord."

"It was no effort at all," Desjardins said, inwardly

thinking that sharing his favorite wine was the
least he could do considering what James would
most likely go through in the weeks ahead.

James worked as secretary to Benjamin Franklin,
a position of prestige that had become a curse. He
accompanied Franklin nearly everywhere and knew
minute details of his life, details *L'Esprit* was determined Desjardins would access. It was a painstak-
ing business, costing a great deal of time and
resources to yield very little. So far he had kept
L'Esprit content, but he did not want the man content. He wanted him dead. In order to make that
happen, he required information so valuable it
would give him an advantage.

Beautiful women were excellent at luring such
commodities from men.

"You have a lovely home," James said.

"*Merci.*"

James was tall and lean with brown hair, dark
eyes framed by brass spectacles, and a strong jaw.
He was not handsome by any definition, but Desjardins's daughter Anne was infatuated with the
man's "intensity" and spoke of him incessantly.
Anne took great pains to join any outing or excursion that included James and noted all the minute
details, such as how he liked his tea. Because of
this, Desjardins felt he had a strong grasp of the
type of man James was. He intended to feed that
information to Lysette, which she could then use
to become perfect for him.

"What are your plans for the rest of the week?"
Desjardins asked.

He listened carefully to James's reply, cataloguing the finer points to include in his notes for Ly-

sette. He hoped the secretary enjoyed his brief time with the lovely blonde who was far above his station.

She would cost him his employment and reputation, if not far more precious things. Such as his life.

Chapter 4

"So, we finally part ways," Lysette murmured.

Simon grinned. If this had been the end of a liaison, he would have affected a more flattering show of melancholy. As it was, such subterfuge wasn't necessary.

"Look how happy you are." A reluctant smile curved her lips and he noted how it transformed her features. Lysette was truly one of the most beautiful women he had ever met. Her glorious tresses were shot with various shadings of pale gold and light browns. Her skin was like the richest ivory satin, her eyes the blue of a clear summer sky, her lips lush and pouty within her heart-shaped face. She was petite and lithe but perfectly proportioned. Not too curvy or too thin. Because of her exterior flawlessness, he found it somewhat unnerving to realize that, aside from the moment he first met her, he had never had any desire to tumble her. Even after the last few weeks of abstinence and near constant proximity to her, he hadn't considered bedding her.

"You must be relieved to be rid of me, as well," he said easily.

"Of course."

The hard glimmer returned to her eyes and he sighed inwardly. Once again, the moment he felt the slightest softening toward her, she reminded him of why he did not like her. It had nothing to do with her lack of affection for him and everything to do with the fact that she was so mutable. At times she seemed confused, at others she appeared to relish her work far too much for his tastes. He suspected she was a bit touched and he had learned to avoid those who suffered afflictions of the mind. They were a danger to themselves and others.

As soon as the carriage rolled to a stop in front of the small home on a quiet street, Simon opened the door and leaped out. Then he extended his gloved hand to assist Lysette down.

Her hat rim came into view first, then it rose as she tilted her head back to gaze at the front of the residence.

"What is this place?" he asked.

"My home."

Simon studied her openly. She seemed pensive and melancholy, her pale blue eyes shadowed with secrets he did not care to know.

Lysette Rousseau was one of the most cutthroat individuals he'd ever had the misfortune to meet, one who took pleasure in the misery of others. It was oftentimes difficult to reconcile her beautiful, fragile exterior with the hardened woman he knew her to be. He'd watched her kill a man with novel ferocity, an act even more disconcerting when committed by a lovely seductress. Yet she had the bearing and tastes of a woman of breeding. The combination of civility and blood thirst was discordant.

Frankly, he could not wait to be rid of her and the mystery she represented. He was weary of prying into other people's lives on behalf of a king he cared little about. He wanted to live his own life and he had—finally—accumulated enough wealth to do so. No longer would he serve the needs of another. The world was his, or it soon would be, once he exchanged the wily Lysette for Richard and the others.

He pivoted and wrapped her arm around his. "Ready?" he asked.

Lysette inhaled sharply, then nodded.

Simon noted that tiny act of gathering courage and felt a brief flare of concern. He almost asked her if there was some assistance she required, but he held his tongue. While the last vestiges of his chivalry urged him to assist a damsel in distress, the blunt truth of the matter was that she had made her own bed and now she must lie in it. His responsibility was not to her but to the dozen men who worked for him. Still, despite thinking so callously, he let kinder words leave his lips.

"I will remain in Paris for a month or so."

The statement was not a romantic appeal and she knew it. He was offering a temporary harbor in case of a possible storm. The startled look she gave him in response afforded him a brief glimpse of an unaffected Lysette. For a moment she glowed from within, a shimmer of wary hope and innocence.

Then it was gone.

He steeled himself for a sharp and jeering rebuke, as was her usual response to any friendly overture.

Instead, her mouth curved slightly and she gave an almost imperceptible nod.

Together they climbed the steps and entered her home. As they walked into the foyer, the lilting notes of a pianoforte greeted them. An elaborate and stunning crystal-covered chandelier hung above the gold-veined marble, and fresh flowers displayed in alcoves contributed their fragrance to the genial welcome.

Lysette led him into a parlor decorated in soothing shades of yellow and gold. Amid the soft palette, the emerald-garbed Comte Desjardins could not be missed.

"*Bonjour*, Mr. Quinn," the comte greeted, rising to his feet from his seat at the pianoforte.

"My lord." Simon once again marveled that such a short and slightly built man would have such a powerful voice. He doubted such volume could be contained in a whisper, a thought even more startling considering the body to which the voice belonged looked as if a stiff wind could topple it over.

"Lysette, *ma petite*." Desjardins approached her with a look of pride and affection on his long face. He caught up her hands and kissed her cheek. "*Comment te sens-tu?*"

"*Bien, merci.*"

Lysette's response was much more subdued, without a hint of warmth. The comte seemed unaffected by her lack of joy at being returned to his care.

"Excellent." He turned back to Simon. "Would you care for some tea, Mr. Quinn?"

"No, thank you." Simon's brows rose slightly at

the ease with which Desjardins appropriated Lysette's home. "I prefer to conclude our transaction and go on my way."

"What of Jacques and Cartland?" Lysette asked.

Desjardins gestured for Lysette to take a seat. "Arrangements will be made."

She glanced at Simon and he answered with a querying lift of his brows. She frowned, apparently as clueless as he was.

"Your men were released when you arrived, Mr. Quinn," the comte said, "as promised."

Simon moved over to the window and looked outside, then he glanced at the clock on the mantel. "I will enjoy your company for a few more moments, if you have no objections."

Lysette's mouth quirked. They all knew Simon would not leave without ensuring his men were safe, objections or not.

The comte shrugged. "As you wish. Stay as long as you desire. I am grateful to you for returning Mademoiselle Rousseau in good health."

"I take no pleasure in wounding others," Simon said grimly. "And I cannot expect to receive my men unharmed if I return damaged goods."

"Very civilized of you. So what are your plans now?" Desjardins asked, rocking back on his heels and smiling innocently.

"None of your damned concern," Simon drawled, growing impatient with the comte's facetiousness. "No offense, my lord."

"None taken."

A short rap on the door heralded the arrival of a tea service delivered by a housekeeper as elderly as the butler. Both looked as if they should have been pensioned off long ago. As Lysette began to strip off her gloves, Simon looked out the window again. Across the street, a flash of red caught his eye. He grinned and turned about.

"I will take my leave now," he said.

"See?" Desjardins gloated. "I am a trustworthy fellow."

Simon choked. He moved to Lysette and she extended her bare hand to him.

"Au revoir, mon amour," she purred.

He bent and kissed the smooth skin, his gaze locking with hers. "Try to stay out of mischief."

"What fun would there be in that?" Although she teased, the lines of strain that rimmed her eyes and mouth belied her nonchalance.

Simon glanced at Desjardins with a scowl, irritated to discover that he was unable to leave Lysette if she felt endangered. But the regard the comte bestowed upon her was affectionate. There was warmth in his eyes and his smile. The inequality of the exchange for her return was also a sign of her value. She would land on her feet, of that Simon was certain. And if there was trouble, she knew where to find him.

With a last squeeze of her hand, he released her, and after bowing to the comte, he departed. There was a slight spring to his step as he returned to his waiting carriage.

When the bars restraining his men had been opened, he had been freed as well. He answered to no one now and nothing held him back.

As Lysette poured tea, she also watched Desjardins. The comte stood at the window, watching as Simon left. He looked thinner and more gaunt, which was disturbing. But when he turned about and faced her, he seemed genuinely happy.

"You look well," he said, assessing her carefully.

"As well as can be expected under the circumstances." She added liberal amounts of sugar and cream to the comte's serving, then held the cup and saucer out to him.

He stepped closer and accepted it. "Tell me what transpired."

Lysette straightened. Her last assignment had gone horribly awry, despite how simple the plan had seemed on the outset. Quinn's closest associate, Colin Mitchell, had left Quinn's employ with the intent to return to England. Jacques had been tasked with befriending Mitchell in an effort to discover the identity of Quinn's superior—the man who took French secrets directly to the English king.

Unfortunately, on the night Mitchell and Jacques were due to board the ship, another of Quinn's men—an Englishman named Cartland—murdered a man closely connected to Agent-General Talleyrand-Périgord. Cartland was apprehended and accused Mitchell of the crime. To add weight to his protestations of innocence, he revealed the names of other men working for Quinn, thereby exposing a broad network of English spies.

At that point, they should have abandoned Mitchell and waited for another opportunity. Instead, Lysette's desperation to be freed from obligation to Desjardins led her to make a reckless offer—she would associate with Quinn and salvage the mission, and in return, Desjardins would release her from further service to him.

"Shortly after arriving in England," she said, "we

were discovered by Mr. Mitchell, which enabled us to place obstacles in his path. We hoped this would lead to his seeking assistance, which might reveal the identity of the man we sought."

The comte sat on a nearby gold velvet chair. "Sounds ideal."

"It would have been, if Mitchell had not been so well connected. He had no need to seek out his superior for help."

"Hmm . . ." Desjardins watched her over the rim of his cup. When he lowered his hands, the smile he revealed was chilling. "An interesting tale."

She shrugged. "It is the truth. No more, no less."

"Is it?"

"Of course." Her tone was casual, but the hairs on her nape prickled with alarm. "What else would it be?"

"An elaborate ruse, perhaps?"

"*Absurde,*" she scoffed. "What purpose would that serve?"

"I've no notion, *ma petite.*" His smile faded and his eyes hardened. "But you have been in the company of Mr. Quinn for some time now. A man rather infamous for his appeal to women. Perhaps you have succumbed to his charm."

Lysette stood in an angry swirl of floral skirts. "And now I seek to betray you?"

"Do you? You told him your real name. Why?"

"Because that was to be my last *favor* for you."

"A curious way to exert your independence."

"Kill me, then," she challenged with a jerk of her chin. "There is no way to prove any denial of your claims."

Desjardins rose with maddening leisure and set

his tea on the table. "As you killed François Depardue? A man working to serve the interests of the agent-general?"

Lysette felt the familiar knot of ice form in her stomach. "He deserved it. You know he did."

"Yes, he was an animal. A vicious, rutting beast who associated with others of his ilk." The comte came to her and wrapped her in his skeletal embrace. She shuddered with revulsion, but did not pull away. He had taken her from Depardue, clothed and fed her, trained her to survive.

"I will help you," he crooned, stroking his hands down her back as a loving father would. "No one will ever learn of your involvement in his death. In return, you will help me. One last time."

The nightmare of her life was never ending. "What do you want?" she asked wearily, her shoulders drooping.

"I have an introduction to make."

"Whom do you want dead now?"

He pulled back and gifted her with a soft smile. "I need a different sort of *femme fatale* for this."

That statement frightened her more than an order to kill.

"I am dreadfully worried about her, Solange," Marguerite said sadly, her fingers pushing needle through cloth by habit more than actual thought. "She has changed so drastically since Lysette passed."

"I noticed."

Marguerite glanced up at her dearest friend, a courtesan she had met years ago during an afternoon of shopping. Solange Tremblay was a lovely brunette, blessed with a girlish laugh and smile that kept her in demand. On the surface, they had little in common. Solange had pulled herself up from the serving class, while Marguerite had fallen from the heights of nobility. Solange was dark, Marguerite was fair. And yet they shared a deep affinity. They had both borne the censure of the world to live their lives as they saw fit.

After the tragic end of her affair with Philippe, Marguerite had wed the steadfast de Grenier and traveled with him to Poland, never to return to France . . . until now. It was only through correspondence that her friendship with Solange had grown and strengthened, and now that they were together again in the flesh, it felt as if no time had passed.

"You described her as so vivacious," Solange murmured, sipping delicately from a half-full goblet of brandy. She was curled atop a ruby red velvet chaise in her decadent boudoir, her long legs bared by the slit in her ivory satin negligee. "All the stories you used to share about your daughters. How different they were, despite the fact they were twins—the elder one so outrageous and wild, the younger one so contemplative and studious. If I did not know better, I would think it was Lysette who came with you, not Lynette."

"That is it exactly," Marguerite said, discarding her needlepoint on the seat beside her. "At times it feels as if she is trying to be Lysette."

"Perhaps she does not want to burden you. Perhaps this is her way of giving you comfort."

Closing her eyes, Marguerite leaned her head back and fought the weight of depression and weariness that had grown more and more oppressive since the night she left Paris with de Grenier twenty-three years ago. "It is no comfort to me to see her so wan and unhappy," she whispered. "It is as if all the life in her died with Lysette. She should have been a wife by now. A mother. Yet she shows so little enthusiasm when courted, the gentlemen soon set their sights elsewhere."

"She used to be quite flirtatious, *oui*?"

"Very much so, but no longer. She is altered. I used to worry about her future; she seemed unable to be serious about anything. Now she is far too solemn about everything."

"I cannot imagine what it would be like to lose the person with whom you have spent the entirety of your life. A person who is identical to you. Perhaps, in truth, a piece of her is forever lost."

Hot tears leaked out from beneath Marguerite's closed lids. "I cannot lose both of my children. I can't bear it."

"*Mon amie . . .*"

Marguerite heard the goblet come to rest on a table, then the rustle of satin as her friend crossed the space between them to join her. She sank gratefully into the offered embrace, finding comfort in the physical closeness. She had been lonely for so long. The birth of her daughters had damaged her womb and prevented future conception. Her barren state had created a rift in her marriage that grew wider with every passing year.

"You are still deeply grieving. Is it any wonder that Lynette is also restrained by mourning?" Solange's delicate hand smoothed over Marguerite's unbound hair. "One of you must return to the land of the living, so that the other may follow."

"How can it be me?" Marguerite asked, wiping at her tears. "I ceased living long ago."

"You've returned to Paris. It is a start."

But it was not an easy one. Marguerite had been content in Poland, despite the gulf between her and de Grenier. There were no specters there, no temptations, no regrets. There were many things to haunt her here.

Straightening to a seated position, she reached for her friend's abandoned glass and downed the expensive contents in one desperate swallow. She inhaled deeply, relishing the sudden warmth brought by the burn of alcohol in her gut, then she glanced over her shoulder. "Tell me how."

"A party." Solange's pretty features transformed with a mischievous smile. The combination of a French mother and Italian father had given her an exotic attractiveness that made her much sought after. "It is no tame affair, I must tell you. Baroness Orlinda revels in bawdy, scandalous parties."

"I cannot take my daughter to an orgy!" Marguerite protested with wide eyes.

"Mon Dieu." Solange laughed her girlish giggle. "It is not so bawdy as that!"

"I do not believe you. Regardless, we cannot allow our presence in Paris to become known. It is too hazardous."

"After all these years, you are still afraid?"

"If you had seen the horror of that day, you would never forget."

"Do you love him still?"

"Everything I have done from that day to this one has been because of my love for Philippe."

Marguerite rose, her gaze roaming along the length of the room's red damask-covered walls. It was a space designed to startle and titillate with its gilded accents and exotic candle scents. Oddly, it

relaxed Marguerite to occupy it. There was no arti-
fice here. The purpose and appeal were clear, just
as it was with Solange.

Marguerite collected the empty glass and moved
over to the console, where several decanters waited.

"I think he still pines for you," Solange said.

Pausing midpour, Marguerite watched her hand
shake violently, an outward sign of the inward jolt
the news brought her. "What kind of woman would
that make me," she asked quietly, "if I wished that
were true?"

"An honest one."

Marguerite exhaled audibly, then continued to
refill the glass. "I am a married woman. I respect
my vows and my husband. It is why de Grenier
must not learn of our visit. He has sacrificed a
great deal for me. I will not have him concerned
that I cuckold him with a former lover."

"I understand. That is why I suggested the
baroness's gathering, which, I assure you, is no more
shocking than this boudoir. I doubt there will be
many of your former acquaintances in attendance.
You can assume another name and wear a mask as
added protection."

"That still does not address the impropriety of
taking my innocent daughter to a gathering of licentious revelry!" Marguerite returned Solange's
goblet to her, then set her hands on her hips.

"She is numb with grief and has been for two
years. Do you imagine jaunts to museums will wake
her?" Solange held up a jewel-encrusted hand to
halt any further protest. "Why don't you ask her if
she would like to attend?"

"Ridiculous!"

"Is it? If she says no, then nothing is lost. If she says yes, does that not imply that some of the Lynette of old still dwells in her? Would that not be worth one night of impropriety?"

Marguerite shook her head.

"Sleep on it," Solange suggested. "You may feel differently when rested."

"Saner, perhaps."

"Sanity, as defined by Society, is overrated, *non*?"

For a moment, Marguerite contemplated arguing further, then she turned about and poured herself a drink instead.

Chapter 5

"**M**r. Quinn."

A cool, tentative hand touched Simon's shoulder. Years of living under duress had made his valet's stealthy approach into the bedchamber impossible to overlook, but exhaustion kept Simon prone on the bed and unmoving.

He opened one eye and met the frown-capped gaze of the servant. The man was blushing. Most likely because of the woman lying beside Simon. With his head turned away, Simon could not be certain, but he would not be surprised if the lovely brunette was baring more of her lush body in slumber than she ever would while awake.

"You have a caller, Mr. Quinn."

"What time is it?"

"Seven."

"Bloody hell." He closed his eye, but he was fully aware now. He was not a man people visited to discuss inanities. "Unless they are ablaze or otherwise mortally wounded, tell whoever it is to return at a decent hour."

"I attempted to. He responded by moving a large quantity of trunks into one of the guest bedrooms."

Simon's eyelids lifted, as did his head. "Beg your pardon?"

"The Earl of Eddington has taken up residence here. He claims you would have it no other way."

"*Eddington?* What in hell is he doing in Paris?"

Careful not to wake his companion, Simon extricated himself from the mass of tangled bedclothes. He sat on the edge of the mattress, and waited for the spinning room to settle. A night of hard drinking and harder sex had left him with only an hour or two of sleep.

The valet shook his head, his gaze darting over Simon's shoulder.

Twisting at the waist, Simon glanced at his companion and found her sprawled lewdly in the very position she had been in when he last dismounted from her—legs spread wide with her fingers curled into the linens.

Apparently, he was not the only one exhausted.

He stood and caught up the counterpane, which had slipped off the end of the bed to puddle atop the carved wooden chest at the foot.

"I need a bath," he said as he covered the woman.

"I will see to it." The valet bowed and asked, "What should I tell his lordship?"

Simon straightened. "Tell him it's damned early and my mood suits my lack of sleep. He has been forewarned."

The servant choked and scurried from the room.

* * *

An hour later, bathed and dressed in a sapphire silk robe, Simon left his suite of rooms and descended the staircase to the foyer.

The early morning light streamed in through the decorative window above the front door, glimmering through the crystal chandelier to cast rainbow light upon the parquet floor. His hair was damp and his bare feet chilled despite the Aubusson runner that lined the stairs. The minor discomfiture kept him alert, which was the intent. Eddington was not a friend. There was no reason for the earl to decide to visit unannounced and uninvited so soon after Simon had left his employ.

Leastwise, no *welcome* reason.

Simon heard the sound of silverware making contact with china at the same moment a footman bowed to him and gestured toward the dining room.

"My lord," Simon greeted as he entered.

The earl looked at him and smiled. "Good morning, Quinn."

"Is it?" Simon moved to the walnut buffet, where covered salvers kept food warm. He briefly wondered what the cook had thought of the menu request. He could not remember the last time he had enjoyed morning fare, as he usually began with the midday meal. "I am not often awake at this time, so I've no notion of what constitutes a 'good' morning or not."

Eddington smiled and resumed eating, supremely casual and confident as if he owned the house he dined in. Like most members of the peerage, he assumed his surroundings were his to control.

"Personally," the earl drawled, "if I find myself

waking with an attractive woman beside me, I consider it a fine morning indeed."

Simon laughed and settled into a chair without a plate of food. The aromatic smells of eggs and kippers made his stomach revolt. He gestured for tea instead. "Why are you here?"

"May I eat first? The food on the ship left much to be desired."

Contemplating why the earl would come here of all places, Simon's gaze moved along the cloth-covered length of the table, then around the room. He frowned as he noted the miniscule floral pattern in the golden damask that covered the walls. He had never noted the flowers before and wasn't certain he liked them. "Can you not eat and speak at the same time?"

"Not while maintaining my dignity," the earl retorted.

Simon's examining perusal returned to his guest. The earl was a figure of some notoriety in England, lauded for his dark handsomeness and exquisite garments. Women flocked to him and he cultivated his libidinous reputation with relish. The nearly foppish façade was brilliantly affected to deflect suspicion. It was difficult to believe that a man so concerned with his appearance would have any time remaining to head an elite organization of English spies.

"I may return to bed, then," Simon said with more than a trace of irritation in his tone. He had no need to await anyone's regard.

"Very well." Eddington sighed and set his utensils down. "Privacy is in order."

Simon nodded to the servant who had poured his tea, then waved the man away. The two footmen by the entrance also retreated, closing the door behind them.

"Since you left Jacques and Cartland in my care," the earl began, "we've had the opportunity to question them at length. Both men have been extremely forthcoming, and Jacques, in particular, has a great deal of valuable information to share."

"How fortunate for you," Simon said dryly.

"Yes, but it also raises a great deal of questions. Mademoiselle Rousseau was traded for a dozen men. In addition to that expense, Jacques and Cartland were forfeited. We need to know why she is so important to the *Illuminés*."

Lysette.

Simon arched a brow. The woman would forever be in trouble of some sort or another. "*You* need to know," he corrected. "I do not care."

"You *will* care," the earl said, "once you understand the stakes involved."

"I highly doubt that. Regardless, it would be wiser for you to stay with someone else. Someone who has no known history of aiding the British Crown."

"But you may require my assistance." Eddington reclined insolently into the high-backed chair.

"With what?" Simon's hands wrapped tightly around the curved arms of his seat. "The only activity I am presently engaged in is carnal pursuit. I assure you, I can manage that task well enough on my own."

Eddington ignored the jibe. "You spent some time with Mademoiselle Rousseau, did you not?"

"Too much time."

"You tired of her?"

"We were never lovers, if that is your hope."

"By all accounts, she is quite lovely."

"Beautiful," Simon agreed, "and a bit touched. I like my bedsport wild, but sane."

"Interesting." Blue eyes narrowed. "Perhaps you could overlook her brain in favor of her body?"

"Perhaps you can fuck her yourself," Simon bit out. "Do not forget, my lord. I no longer work for you."

The earl smiled. "I have not forgotten."

"Good." With his mood souring by the moment, Simon pushed back from the table and stood. Putting distance between him and Eddington was suddenly of primary importance. There were very few things as dangerous as a politically minded, ambitious man. "Enjoy the house. I believe I will quit France in favor of Spain."

"You would be paid handsomely," Eddington offered.

"You do not understand." Simon set both hands palms-down atop the table. "Lysette is no fool. She knows I disdain her. If I approach her for sex, she would see straightaway that I had ulterior motives. There is no chance she would trust me."

"She might, if you tell her that you have been betrayed by those you once worked for. Tell her that your accounts have been seized, and you thirst for revenge and restitution."

Simon snorted. "Why in hell would she believe such a tale?"

"Because it's true?"

Shock held Simon frozen for the length of several heartbeats, then he growled, "Surely you would not be so imprudent."

"Desperate times lead to desperate measures." The earl maintained his leisurely pose, but Simon felt the tension in him. He knew he'd provoked a dangerous enmity. "England is beset on all sides. I would do anything to protect her."

"Spare me. This has nothing to do with the good of England and everything to do with your own lofty aspirations."

"If my aspirations are achieved by assisting my country, what harm is there in that?"

Simon's fist slammed into the table, rattling everything that rested upon it. Eddington flinched.

"What harm is there?" Simon barked. "You force me to risk my life when your own would do as well? You are comely enough. Why not manage the deed yourself?"

"I am at a disadvantage from the start. Since I lack even an introduction to Mademoiselle Rousseau, I have months of acclimation ahead of me. The same difficulty faces every other alternate I considered. I am left with no choice but you."

"Just as I have no choice?" Simon snapped. "You drag me into your mire with a smile."

Eddington attempted a more serious mien, but it was too late. Simon was infuriated as he had never been before. The whole of his life he had made every move by necessity, never having an option if he wanted to survive. The thought of finally achieving independence had been dear to him. Never looking over his shoulder, never fearing he would be discovered with something to hide.

. . . to be thrust back into that life against his will . . .

He realized he'd never had any power at all.

He should have followed Mitchell's example—gathered his coin, changed his name, and traveled to a distant land.

Although he collected his error too late, Simon was a man who lived by his wits. He never made the same mistake twice. Eddington had him on a leash now, but he would not always. When all was said and done, Simon intended to ensure that he was never under anyone's thumb again.

And Eddington would rue the day he set this plan in motion.

Pulling out his chair again, Simon sat. "Tell me everything you know."

Lynette turned back and forth before the mirror with wide eyes.

"I am not certain I possess the aplomb to carry this garment," she said, her gaze meeting Solange's reflected perusal.

"*Absurde.* You are a vision." Solange stood at her back, fluffing out the many layers of lace and shimmering blue-green silk. "You remind me of your mother when we first met."

It seemed not long ago that Lynette had enjoyed nothing so much as shopping (except, perhaps, flirting). Her modiste expenditures had been exorbitant, a fact her father often scolded her about. It could not be avoided, she used to say, pointing out how the richer colors and fabrics she favored were costlier than the pastels Lysette preferred.

The gown she presently wore would once have been a delight. The glorious color, accented with layers of gold lace and satin, was alluringly cut to accent her slender waist and full bosom. As she moved from side to side, the veriest hint of rosy areola peeked above the dangerously low bodice.

It was the garb of a seductress, a role she had once prided herself on aspiring to.

Now she felt her cheeks flushing and her hands tugged at the material trying to pull it into a less revealing position. She could not help but hear Lysette's admonishment that the brain was as much a sexual organ as the breasts and hips.

"You are more than beauty, Lynette," her sister would say.

"You are the brilliant one," Lynette would retort without heat. She loved her sister too much to compete with her. It was simply the way things were. Lysette was a creature of calculated reason; Lynette was more tactile and emotional.

At least she had been. She was not that girl any longer.

Since Lysette's passing, Lynette had taken to reading the many books her sister had left behind, finding comfort in the feeling of closeness the activity engendered. She also found comfort in the changes wrought by her new awareness of mortality. There had been so much remaining for Lysette to accomplish. Lynette—too long aimless and frivolous—realized that life was finite and she wished hers to be filled with more than mere flirtations and parties.

"You met *Maman* while visiting a modiste, did you not?" Lynette asked, gesturing for her mother's maid, Celie, to approach and undress her.

"Twirling before a mirror, just as you are doing now," Solange agreed, moving to her open armoire in search of another gown. "Of course, the attire she was fitted for that afternoon was not suitable for more than a lover's eyes."

For a moment, Lynette considered asking more

questions, then she shuddered and thought better of it. She did not want to think of her mother and father in carnal congress.

"How about this?" Solange asked, shaking out a pure white gown. It was lovely, if demure, with elbow-length sleeves and cream satin bows. "I commissioned this gown as a jest."

"A jest?"

"A paramour once protested the cost of my gowns, saying that he preferred me naked, therefore why should he pay to dress me?" Solange handed the gown to Celie. "I wore this to prove that garments can have various effects, depending on the wearer and the occasion."

Lynette studied the dress as she donned it, admiring the costly pearl accents. " 'Tis beautiful."

"I think so, too. Although I wore it only the one time." Solange stepped closer and set her hands on Lynette's shoulders. "You look a vision in white. Many women with your hair would be unable to forgo color; they would look pallid. Your skin, however, has a lovely rosy hue."

"Thank you."

Lynette thought it was just the sort of gown her sister would have worn. This impression was confirmed when a loud gasp from the doorway announced Marguerite's arrival.

Turning, Lynette faced her mother, wincing when she noted how pale she was. Still, the vicomtess managed a shaky smile. "You look lovely, Lynette."

"I look like Lysette."

"*Oui*. That, too." Marguerite approached in an elegant cloud of swaying blue satin and examined her daughter from head to toe. "Does this gown please you?"

"Of course, *Maman*. I would not choose it otherwise."

"As long as you are happy," Marguerite said. Then she gave a shaky laugh. "I am slowly adjusting to this new woman you have become."

"She is not completely changed," Solange pointed out gently. "She is quite eager to attend the baroness's ball."

Lynette nodded and smiled wide, hoping to relieve her mother's melancholy. "I would not miss it for anything. I have heard tales of such events, but never thought to attend one."

"*Mon Dieu.*" Marguerite winced. "De Grenier will think I've gone mad if he hears of this."

"He won't," Lynette assured her, walking to Solange's bed, where a proliferation of masks were laid out. The array of colors, ribbons, and feathers was impressive. Her gaze raked over the lot and settled upon a half-mask of crimson silk. Scooping it up, she held it aloft. "My face will be covered with this."

For the space of a breath, there was silence, then the vicomtess's face lit up with a genuine grin. "That is just the color I would have picked for you!"

Solange reached over and squeezed Marguerite's hand. "It will be great fun for all of us. And the baroness has admirable taste in men."

Marguerite snorted. "No man attending such an event would be suitable for my daughter."

Lynette hid a smile, briefly thinking of the man on horseback and others like him whom she had met over the years. Dark and dangerous. Delicious. As much as grief had changed her, that was one thing that remained the same.

"I see that smile," her mother accused.

But there was a sparkle in Marguerite's blue eyes that had been absent for years.

It warmed Lynette from the inside. Perhaps the time for healing had finally begun.

From the shadowed depths of the parked carriage, Lysette studied the man strolling briskly down the street.

The flow of carts and pedestrians was steady, often impeding her view. Regardless, Edward James was difficult to miss due to the purposefulness of his stride. He moved through the milling crowd with ease, his hand touching the brim of his hat repeatedly as he greeted those he passed.

Tall and almost slender, Mr. James was definitely of the bookish variety of male, yet he was blessed with a confident bearing and long, muscular legs. His hair was a lustrous brown, nothing extraordinary but not lamentable either. The color of his ensemble was a dark green that was more sensible than noteworthy. His garments were nicely tailored and well maintained, though inexpensive. In short, Edward James was an average man leading an average life . . . if not for his employer.

"Did you study the notes I provided you?" Desjardins asked from his seat opposite her.

"Naturellement."

Mr. James led a quiet life. He spent his free time reading or visiting with friends. While he occasionally accompanied Mr. Franklin to elevated social events, he was said to be subdued, yet charming on those occasions, displaying no signs of avarice or a surfeit of ambition.

"James appears to have no aspirations," the comte

said with obvious disdain. "It is hard to lure a man to vice when you do not know what motivates him."

"I agree."

"That is why we must provide the motivation."

Lysette watched Mr. James disappear from view into a shop. "And what will that be?"

"Love."

Her brows rose and she glanced at him. "For *me*?"

"Of course."

"Your faith is touching," she murmured, "but misplaced. No one has ever loved me."

"I love you." Desjardins smiled when she snorted. "Beyond that, you cannot say for a certainty, can you? You have no recollection."

"If I had been loved, someone would have come for me." Her fists clenched. "Someone would have searched until they found me."

"I gave up fourteen men for you, *ma petite*. Is that not love?"

For himself, perhaps. She served a purpose, that was all.

"Are we here for a reason?" she asked crossly, irritated by the feeling of being a pawn. "Or are we merely spying?"

"I want you to cross paths with him." Desjardins rapped on the roof to signal their intent to alight.

"And then?" She was often fascinated by the workings of the comte's mind. It was the one thing about him that she admired.

"Then you will continue on your way and I will appear. I shall offer him a chance to indulge his fascination."

The carriage door opened and the comte stepped down first, then extended his hand to her.

"Fascination?" she queried, pausing in the doorway.

"With you. After he sees you, thoughts of you will linger with him all day. He will be desperate to see you again."

"And what chance for indulgence do you have in mind?" She took his hand and stepped carefully down to the street.

"Baroness Orlinda is having a fête this evening."

"But . . ." Her eyes widened. "What of Depardue's associates? You know it is not wise for me to be too visible!"

"It will be a brief sojourn, and visibility is not our aim. We want him to pursue you, not find you easily."

"He will not enjoy such a gathering," she pointed out, "if your study of him is correct."

As Lysette shook out her skirts, she tried to imagine the understated James enjoying the shocking revelry of an Orlinda party and failed. She also searched inwardly for any feelings of guilt and found only determination. James was her last impediment to freedom. Desjardins had promised her emancipation, if she could succeed in gaining information about Franklin through his secretary.

"No, he will be uncomfortable, as you will be." Desjardins smiled. "You will suggest departing and James—already enamored with you from your meeting this morning—will arrange to take you away. That will begin a series of shared memories that will build the foundation of your romance."

"Or so you hope."

"Trust me." The comte kissed her on the temple and gave her a gentle push. "I will join you in a few moments."

Straightening her shoulders and steeling her resolve, Lysette looked both ways, then weaved through the carts traversing the busy thoroughfare. Her focus narrowed, a huntress closing in for the kill. Because of this preoccupation with her quarry, she did not notice the Irishman who lounged insolently within the recessed entryway of a nearby merchant.

But then, Simon Quinn had spent the entirety of his life perfecting the art of fading into shadows. It was a skill that had saved his life many times.

"Poor bastard," Simon muttered, commiserating with the unfortunate Mr. James.

He watched Lysette assume a casual stance before a shop window, then he straightened. From his vantage, he'd heard enough to begin a hunt of his own.

Tugging down his tricorn, he passed Desjardins's unmarked equipage and set off toward the Baroness Orlinda's residence. Months ago, he'd met the lovely baroness while playing a game of cards and they had struck up a flirtation. She would be pleased to learn that he had returned to France.

And he would be pleased to attend her ball.

Through a storefront reflection, Lysette watched Mr. James approach. He appeared distracted—his head was bent and his lips moved as if he spoke to himself. Beneath one arm, he carried a wrapped bundle. He raised his other hand to adjust his spectacles for a better fit.

She waited until he was nearly behind her, then she stepped back abruptly, placing herself directly in his path. He hit her with the force of a falling bag of rice, hard and impossible to withstand. She cried out in surprise, stumbling, nearly falling. Distantly, she heard him curse under his breath, then she was snatched close with such speed and strength that she lost her breath.

"Are you all right, mademoiselle?" he asked, startling her anew with the sound of his voice. It was deep and slightly rumbling.

Clinging to his sinewy forearms, Lysette lifted a hand to straighten her skewed hat and found herself gazing raptly up into his face.

He was scowling, and glancing up and down the street. Still, his profile arrested her. His jaw was square and strong, his skin kissed by the sun. The knot of his cravat was simple, yet perfect.

To add to her already overwhelming astonishment, James seemed completely unaffected by their public embrace. Truly, he appeared to have forgotten she was there. He stepped back and released her, bringing her attention to the fact that he had dropped his purchases in order to catch her.

Lysette sensed that the time when she could capture his attention was nearly at an end. She acted on instinct, reaching out and sliding her hand between his coat and waistcoat, her palm pressing firmly over his heart.

"Forgive me," she breathed. "I am so clumsy."

James's hand caught her wrist in a lightning-quick movement, his head swiveling to face her, revealing astonished brown eyes behind his brass-rimmed spectacles. She could see the moment when he became aware of her as an individual woman, rather than merely an anonymous intrusion into his path.

As she gazed into his luxuriously lashed eyes, Lysette realized how hard he felt beneath her hand. She gave a tentative squeeze and a dark rumble vibrated beneath her touch.

"I was not minding my direction," he said, pulling her hand away. He lifted it to his lips and kissed the back. "Edward James."

"Corinne Marchant." She smiled and he flushed slightly, the crest of his cheekbones darkening with high color.

That response soothed her jangled nerves slightly.

"It is a pleasure to meet you," James said. "Although I would have preferred to introduce myself in a more refined manner."

In any other instance, she would have flirted more heavily; perhaps she would have said the collision was worth it in order to meet him. But Mr. James was not the type of man women lured in that manner. He was too . . . *intense* for such play. He was also lacking the very qualities that enticed women to try and win a man's regard. He was in trade and he was not handsome.

So she backed up to a more appropriate distance and busied herself with resettling her hat back into its former jaunty angle. "I am a featherhead to have been so absorbed in a pair of shoes."

His gaze narrowed on her, then he turned his head to look at the slippers she referenced. Pale pink and studded with diamonds, the cost for such detailed craftsmanship was unquestionable.

"No one would notice such extravagance when worn by a woman so lovely as you," he said gruffly. "They would not be looking at your feet."

Lysette smiled. The compliment was difficult for

him to voice, which made it all the more charming. "Thank you."

She was not sure why he did not move away. His eyes were not lit with the masculine appreciation she was accustomed to seeing. Instead he examined her, as if she were an anomaly he wished to classify. His dropped package rested at his feet, but he seemed in no hurry to reclaim it. Pedestrians brushed past them as they completed their errands, yet he seemed not to be aware of any of them.

Afraid that her unabashed perusal of him was causing the suspicion, she tilted her head and said, "I hope the rest of your afternoon is less eventful."

James bowed slightly. "And yours as well."

They parted. As she walked away, she did not feel him looking after her. Curious, and hoping that if he sighted her glancing back at him, it would spark interest, she paused and turned. Edward James was striding away briskly.

Shrugging, she continued on to Desjardins's carriage to wait.

Chapter 6

The Baroness Orlinda was infamous for the scope and grandeur of her bawdy gatherings. Still, Simon was fairly certain that tonight's mythological theme would be difficult to surpass in sheer audacity and imagination.

The large ballroom was littered with potted trees and bushes to re-create the feeling of being in a forest. The four sets of French doors leading out to the balcony were thrown wide, allowing the evening breeze and the splashing sounds of the massive courtyard fountain to waft in. Sheer blue panels were draped between select pillars, simulating an afternoon sky and providing clever shielding for the occasional hidden chaise. Even the servants were dressed to enhance the mood, their bodies draped in white linen and their heads crowned with rings of leaves. The air was redolent with the scent of exotic candles and filled with the flirtatious laughter of reveling guests.

Simon found the whole affair highly diverting,

yet he did not partake. He was not one to enjoy providing voyeuristic entertainment and his fouled mood from the morning continued into the evening. The sensation of being a puppet on Eddington's strings was not a pleasant one. More than ever, Simon wanted to start anew and find a calling that soothed his restless spirit.

Perhaps his age was wearing on him. Where once he'd found his livelihood and its lack of structure to be liberating, now he found it stifling. He had no home, no roots, no family. He could do nothing about the latter things, but he could purchase a home. Ireland called to him, as it did to all her sons. If he reclaimed his wealth and rid himself of Eddington, he could return to her verdant shores and establish the roots denied him by his parentage.

A sharp trill of feminine laughter drew his gaze to a draped alcove where two women watched an amorous couple make use of a convenient chaise. From there his gaze roamed in a slow sweep of the ballroom, searching for Lysette, Desjardins, or the unfortunate Mr. James. The riot of colors on display was distracting, as was the creativity displayed in the masks most guests wore. It was odd that such a small shield could create the feeling of anonymity, but there was no denying that it did. Many of the guests in attendance would show much more restraint were they to expose their faces to view. And censure.

As he looked toward the main entrance to the ballroom, Simon stilled. An angel peaked out from behind a large fern, her pearlescent gown glimmering with the glow of blazing candlelight.

Watching him.

She stiffened when he spotted her, then side-stepped into full view. A silent challenge.

You may have found me, her pose said, *but I am not ashamed to be caught staring.*

Simon grinned.

Lysette.

Unwigged, her golden tresses were instantly recognizable, as were the enticing curves of her figure.

Then he frowned, confused.

She was . . . different; he could sense that straightaway. There was an air of expectation about her, a vibrating excitement that he detected from across the room. He had seen her become enlivened by only two things: death and drama. And truly, that had been more akin to morbid glee.

Then there was the mask she wore . . .

Crimson. Vibrant. He would never have chosen that color for her. In the months they had spent together, she had worn either pastels or dark colors. Lysette did not like to attract attention, a wise predilection when one's livelihood consisted of secrets and lies.

Intrigued, Simon moved to a nearby pillar and leaned his shoulder against it. He smiled. She froze. He imagined her breath caught, a guess reinforced when her lips parted on a gasp. Her reaction and the subtle alteration of her stance were further curiosities.

She was attracted to him.

He watched her return his stare with unabashed frankness, which was not surprising. She had always challenged and annoyed him deliberately. Yet now, that did not appear to be her aim. Lysette's hands rubbed nervously at the sides of her gown, her breasts lifted and fell with rapid breaths, her tongue stroked like a lover's caress along her full bottom lip. All the while she looked at *him*. Rarely blinking, as if entranced.

Long minutes passed, yet he could not look away. She was a vision of heaven and hell, a devilish angel who apparently could fascinate men at will.

The question was: Why did she decide to fascinate him now?

And there was no denying that he was fascinated.

His smile faltered as his body tensed. Bloody hell. What was she doing? More to the point, what was she doing to *him*? The woman had bluntly offered him sex once and he had felt no interest at all. Now, he was fighting the urge to snatch her close and claim that lush mouth he'd previously found incapable of more than frustrating him.

There had always been an invisible cloak around her that discouraged intrusion. *Stay away*, it said, and he'd been only too happy to oblige. Now the mantle she wore was an enticing one. *Surprise me*, it whispered. *Thrill me*. The change was drastic. Wariness turned to eager anticipation.

It seduced him. *She* was seducing him.

Her perusal was heating his skin, creating the urge to shift uncomfortably, which he refused to do.

Her assignment was to lure Mr. James, damn her. Why, then, was she luring him instead?

The only way to find out was to ask her.

He straightened abruptly and strode toward her

in a direct path, his purpose so determined that other guests moved out of his way.

"Mademoiselle."

His voice came out lower, more intimate than he had intended, and she shivered, a sure sign of her cognizance of the growing sensual awareness between them.

"Mr. Quinn," she greeted in return, her voice husky and inviting.

As his blood thickened, Simon's gaze narrowed. He caught her elbow abruptly and pulled her toward the exit. Wisely, she did not protest.

He led her through the crowd and down a hallway, opening a closed door and pushing her ahead of him into the room. The interior was dark, and for a moment, her resemblance to an angel was magnified by the contrast of her white gown in the darkened room.

Lysette stepped farther into the large, liberally furnished library. Simon entered behind her, aroused by the exotic scent of her skin, a new fragrance he'd never smelled on her before.

He was infuriated by her effect on him. Despite his doubting of his sanity and his wariness of her motives, he was hot for her. The feeling of acting outside of his will was too similar to his situation with Eddington.

He pushed the door closed and the latch clicked into place, securing them alone together.

"What game are you playing?" he asked gruffly.

As the unmistakable sounds of sexual congress reached her ears, Lysette altered the use of her fan from a shield to its intended purpose, that of cooling her heated cheeks.

She stood in the far corner of the Orlinda ballroom, her back to the wall, her front shielded by a fern. As far as hiding places went, it was superb. She had a clear view of the main entrance to the ballroom, yet no one could see her unless they came within a few feet. The only reason for Edward James's attendance would be to see her again. He would seek her out. *If* he came.

Lysette doubted he would. When Desjardins related the details of his conversation with James, it did not sound hopeful. James had been dismissive of such entertainments and claimed to be too busy to spare the time. The comte was certain the protests were no more than tokens. He claimed James had appeared flustered and distracted.

"I think that is his normal deportment," she argued. "He seemed to find me interesting in the way one would a pretty butterfly—fleeting and not the least bit absorbing."

"We shall see," Desjardins said smugly. "I am rarely in error about such things."

So here she was, concealed in a corner of the crowded ballroom to avoid unwanted attention, forced to listen to the sounds of an overly amorous couple.

Although she knew that many considered lovemaking to be pleasant, she could not agree. It was painful and degrading at worst. Unsavory at best. It was an invasion, an act of domination. She could not collect why some women enjoyed it. She assumed it was the thought of possible tangible gain, for a happy man was often a generous man.

As the moaning intensified, Lysette cringed, feeling painfully awkward despite being armored in her favorite pale yellow gown. The sleeves were longer and the bodice higher than current fashion dictated, yet it was undeniably a lovely confection. She had hoped it would deter those seeking easy sport, but it appeared that mere attendance was a statement of willingness.

"Mademoiselle Marchant."

The deep, coarse rumble of James's voice rippled down her back like heated water, sensual and saturating.

She pivoted with wide eyes, startled by his stealthy approach. It had been a long time since anyone caught her unawares.

Her mouth curved in a genuine smile. "Mr. James, what a pleasant surprise."

He wore an evening ensemble of blue velvet so dark it was nearly black. His cravat was once again modestly tied, yet perfect. He was wigged, but the style was simple. His mouth was hard, his gaze harder. She should have been intimidated by such severity or frightened by his intensity. Instead she felt a different kind of stirring. Something hotter, more disturbing.

"Why are you here?" he asked.

Lysette blinked. "Beg your pardon?"

"You do not wish to be here."

"What gives you that impression?"

"I have been watching you squirm for the last ten minutes."

A laugh escaped her. "Why not approach me?"

"Answer my question first."

"I felt compelled to come."

His dark eyes narrowed behind his spectacles. She grinned, beginning to enjoy his examining perusals. He was confused by his fascination with her, and she suspected he did not enjoy it.

"I have no notion of why I am here," he murmured.

"Should we leave?" she suggested, wondering if her assignment could be so easily won. Perhaps Desjardins was correct about Mr. James.

"What would we do?" There was danger in his voice, warning.

"You assume I meant for us to leave together."

A flush spread across the crests of his cheekbones. "What is the comte to you?"

"Is this an inquisition?" she drawled.

"A lover?"

Lysette stiffened. "You are too bold." She turned away, her heart racing with the mad hope that he would chase her.

She was not disappointed.

The clicking of his heels upon marble was impatient, reckless. He caught her arm and tugged her back, yanking her behind the fern, rather than beside it. When she gaped at him, his lips tightened into a thin white line.

"Why did he go to so much trouble to pair us here?"

Lysette's brows rose. "Perhaps he thinks I am in need of a man-of-affairs since my husband passed."

James's eyes burned with an inner fire. "I am not for sale."

"What an odd thing to say." The beat of her heart leaped into a mad rhythm. Nothing in Desjardins's notes could have prepared her for Edward James.

"Nevertheless, it is true," he said briskly. His hands flexed around her forearms, kneading.

"What a relief to have dismissed that misapprehension," she whispered, her voice husky from the heat of the air around them.

"I have a different theory," James rumbled. "One more suited to this venue."

"Do I wish to hear it?" Becoming short of breath, she stepped back, half afraid he would restrain her. There was an air of frustration and determination about him that seemed to brook no refusal. But her fears were groundless. The moment she pulled away, he released her.

"I am not what you want me to be."

Lysette forced her lips to curve in a careless smile. "This grows more intriguing by the moment."

"I do not provide stud service," he snapped.

"Well," she swallowed hard, "that is probably wise, considering your charm leaves much to be desired. You might starve to death if that were your occupation."

The glittering of his dark eyes should have alerted her. But frankly, she had not even considered him *capable* of grabbing her and kissing her senseless. When he did—arching her back over his forearms, mantling her body with his larger one—she lay motionless for too long, shocked by the feel of his firm mouth on hers. Though his approach had been rough, his kiss was not. It was as perfect and deliberate as his clothing.

Then, shock solidified into fear. Her lungs seized, cutting off her air. She struggled and pushed at his shoulders. Then bit his lower lip.

James released her with a curse, nostrils flaring,

mouth bleeding. He radiated lust and the need to dominate, two things that were highly dangerous when mixed, as she knew all too well.

Lysette struck him full on his cheek.

"If you ever lay a hand on me again," she bit out, "I will sever it."

The blow turned his head not at all, though a reddened imprint betrayed the force of the hit and his spectacles were askew. She set off at a near run, crossing the ballroom in a diagonal direction toward the door, pushing through those who stood in her way.

This time, no footsteps followed her and she burst out to the gallery with a gasp of relief. She turned on her heel and moved toward the front foyer, determined to send a footman in search of a hackney. The hallway was dimly lit on purpose, another affectation to lend to the sensual atmosphere. She relished the near-darkness, finding comfort in the anonymity it afforded.

"Lysette."

She paused at the sound of her name. It was said in a murmur, but it was audible even over her labored breathing. Spinning, she faced Desjardins as he exited the ballroom, his thin frame backlit with the light of the ballroom's chandeliers.

"Where are you going?"

"Home. You had better find someone else to woo Mr. James. Someone who prefers boorish manners and lack of finesse."

To her chagrin, the comte threw his head back and laughed. *"Ma petite,"* he said, approaching her with a wide smile, "you are a delight."

When he reached her, he linked his arm with hers. "You are far too agitated. You should take a moment to collect yourself while I will order the carriage brought around."

Lysette stood unmoving. She could not believe Desjardins was not insisting she return to the ballroom.

"Come now," he said, linking arms with her and leading her back down the darkened hallway toward the retiring rooms. "You know my carriage is far more comfortable—and cleaner—than a hackney."

There was no protest she could make to that. As it was, she had failed to satisfy his request for her help. Inhaling sharply, she nodded her agreement and disengaged to continue on without him. Her nerves were stretched taut, and when her rapid stride threatened to overtake a couple ahead of her, she slipped into an alcove, reluctant to witness another amorous pairing.

As they disappeared into a private room, Lysette briefly admired the beauty of the woman's pure white gown, which glimmered in the low lighting. The modest cut along with the feminine bows was just the sort of design she favored. The male half of the couple was dressed in dark colors, his body blending into the surrounding shadows. Lysette admired the woman's daring in retreating alone with a large man. Lord knew she could not have done it. A mere kiss had sent her fleeing.

When she was once again alone, she withdrew from concealment and slipped into a retiring room, eager to restore her bearings and return to the safety of her house.

* * *

Desjardins watched Lysette walk away and laughed silently. He did not believe he had ever seen her so flustered. And Mr. James . . . Who knew the staid exterior restrained such passion? Of course, that was why the comte enjoyed spying. There were so many things people would do in private that they would never do in public.

Sadly, Depardue had ensured that Lysette would never appreciate the amorous attentions of a man. Certainly not attentions with the fervency James had displayed in the ballroom.

But there was a solution. Lysette felt a deep sense of obligation when someone did her a kindness. Every unsavory act she had committed for him over the last two years had been because he'd taken her away from Depardue and his men. If he could orchestrate a way for James to rescue Lysette from some hazard or another, she would be grateful to the man and forgive him many of his foibles. However, it would have to be a grave matter in order to make the attachment deep enough to facilitate sex.

Since the stakes involved with corrupting James included Desjardins's own viability, the comte considered it suitably worthy of his next drastic action.

He moved down the hallway to the retiring rooms. On the wall behind him, a turned-down oil lamp cast barely enough glow to act as a beacon. He glanced both ways to ensure he was alone, then he spilled the oil down the wall to pool between the stained wood trim and the edge of the burgundy and gold runner. He set the corner of his kerchief ablaze and dropped it in the direct path of the spreading puddle.

Desjardins was whistling as he walked away, inwardly applauding his own genius. He jumped when the oil caught fire, the sudden whoosh of combustion loud in the stillness of the hallway. He hurried toward the ballroom to find James, his pathway lit by the orange glow of flames behind him.

Simon did not understand how one moment Lysette was standing across the room and the other she was sprawled between his legs, her mouth moving with checked hunger beneath his. He did not comprehend why she was so very different tonight or why that alteration had such a potent impact on him.

He only knew that he was hard and aching, his heartbeat thundering, his skin damp with sweat. He wanted her, with the innate need one felt for food and water.

"Why now?" he asked, nibbling his way to her ear.

She wrapped her arms around his shoulders and bared her throat. He pressed his open mouth to the tender skin and sucked gently.

In response, she writhed against his throbbing cock, inciting his lust to greater heights. "Mr. Quinn . . ."

He chuckled, enjoying the game. "Who knew you burned so hotly beneath all that ice?"

"Kiss me again," she begged, her throaty voice inspiring thoughts of her twisting and arching beneath him in his bed, the kiss she pleaded for being bestowed to more intimate lips.

"We must leave, before I lift your skirts and take you here."

If his desire had been even a modicum less, he would fuck her right here, right now, and clear his mind enough to take her home. As it was, he was familiar with the need that rode him so hard. Rare as it was, it was still recognizable.

Once he started, he would be at her all night.

"No—"

He suckled her lower lip to stem any protest and her lush body rested more fully against his. "Then let us retire to a more private venue, Lysette. Before lust rules my better sense."

She stiffened against him, apparently becoming aware of how impatient he was. She pulled back with a frown, her eyes wide and glittering in the near darkness. Her mouth opened to speak, then her head swiveled to the side, her gaze locking on the door.

"Do you smell that?" she asked, pushing against his chest to put distance between them.

Simon inhaled deeply, searching for the scent of exotic lilies. Instead, he smelled acrid smoke. It took a heartbeat's length of time for the danger that odor implied to penetrate the haze of carnal hunger. At the exact moment he realized it, a scream from the ballroom confirmed his fear.

"Hell's teeth!" He leaped to his feet, steadying Lysette before he ran to the door.

The flickering orange glow visible through the gaps around the portal was ominous. Simon reached for the glass knob, then yanked his hand away with a curse.

"If I was not gloved," he said, turning to face Lysette, who was securing her mask to her face, "I would be burned. The fire is directly outside the door."

"*Mon Dieu.* What will we do?"

He found the question an odd one, coming from a woman so well versed in subterfuge, but he had no time to contemplate it. "The window."

"What of the others?" She followed him without hesitation.

"They have the doors to the garden." The multitude of screams from the ballroom bore witness to the guests' cognizance of the blaze.

Simon thumbed the window lock and pushed up the sash, poking his head outside to ensure the way was clear. Overgrown spearmint lined the flowerbed that bordered the house, an innocuous landing. The air was clear and cool, which contrasted sharply with the smoke rapidly filling the library they occupied. "Give me your hand."

He glanced over his shoulder, his brows rising when he saw her searching under her gown with both hands. When her panniers and underskirts fell to rest at her feet, he smiled. Pragmatic Lysette. He suddenly found the trait admirable, rather than coldhearted.

She set her hand in his and managed a tense smile. "Would you find it strange for me to say that I am glad I was with you when this happened?"

With a tug, he pulled her into him, pressing his lips to hers in a quick, hard kiss. "You can show me how much later."

He helped her out, holding her hands in his until he was certain she was settled firmly on the ground. Then, he tossed one leg over the sill and prepared to follow.

A woman's panicked scream arrested him midegress, knotting his gut with commiserating fear.

This one sounded closer to his location than the ballroom. Much closer. Simon glanced again at the door, scrambling to think of a way to reach whomever he heard.

There was no way. His eyes were watering, his lungs were burning. There were only two exits from the room—the door, now bowing from the heat, and the windows, one of which he was hanging outside of. He would have to search from the exterior of the manse.

With this thought in mind, Simon dropped out of the window, landing in a crouch amid the profusion of mint. After the polluted air in the library, the crisp scent was a welcome relief.

He looked around for Lysette, but she was gone, most likely to join the others. He was glad, relieved that she was safe.

Freed from his concern for her, Simon ran along the wall in search of others who might need rescue.

Chapter 7

"Vexing woman," Edward muttered as he descended the front steps of the Orlinda manse. He had hoped to leave Corinne Marchant behind, but she remained with him—the feel of her in his arms, the sweetly floral scent of her, the sting of her palm against his cheek.

And the way she spoke to him . . .

"Contrary female." His fists clenched along with his jaw.

He almost reconsidered his decision to walk home in lieu of splurging on a hackney. Although a long walk would clear his mind and take the edge off his lust, a carriage would put greater distance between him and Corinne in a shorter amount of time. Distance that might temper the urge to go back inside and apologize. The itch to charm her properly and win her regard was nearly overwhelming.

Despite knowing her motives were impure, he wanted to scratch that itch.

There was no possibility that her interest was genuine. She was too beautiful, too wealthy, too well connected to find anything noteworthy about him—other than his work for Mr. Franklin.

It was not the first time he had been approached as a gateway to Franklin. It was, however, the first time he considered allowing it to happen for personal gain.

As his feet hit the front drive, his pace increased. His conscience told him to put any thoughts of a possible liaison between himself and Corinne far from his mind. If he did not seek her out, he doubted she would approach him again. The thought caused a sharp pang of regret.

"Damn you."

He had never seen a woman more lovely. She had the face of an angel and a body built for sin. If anyone asked him to describe his epitome of perfection, he would point to Corinne Marchant. But that was not the problem. He could resist the lure of the flesh; his cock did not rule his head.

No, it was not the drive to rut with beauty that drove him mad. It was her eyes. So hard at moments, as if she had lost all feeling. Then, suddenly warm and lit with wry amusement. Some part of him believed he was responsible for those glimpses of the private woman. Those ephemeral sightings made him want to see more of her, all of her.

Edward growled. He was used to having what he wanted. A modest man, he rarely wanted much and never anything beyond his means. The attraction he felt toward Corinne defied reason. They had nothing in common. What was the lure?

She was damaged. The bruised and haunted look that wracked her features after he'd kissed her bespoke deep scarring.

Someone had abused her terribly.

Fury coiled tight within him. Her past was no deterrent. Instead, it made him want her more. The desire to protect her was as powerful as the desire to mate with her. He wanted rights to her. More precisely, he wanted the right to find those responsible and mete out the justice they deserved for damaging such perfection.

Dangerous thoughts, dangerous feelings. They had no place in his regimented and orderly life, just as Corinne had no place there.

A scream rent the night, one so filled with terror it stopped him midstride.

He turned to face the manse again, seeing nothing amiss from the front, but certain the sound had emanated from there. He was frowning at the elegant, columned façade when more screams disturbed the peaceful eventide. He set off at a run.

The liveried footmen and groomsmen standing at the front drive left their stations and sprinted up the stairs before him. The moment the door opened, thick, black smoke roiled out. The four servants paused on the threshold, gaping.

"Fetch buckets from the stables!" Edward ordered.

"Yes, sir." The two groomsmen ran back down the stairs and around the side.

He shouldered his way in front of the remaining horrified footmen. "You two, come with me. We must make certain everyone vacates the house."

Together, they plunged into the wall of smoke. Intolerable heat assailed them, the flames fed by the newly opened door. Struggling to see through watering eyes, Edward drew in a choked breath and stumbled as scorching, soot-filled air burned his throat and singed his lungs.

He was suffocating by the time they reached the ballroom, a journey hampered by the need to feel along the wall to find their way. They split up when they reached their destination, groping their way through the many planters and columns in search of anyone yet to flee. Black smoke rolled in through the doorway behind them in ever-expanding plumes. It tumbled across the soaring ceiling and began to lower in a malevolent cloud. Edward's heart raced madly, his hands swiping impatiently at the tears that stung his heat-sensitized cheeks.

Surely Corinne would be safe. She'd left when he did. She was most likely home now, cursing him to Hades.

Thank God. He would be insane if she was here.

"Mr. James! Mr. James!"

Edward altered course, moving in the direction of the hoarse, unrecognizable voice calling out to him. A moment later, Comte Desjardins lurched into view from the depths of the cloying, burning smoke. His thin frame was wracked by violent coughing and he lunged at Edward, catching him by the shoulders.

"Corinne," the comte gasped, his reddened eyes glistening with near-hysteria. "Is she with you?"

A chill swept down Edward's spine, in spite of the intense heat. "No, she left."

"Are you certain? S-she was . . . to ride with me—" Desjardins coughed so forcibly that black spittle coated his lips. ". . . retiring room . . ." he wheezed. ". . . have not seen her . . ."

"Dear God."

Edward grabbed the comte's arm and dragged him out to the terrace, where the rest of the guests gathered. Then, he ran around the side of the manse, searching for windows with light, fighting a rising panic that threatened to paralyze him.

A woman in white stood outside an open window from which tendrils of smoke wafted.

"Go to the others," he ordered. "On the rear lawn."

She hesitated, her masked face gazing up at the window.

"Now!" he barked, in a tone no sane person refused.

Nodding reluctantly, the masked woman lifted her skirts and moved toward the rear of the house. Edward heard a distant scream at the same moment a masculine leg appeared over the sill. Assured of the safety of the woman's paramour, he darted for the side gate.

No Corinne. Where in hell was she?

Edward sprinted around the front of the manse and burst through the gate on the other side, narrowly skirting the stairs that led down to the delivery entrance. He was halfway along the length of the manse when he spotted Desjardins gesturing frantically before a window.

"Is she in there?" Edward rasped through his burned throat, skidding to a halt.

He studied the window through gritty eyes. Shadows danced sinuously against the glass.

Smoke. Too much of it. He could not see into the room.

"I saw movement," the comte croaked. "Perhaps—"

The window exploded outward in a shower of broken glass, forcing them to duck beneath crossed forearms. A chair crashed to the ground with a splintering thud and smoke poured out the newly created orifice. A second later, flames that had been hugging the ceiling of the room lunged for the night air, licking outward along the manse walls.

"Corinne!" Edward roared.

The only reply was the crackle of fire eating everything in its path. After the initial burst of oxygen-starved flames, the blaze retreated back into the room, spurring him into action.

Edward spun around and caught up the damaged chair. With a mighty heave, he thrust the cracked rear legs into the flower bed and supported the padded damask back against the manse wall. He shrugged out of his coat and wrapped it around his forearm, then climbed atop the wobbly seat.

"Corinne!" he yelled, his damaged lungs seizing in protest.

Turning his head away to protect his face, Edward used his shielded arm to knock away the jagged glass that rimmed the broken sash frame. One thick piece was too firmly anchored and it sliced through his coat, shirtsleeves, and into the flesh beneath. He hissed, but refused to turn away.

"Corinne!"

Her precious face appeared, streaked with soot and trailed with tears. Corinne's pale hair clung to her reddened skin in sweat-soaked tendrils and her nose ran copiously.

He had never seen anything so lovely.

"Christ," he gasped, near dizzy with relief. "Come out of there."

"James," she whispered, her shoulders coming into view as she pushed weakly to her feet.

Admiration for her strength filled him. He knew how much it must have taxed her to break the glass.

"Yes, love. Come to me." He held his arms out to her.

She swayed haphazardly and toppled out the window in a dead faint, her voluminous skirts catching in the protruding shards of the broken pane and tearing with a hideous rending noise.

Edward caught her and tumbled off the collapsing chair, twisting his body to absorb the entirety of the impact on his back. The breath was knocked from his beleaguered lungs. His spectacles were knocked from his head and, if he was not mistaken, presently crushed beneath him, but Corinne was in his arms, alive.

For now. She required the care of a physician immediately. Every breath she took rattled in her lungs and bubbled back out in black ooze upon her bloodless lips.

Coughing through his charred throat, Edward accepted the comte's minimal assistance to regain his footing with Corinne held securely in his arms.

He gathered the tattered remnants of her gown and strode quickly toward the front of the house.

Simon raced toward the rear of the manse. He had checked every window as he passed it, searching for the source of the scream he'd heard just moments ago. He could not reach her through the door, but perhaps he could find her still. He had to try.

The clanging of bells carried news of the fire

through the city. The night air smelled of char and heat, and sobbing told the tale of woe that ended an event meant for revelry.

He reached the rear lawn and saw a handful of servants running to and fro with sloshing buckets of water from the stables. The stunned and terrified guests huddled in various-sized groups, paralyzed and useless.

"Halt!" Simon roared, his voice carrying through the night.

The servants paused, gasping, their buckets more than half-empty from the jostling required to cover the distance from the mew to the manse.

Simon gained the terrace, then leaped atop the wide marble edge of the fountain.

"They cannot battle this blaze alone," he yelled, gesturing to the servants. "Every able-bodied man must assist if we are to end this! There are others trapped inside in need of rescue."

No one moved at first. Simon searched the huddled mass and spotted a young man of seemingly fine physical condition. "You," he ordered, pointing with his finger, "come here."

There was a brief hesitation before the man came forward. He was disheveled, his shirtsleeves hastily tucked into his doeskin breeches, his waistcoat and coat unbuttoned. From the cut and quality of his garments, Simon was certain he was a member of the peerage. But Simon did not care. Rank had no bearing in his mind when lives were at stake.

Grabbing his elbow, Simon lined him up by the terrace doors. He looked about and more men approached under the weight of his condemning stare. Some were sluggish and reluctant, but as the line formed from the door to the fountain, the level of enthusiasm displayed increased.

Simon grabbed a bucket from a servant, plunged it into the fountain, and passed it to the first man in line. It moved down, man-to-man, the participants gradually moving forward until the procession stretched from the interior gallery door where the fire raged to the terrace.

Of their own accord, the men changed positions—the lead man retreating to the cool air of the outdoors with an empty bucket, while the second man stepped up and discharged his ration of water before retreating to collect more and pass it along the line.

Once the water was flowing steadily into the house, Simon risked a glance toward the lawn and saw Lysette standing with two other women, watching him from behind the crimson mask. Relief filled him at the sight of her safe and unharmed, her white gown glimmering like a pearl in the moonlight. Then his relief was replaced by fear.

Her presence goaded him like a painful spur in his flank. There was danger here and he could not fight it while concerned for her safety.

He abandoned his post without thought, striding toward her with a clenched jaw.

"I need you to go home," he said when he reached her, sparing a brief nod of acknowledgment to her two companions—one wigged, the other a brunette.

The wigged woman grabbed Lysette's elbow. "I was just saying the same to her."

Lysette opened her mouth to reply, but the set

of her shoulders forewarned him of her intention
to argue.

"Now," he ordered brusquely. "I cannot think
while you are here."

Simon led the way along the side of the manse,
his gait so long and rapid that the three women
had to scamper to keep up with him.

They reached the drive and Simon whistled
sharply, drawing the eye of every coachman. The
brunette took the lead then, hurrying to a well-
appointed equipage and herding the other two
inside.

Lysette reached out to him. "Come with us," she
begged.

Simon caught her gloved hand and kissed the
back. "I am needed here." He retreated and closed
the door, glancing at the coachman with a silent
order to set off. "Godspeed."

With a crack of the whip, the carriage rolled forward. The other coaches moved to open a pathway
and within a few moments it was out of sight.

The knots of tension in Simon's shoulders loosened appreciably. Now he could focus on the grim
task ahead.

He pivoted on his heel and headed back.

"Mon Dieu!" Marguerite gasped, staring out the
window at the smoke rising from the Orlinda
manse. "Who was that?"

"Simon Quinn," Lynette and Solange answered
in unison.

Lynette glanced at Solange with raised brows.

"I would be remiss if I did not know the name of

so handsome a man." Solange smiled lightly, and Lynette was pricked by jealousy.

It was obvious from the conversations she'd overheard that Mr. Quinn was the object of an inordinate amount of female lust, but now that she had held him intimately, she had no desire to share even a small piece of him. His passion was addicting and she wanted the whole of it for herself.

Marguerite's gaze moved from the window. "*What* is he?"

"No one knows for a certainty." Solange shrugged. "However, I had a paramour who had the ear of Talleyrand and he was convinced the man is an English spy."

"He is Irish!" Lynette protested.

"He is a mercenary," Solange corrected. "His loyalty is for sale."

Perhaps that should have mitigated Lynette's fascination. It did not.

"Why did he act as if he knew you?" Marguerite queried with an accusatory note in her tone.

Lynette leaned forward. "It is not me he knows. It is Lysette."

Her mother's face paled. "What are you saying?"

"He called me Lysette, *Maman,* and acted as if we knew each other well."

"That is impossible."

"Is it?" Lynette removed her mask. "He looked at me directly and called me Lysette. How can that be a coincidence?"

"You removed your mask for him?" Marguerite whispered, her eyes wide.

"Well . . ." Lynette's face heated. "He removed it."

"Lynette!" her mother cried, her spine straightening with indignation. "How could you? I should have dragged you with me to the kitchen when that oaf spilled wine on my gown. I trusted you to behave in my absence."

"Marguerite . . ." Solange began soothingly.

"And you!" Marguerite glared at her dearest friend. "This evening was your idea. You should have kept a better eye on her."

"Mon amie." Solange laughed softly. "Nothing can deter true determination."

"That is a poor excuse for lack of supervision."

"Did supervision deter you? Seems to me the daughter has the same taste in men as her mother."

Marguerite's mouth opened, then closed. A flush spread across her cheekbones.

Lynette's gaze darted back and forth between the two women, uncomprehending. Her father was nothing like Simon Quinn.

"About Lysette . . ." she began tentatively.

"How would he know her?" her mother snapped, her foul mood escalating.

"That is the question I intend to ask him," Lynette replied.

"No." The word was uttered with such finality it took Lynette aback. "You will stay away from him."

"We have to know!" Lynette protested. "*I* must know!"

"I said no, Lynette. There will be no further discussion on the matter. Your sister is gone."

"But wasn't Quinn dashing when he spirited us away?" Solange murmured.

Marguerite glared at her.

Lynette knew when it was time to hold her tongue and she did so, but the uncommonly vehement refusal created a deep-seated unease.

She *would* seek out Mr. Quinn.

Nothing could stop her from discovering if there was something about her twin that she did not know.

Especially if the secret kept was Simon Quinn.

Edward reached the gate leading to the front drive and paused with the unconscious Corinne tucked securely in his arms. Impatience and concern rode him hard as he waited for the struggling Desjardins to overtake him and release the catch.

Just as the comte gained the distance between them, the portal swung open of its own accord. A tall, dark-haired man stood on the threshold, coming to a halt at the sight of them.

"My lord," the gentleman greeted in a hoarse voice.

"Quinn," Desjardins returned.

Edward sensed a wary tension emanating from the man called Quinn. It caused him to hold Corinne more securely, her face turned in toward his chest.

Quinn glanced at the back of Corinne's disheveled head, then rested a moment on the shredded skirts of her once-bright yellow gown.

"Do you require assistance?"

"At this point, only a physician can help her."

With a nod, Quinn stepped aside, facilitating their departure.

The comte hurried forward, waving madly for his carriage, which waited with a dozen others clogging the drive. The various drivers spotted Edward's burden, and they began the arduous task of clearing a path for their departure.

As they approached, Desjardins's footman opened the door and Edward used the last of his waning strength to carry both himself and Corinne into the interior. He laid her carefully along the leather squab and turned to exit, only to find the comte blocking the doorway.

Saying nothing, Edward sat, grateful for the ride and the opportunity to remain with Corinne a little longer.

The equipage lurched into motion, and Edward closed his eyes and rested his head wearily against the back of the squab. The shallow, rapid wheezing that afflicted all of them echoed within the small confines. He thought of the day and how he had awakened that morning in completely different circumstances. Unencumbered. Focused.

Now, mere hours later, he was embroiled in the life of a woman who would certainly bring him nothing but grief.

However, there was no help for it at this point. He was fascinated and he had never been able to resist exposing the cause of any fascination.

Mysteries were meant to be solved.

Simon watched Desjardins and Mr. James settle the injured woman into a carriage, and wondered why and how the comte's plans had altered so drastically over the course of the day. That morning the comte had enlisted Lysette's assistance in reaching James, but tonight Lysette had been in *his* arms, while Desjardins and James appeared to be rubbing along well on their own.

The situation unsettled Simon, causing the hairs on his nape to stand on end and tension to stiffen his spine. Something was amiss and Lysette's sudden change of heart was beyond suspicious. Mindless with lust, he had not cared about her motivations. He'd cared only about pushing inside her and staying there until he could think again.

Frustrated by the sudden sensation of being played the fool, Simon growled and continued his journey to the back of the manse. He glanced at every window as he passed it, searching for any signs of occupation. He hoped everyone was safely free of entrapment. His eyes lit on the destruction of one window and a shattered chair beneath it. Glass littered the gravel pathway and bore testament of a desperate attempt to stay alive.

How in hell had this happened?

Simon gained the terrace and was relieved to see that the line of water carriers continued to work industriously.

He rejoined them, working past the sunrise, his thoughts actively occupied with the mystery Lysette, Desjardins, and James presented.

Chapter 8

"What in bloody hell happened to you?" Eddington queried as Simon stumbled through the front door shortly after nine in the morning.

The fresh, clean fragrance of the interior of his home was a welcome relief after smelling nothing but smoke the entirety of the long night. Simon glanced at his sweat-soaked and soot-covered garments and knew the entire lot would have to be destroyed. The burnt odor was now permanently ingrained in the cloth. In contrast, the earl was freshly bathed and wearing a comfortable robe.

"You are buying me a new wardrobe," Simon growled, shrugging out of his coat, an action that caused ash to sprinkle down to the rug.

Eddington's nose wrinkled. "Good God. You are a disaster."

"The Baroness Orlinda's home caught fire during the ball." Simon brushed past the earl on his way to the stairs.

"An accident?" Eddington fell into step behind him.

"So it would appear. A poorly secured lamp in the gallery."

"What are the odds?"

Simon snorted.

"Was anyone injured?"

"Smoke inhalation and some minor burns. Miraculous, really, if you saw the state of the manse."

Pushing open the door to his room, Simon absorbed the familiar feeling of homecoming. He had purchased the house as is, with furniture and art included. The man who had owned the place previously must have had an affection for slumber. The bed was massive and comfortable, the drapes thick and dark, the rugs plush and warm. The palate of dark reds, greens, and stained walnut furnishings created a soothing, masculine retreat.

"That is not the worst of it," Simon muttered, stifling a yawn and shooting a longing glance at his turned-down bed. His valet took one look at him and quickly tossed a towel over a footstool, so that Simon could sit and remove his boots. Then the servant excused himself to arrange a bath.

"There is more?" Eddington asked, wide-eyed. The elegantly tall earl moved to one of the wing-backs in front of the grate and smiled at the pretty maid who was stoking the fire into a hearty, welcoming blaze. She flushed prettily and bobbed a quick curtsy before retreating, leaving the two men alone.

"Mademoiselle Rousseau attempted to seduce me."

"Attempted?" There was laughter in the earl's voice and Simon glared at him.

"Yesterday morning she was set on luring Mr.

James to an ignoble end, and last night James and Desjardins were working in tandem while she was after me."

"Interesting," the earl murmured. "What are your thoughts?"

Arching a brow, Simon stood to remove his waistcoat and shirtsleeves. "My thoughts are that you will return my coin to me whether I complete the task agreed to or not. If they have set me as a target, our agreement will not be forfeit nor substituted."

"What leverage do you have to enforce this?"

Simon raised his fists.

Eddington shuddered. "Point taken."

It was Simon's pugilistic expertise that had first caught the earl's attention. Simon had taken down nearly a dozen men with only minor bruising to show for his efforts, and Eddington had immediately decided that he could use a man of such talent. Since Simon's position as Lady Winter's paramour was eliminated by her marriage, he gratefully accepted the employment. In short order, Simon proved he was as agile of mind as he was on his feet.

"You think they mean to implicate you?" Eddington asked thoughtfully. "If you were accused of crimes against Franklin and your work for the English Crown was to become known, it would increase the animosity toward England with both the French and the Revolutionaries."

"That is certainly possible," Simon agreed, pulling his shirt over his head and reaching for the fastenings of his breeches. "There were other oddities last night. While Desjardins and James were occupied with each other, Lysette waited with two other females."

"Who were they?"

"I am not certain. Truly, I did not pay much attention to either of them, other than that they surrounded her as mother hens would. Lysette is not the type of woman that other women like. I know you collect what I mean."

"Curious." Eddington set his elbows on the armrests and brought his steepled fingertips to his lips. "What do you intend to do?"

"I am going to bathe, then sleep." Simon moved toward the bathing chamber, where the splashing of water told him the tub was being readied. "After that, I will visit Mademoiselle Rousseau and ask her outright."

"You think she will tell you?" the earl called after him.

"No. But at least she will know that I am not ignorant of something being amiss."

"You might wish to enlist aid."

"I might," Simon said evasively, having already planned to do just that. However, that was not information he wished to share with the earl.

"I will see to it," Eddington offered. "I have asked Becking to remain in France while I am here. Might as well put him to good use."

"Excellent, my lord."

He shut the door behind him.

Edward awoke due to a ferocious spate of coughing. He sat up from his reclined position in a chair and glanced around the room, briefly surprised to find himself still in Corinne's house. The last thing he remembered was listening to the physician's orders to keep her cool if she turned feverish and to suction out her mouth and nose at regular intervals so that she could breathe.

He glanced at the clock on the mantel. It was shortly after nine in the morning.

Pushing to his feet, Edward stretched muscles cramped by hours spent sleeping in a wingback. He was late for work, something he had never been in the entirety of his life. He needed to return home immediately, where he could draft a note to Franklin in explanation, bathe, and prepare for the day.

Glancing quickly around the room for any of his belongings, Edward then moved to the door that separated the private sitting room he occupied from Corinne's bedchamber. He knocked lightly, waited for an acknowledgment that did not come, and opened the door regardless.

While the sitting room was decorated in a mixture of various shades of cream and brown with stained wood molding and furnishings, the bedroom was far more feminine with its palette of pale pinks and burgundy with whitewashed wood and gilt. But both rooms were permeated with the soft floral scent that belonged to Corinne alone. It was innocent, not seductive, yet he was drawn to it.

As he stepped deeper into the space, Edward's gaze locked on the tiny form in the middle of the large four-poster bed. Her chest rose and fell in rapid, shallow breaths and black mucus bubbled from her nostrils. Furious, he rounded the chair where the housekeeper sat, intent on a scolding, and found the elderly woman sleeping and completely oblivious to the needs of her employer. The woman's lace-fringed cap was askew and covering her lined brow, allowing messy gray curls to peek out from the left side.

Growling his frustration, Edward approached the bed and managed the onerous task of suctioning Corinne's airways, inwardly thinking that he'd never been a nursemaid in his life. Even when he was the patient, he did not nurse himself to health. He hadn't the time or funds to do more than work through whatever illness affected him.

When he had finished, Edward dipped a clean cloth into the bowl of water on the nightstand and wiped it gently over Corinne's pale face, admiring how beautiful she was even when afflicted. Her brows were perfectly arched, her mouth lushly curved, her cheekbones high and elegant.

It pained him to see her so helpless and he knew that her staff of three servants—housekeeper, butler, and their son, the footman—were not enough to provide the care Corinne needed. If he wanted her alive, which there was no doubt he did, he would have to care for her himself. He could not afford to supplement her staff, even briefly, and he did not understand the nature of Comte Desjardins's relationship with her enough to ask for assistance. It was also not his place to speak on Corinne's behalf. They were strangers.

"Damn you," he whispered, agitated by the complication she presented. A frown marred her brow in response to his gruff tone and he touched the line with the pad of his thumb, smoothing it away.

Edward sighed and left the room, taking the stairs to the main floor and searching out the kitchen. There, he found the butler and footman dealing with a driver making deliveries at the service door.

"Mr. James," the butler said, bowing. It was a lame bow, the man's old frame twisted by what Edward suspected was arthritic pain. He doubted they would be able to manage the household, small as it was, without the assistance of their strapping son.

"Madame Fouche is sleeping upstairs," Edward replied in a curt tone. "I saw to Mademoiselle Marchant myself, but she will need to be watched by someone awake and the orders of the physician followed every half hour."

"Yes, of course." The servant had the grace to flush, but not the sense to admit that he needed help.

"If you can tend to her during the day, I will return to see to her at night."

"Sir," the butler began, straightening as best he could. "Your offer, while generous, is not necessary, I assure you. There is no need to trouble yourself."

Edward smiled grimly. "I will return this evening. If you still feel the same, I will leave."

There was nothing the man could say to that beyond repetitious protestations, so he simply bowed his head again and shot a warning look at his son.

For his part, Edward strode from the room at his customary brisk pace and collected his jacket from the foyer.

He glanced at the clock again on his way out and sighed. He hated to be late.

The courtesan's house was small but elegant and located in an area of the city where only the most successful purveyors of the trade could afford to live.

The procession of carriages and riders on the street was steady, though not heavy, so lengthy observance of any household would be noted in short order. Because of this, the upper-floor chambermaid was hard pressed to slip from Solange Tremblay's home and reach the unmarked carriage across the road in a timely manner. It was not easy, not with the housekeeper forever scolding her to complete three chores at once. Still, she was nothing if not wily.

Keeping her head bent low, she walked a small distance up the street, then crossed it and backtracked to the nondescript black equipage. She paused outside the door.

"Well?"

The black curtains were closed, preventing her from seeing who spoke to her. Not that she cared what he looked like. His coin was good and that was all she needed to know.

"They have made no plans to leave."

"I see."

There was something sinister in the tone used to say the two words. It made her shiver.

A gloved hand was extended and in its palm rested a small purse. She accepted it and dipped a quick curtsy, although she doubted he could see it. *"Merci beaucoup, m'sieur."*

It always paid to be polite to those who paid you. She might argue with the housekeeper, but she was nothing but smiles to Mademoiselle Tremblay. If she was released from her position due to insubordination, *L'Esprit* would have no further use for her and she would lose both wages at once.

She began walking back the way she had come, her steps hurried in an effort to return to her station before her absence was noted.

L'Esprit watched the woman until she disappeared through the side gate leading to the servants' entrance. She did not look back at him, a tiny detail he appreciated. It was so hard to find good help.

He leaned back against the squab and rapped on the roof. The coachman set the carriage into motion with a sharp whistle.

Marguerite had returned to Paris.

He had expected as much, which was why he'd paid the maid to join Solange's household so many years ago. It was a simple, relatively inexpensive thing to keep the woman on retainer, and he had known that one day the expense would prove valuable.

Nothing could be allowed to alter the course of events put into motion two decades ago.

Most especially not Marguerite Baillon.

Corinne's house was quiet as a tomb by five o'clock in the evening.

Edward sat at her dainty escritoire and worked quietly, his gaze moving to the bed at regular intervals to monitor her breathing. He had returned just a little past four and found her raging with fever and incoherent. The staff was exhausted. The footman had run to and fro for water all day and the housekeeper had given Corinne cooled cloth baths until her arms were protesting their exhaustion with tingling aches. When Edward arrived, they had conceded Corinne's care to him with undisguised gratitude. He in turn, appreciated the many hours he had spent researching how best to care for an invalid in her condition.

He had immediately relocated her to a guest room. There, Madame Fouche removed the soiled night rail from her body, while Edward stripped her bed and remade it with fresh linens. He'd ordered that Corinne be bathed again and that vodka should be rubbed beneath her arms, behind her neck, and into the soles of her feet. She smelled like a drunkard now, but her temperature had cooled considerably. She'd then been swaddled like a child and he had returned her to the comfort of her freshly made bed.

In appreciation for their efforts, the Fouches had been dismissed early. Their son, Thierry—who was around the same age as Edward's score, ten, and three years—remained in service. With only two people left awake in the house, it was eerily silent in contrast to the explosion of activity just an hour ago. The thick blanket of peace left Edward with too much time to contemplate his involvement in Corinne's life and too little in the way of answers.

That was why, when the door knocker was rapped impatiently, Edward felt relief. It was a distraction when he felt in desperate need of one.

He paused with his quill suspended above parchment, his hearing alert. A moment later he heard voices, too distant to be distinguished. Expecting Desjardins, he waited for the sound of footsteps approaching. When they did not come, Edward pushed to his feet and walked through the open door into the gallery.

From there, he looked directly down the stairs into the small, marble-lined entry. Thierry stood in the front doorway, speaking at length with whoever stood there. Finally, the servant retreated into the house and closed the door.

Curious as to who else occupied Corinne's life, Edward rounded the landing and entered the upper parlor. He moved to the window and pushed the curtains aside, affording him a clear view of the street in front of the house.

The man named Quinn was unhitching his horse from the post with casual ease. The cut and quality of the man's garments spoke of wealth and privilege, as did the beautiful lines of his mount.

How did he know Corinne?

Quinn stilled just before placing his booted foot into the stirrup. He glanced over his shoulder at the house, lifting his gaze until it met with Edward's. The tension that gripped the man's large frame was tangible even across the distance between them.

There had been a brief moment when Edward considered backing up and out of view. It was not his place to intrude in Corinne's life. They were nothing to each other, not even true acquaintances. When she awoke, she might rail at his arrogance in taking charge of her household—and her—while she was helpless to protest.

But a long-buried part of him reared up and exerted a claim on the lovely Corinne, and he was unable to resist it. He *would* have her. It was the only reason for the madness of his actions since meeting her.

Edward's eyes examined the man who might be a rival, noting every detail. They were as opposite as opposite could be, except for their facial expressions. Quinn looked the way Edward felt—taut, challenged, and malevolent.

Was this the man who had so wounded Corinne? Who had made her fearful and given her that haunted look in her eyes?

His fists clenched at his sides. "I will know who you are," Edward warned softly.

Quinn touched the brim of his hat, smiled in a near sneer, and mounted his horse. He could not have heard Edward or even seen his lips moving, but the fact that he'd picked up the gauntlet was clear.

Another complication in an already tangled affair.

Edward lowered the curtain and returned to Corinne.

Simon stood in the entryway of his home and pulled off his gloves one fingertip at a time, his movements deliberate and evenly paced. The action was meant to calm him, but it was ineffectual. His breath heaved with his anger, and his neck ached with tension.

Edward James had been visiting Lysette while she was "indisposed." The man had stood in the window *sans* coat and waistcoat as if he were at home, his posture both defensive and possessive.

Simon had played this game before, coming to a head with a man over a desirable female. It was a diverting activity and Simon rarely had a true stake in the outcome. If he won the lady's regard, the sex was wild and hot. If he lost it, he conceded with a smile and caught another.

This time, he was incensed. He would like to think it was only his pride that was bruised, but the truth was more disturbing than that. He had been happy those brief, passionate moments in the library. Not merely content or distracted but happy.

To know that it had been nothing noteworthy to Lysette was a bitter realization to reach.

And then there was the feeling that he was losing his mind. He had *disliked* Lysette until last night. Now, suddenly, he felt murderous over the thought of her with another man.

Right now.

He growled and bounded up the stairs to his room, determined to change from his riding clothes to something more suitable for a night of bawdy delights. A hard fuck would get her out of his blood. Tomorrow he would be clear headed and ready to deal with her as he must.

"Mr. Quinn, you have a caller."

Simon paused in the act of removing his cravat. He met his butler's gaze in the mirror attached to the inside of his armoire door. "Who is it?"

"She would not give me her name, sir."

Tensing at the news that his caller was female, he asked, "Is she blonde and beautiful?"

The butler's mouth twitched. "Yes, sir."

All of Simon's simmering anger and frustration reheated to boiling. He yanked off the loosened linen and tossed it on the floor. She must have come haring directly after him in order to reach him so soon. Perhaps she realized how James's show of propriety had ruined her plans for him, whatever they were.

For a moment, he debated sending her away without seeing her just to aggravate her in kind, but the thought of Eddington's hold over him stayed his tongue. The sooner he knew what she was up to, the sooner he could be rid of her and away from the damnable lot of mischief makers.

"Where is his lordship?" he asked.

"Out for the evening, sir."

With a long, rapid stride, Simon quit his chambers and descended to the lower floor. He was vaguely aware of his butler scrambling after him, but he paid the man no mind. He would not be needing tea or refreshments. If anything, he needed a stiff drink.

He paused on the threshold of the receiving parlor and found Lysette seated delicately on the edge of his yellow brocade settee. She was dressed in a bold burgundy gown, another color choice he would not have anticipated her to select but one he found potently alluring against her creamy skin. An elaborately decorated hat rested on the carved wooden side table and she twisted the strings of a matching reticule in her lap.

She was the picture of elegance and gentility . . .

. . . until she looked at him with the blue eyes that had lured him across a ballroom and into her arms.

Something akin to lightning raced across his skin. Burning. Tingling. Making him perspire. His heart rate picked up its pace and his chest rose and fell unevenly.

As he entered, her expression of hesitation and wariness was swiftly replaced with heated feminine appreciation. Her gaze lowered to his bared throat and her tongue darted out to caress her lush lower lip.

When her eyes met his again, the raw, carnal hunger he saw in the crystalline depths hardened every muscle in his body, tightening his frame with coiling lust. A quarter of an hour ago he had wanted to strangle her. Now, he wanted nothing more than to lift her skirts and ride her to a screaming climax.

Again and again.

He growled and snapped, "Bah! You are not worth the trouble."

Pivoting, he left the room.

"Mr. Quinn . . . Wait!"

He turned about again and found her chasing after him. "The name is Simon, curse you, as you well know."

She drew up short, her breathing as rapid as his. "Please. Allow me to introduce myself. I am—"

"I know bloody well who you are, you addlepated female!"

"Lynette Baillon," she continued stubbornly, "daughter of the Vicomte de Grenier. I believe you may have known my sister, Lysette Baillon. Perhaps intimately . . . i-if last night was any indication."

Simon stood frozen, unblinking. "What the devil are you talking about?"

"You do not know me," she said softly. "Until last night, you and I had never met."

Chapter 9

The woman was either daft as you please, or the answer to a prayer.

Simon's gaze narrowed and became examining, moving from the top of Lysette's—*Lynette's*—golden head down to the hem of her gown. He noted the artfully revealed lacey underskirts, the tightly cinched waist, and the low bodice, which displayed a tempting swell of luscious breasts. It was an ensemble designed to display the feminine charms of the wearer to best advantage. The Lysette he knew did not dress to arouse. If anything, her gowns were remarkably understated.

But beyond this woman's outward appearance were deeper, more complex signs—there was no torment in her eyes and no brittle tension in her delicate frame.

Lynette. Lysette.

"Twins," he said, near dizzy with the sudden rush of understanding.

"Yes."

Out of all the things that should have come to

Simon's mind in that moment, the only one that gained prominence was the realization that he was not insane. He did not dislike and desire the same woman with equal vehemence. He disliked Lysette. He lusted for Lynette.

Simon lunged into motion without warning, catching Lynette's elbow and dragging her back into the parlor. He kicked the door shut and tugged her about to face him. Before common sense reared its head or she regained her wits enough to protest, he cupped her head in both hands and took her mouth with savage intensity.

She tensed briefly, then melted. Her body leaned into his, her hands circled his wrists. She whimpered and surged into him, her voluminous skirts pushing into the hardened ridge of his cock and urging him into a frenzy of need.

He spun and pinned her to the door, his knees bending and then straightening, stroking the length of her body with his own. She gasped and his tongue stroked deep into her mouth, licking and tasting, drinking her in. As her skin heated with arousal, the scent of some exotic flower intoxicated him and made him drunk with desire. She did not smell like Lysette. She was unique.

She was his.

"*A thiasce,*" he breathed, lost in the feel of her.

Lynette released his wrists and reached for his waist, the feel of her small hands through the linen of his shirt inciting a ferocious, gnawing need.

Never in his life had he been so desperate to be inside a woman. And it was going to happen. *Now.* Nothing could stop him.

He fumbled for the key to turn the lock, but his

hands shook with such violence that he could not grasp it. With a muttered curse, Simon turned his head away to see what he was doing.

"Were you lovers?" she asked in a husky whisper.

He glanced at her as the lock clicked audibly into place. She was flushed and disheveled and achingly beautiful. Although her features were a mirror of Lysette's, she looked nothing like her. Lynette was soft and warm in his arms, her scent alluring instead of subdued, her passion hot and powerful.

"No," he answered, absently thinking that there were a hundred questions to ask, while simultaneously realizing that he didn't give a damn what the answers were. At least, not at the moment.

"Then why?"

"Why what?" What in hell was she talking about?

He reached between them for the placket of his breeches.

She stilled his movements with her hands. "Why are you so . . . *ardent?*"

Simon laughed and nuzzled his cheek against hers. "Such an elegant way to say I am acting like a rutting beast."

Lynette flushed, but did not release him.

"I usually have more finesse," he promised, forcing himself to take a step back. "Unfortunately, I am out of sorts at the moment."

"Out of sorts? You?" She smiled and his chest tightened. "The man who had a house burning down around him, yet had the presence of mind to rally the guests to douse the blaze?"

"Lust wants quenching like a fire. I rally to that cause with equal gusto."

"You are wicked, Mr. Quinn."

Simon debated whether he should seduce her in the parlor or take her up to bed, but a touch of sadness marred the angelic beauty of her features and reined in his lust as logic could not.

Exhaling harshly, he ran his hands through his hair and fought to tamp down his unruly appetite for her touch, her taste, her smell. *Her.*

He gestured for her to return to her seat.

"How did you know Lysette?" she asked, sitting with a perfectly straight spine and hands folded delicately in her lap.

A peer's daughter, she had said. That would explain the similar elegance of deportment Simon had witnessed in her sister.

It did not, however, explain why Lysette was an assassin.

"Our acquaintance is a difficult one to categorize," he murmured. "But it is not romantic by any definition."

Lynette blushed, but her gaze did not waver from his. "Last night . . ."

He smiled ruefully. "The first time I have ever felt an inkling of attraction to her. I suspected madness was the culprit, because the change was so drastic I could hardly credit it. I cannot tell you what a relief it is to learn that you are two women and not one."

"So you are unaware that she passed," Lynette said gently.

Simon frowned. "Passed what?"

"Passed on."

"Bloody hell." He paced, his thoughts returning to the events of the night before. Desjardins. James. Carrying an injured woman in yellow out to the comte's carriage. The posturing of James in the window had been protective, not possessive. "When? This afternoon?"

Lynette's frown matched his. "Beg your pardon?"

"When did she die?" he asked slowly, feeling disoriented.

"Two years ago."

"That is not possible, Lynette. I saw her alive and well just yesterday."

Lynette's stomach clenched hard and violently. She reached for the armrest of the settee for support and then Quinn—*Simon*—was crouched before her, studying her face with a worried frown.

"I think there is a great deal that you and I do not understand," he said, his Irish lilt soothing and gentle. "Perhaps you should tell me about your Lysette, then I shall tell you about mine."

Inhaling and exhaling in measured rhythm, Lynette attempted to calm her racing pulse. In the space of only moments, she had been barked at, kissed senseless, and now told that her sister was alive and well as recently as yesterday. She knew that was impossible, that there must be some grievous error, but some tiny part of her shouted in vindicated exaltation. The part of her that still felt Lysette as keenly today as it had the last time they had been together.

"Two years ago," she whispered, "my sister was killed when the carriage she occupied overturned and the lamps set fire to the whole."

Simon moved to take a seat beside her. "You have only the one sister?"

"Yes. No other siblings."

"What are the odds that there would be a woman of identical appearance to you who is not a relation?"

"With the name *Lysette*? Impossible." She turned slightly to face him. "I must see her."

"I should like to be there when you do."

Lynette stared at Simon's breathtaking features and felt calmed by his mere presence. It was astonishing to feel such a connection to a stranger, but she did not doubt it.

Simon would not allow harm to befall her. She was convinced of that.

"This woman cannot be my sister." Her voice quavered and she cleared her throat. "In addition to the fact that I was there when Lysette was buried, the simple truth is that she and I were very close. There is no chance that two years would pass without a word from her."

"I do not understand any of this." He rubbed the back of his neck. "But I can tell you the Lysette I know is not . . . well."

"Not well?"

"A bit touched."

"Oh . . ." Lynette worried her lower lip between her teeth. "How did you become acquainted with her?"

"My life is not one you wish to delve too deeply into, Mademoiselle . . ."

"Baillon."

His frown deepened. "Lysette goes by the name *Rousseau*. Does that sound familiar to you?"

"Rousseau?" Lynette frowned, trying to recall if she knew anyone by that name and finding that she did not.

"Mademoiselle—"

"Please," she interjected, "call me Lynette. After

last night . . . and now. You almost . . . against the door . . ." Her face heated.

His large hand rose to cup her cheek with something akin to reverence. "You cannot even say it, can you?"

She swallowed hard, riveted by his tenderness and the way the stroking of his thumb over her cheekbone reverberated all over her body.

A half-smile curved his beautiful mouth and made her stomach flutter. His glance moved over her, from the top of her head to her feet. "You mentioned a father, but not a spouse."

"I am not married."

"Of course not." Simon shook his head. "You are innocent. The daughter of a peer."

The way he said the words, so flatly and resigned, struck her like a blow. She realized he no longer intended to ravish her. She knew she should be relieved, but she was profoundly disappointed. All of her life, she had led the way with men. Teasing, flirting, and steering their conversations in the direction she wished them to go. With Simon Quinn, she was swept away, in control of nothing at all. It was a heady sensation to be so lost in a man, and to know that he was equally lost in her.

"Give me some time," he said, "to investigate this a little further before you proceed. You have no reason to trust me—"

"But I do!"

"You shouldn't." The rueful little smile touched his mouth again, and unable to help it, she lifted her fingers to it. The muscle in his jaw ticked beneath her caress and his blue eyes burned so hot her skin flushed in response.

He caught her hand and pressed a kiss to her palm. The feel of his lips sent tingles up her arm and made her shiver. "I have never known innocence, Lynette. I have no notion of what to do with it beyond corrupt it."

"What are you saying?"

"I am saying that if you do not put as much distance as possible between us and maintain it, I will ruin you." The deep timbre of his voice added credence to his threat. "You will find yourself in my bed and your life deeply entangled in a web of deceit, lies, and danger. As bright as your future is now, it would be equally dark."

"Yet Lysette Rousseau occupies this world you speak of?" she queried, lifting her chin.

"Yes, she does."

"Are you an English spy?" Her gaze moved around the room as it had when she'd arrived. Again, she admired the obvious expense of the design and décor. The palette was one of deep reds balanced by lighter-stained woods. It was both deeply masculine, yet welcoming to all.

"I was," he said easily. But when she returned her gaze to his, his focus on her was sharp.

"You want to know how I would gain such knowledge." She smiled. "By no nefarious means, I assure you. One of the women with me last night is a courtesan. A well-connected paramour of hers once said something of that nature to her."

"How is it that a peer's daughter would be associating with a courtesan?" Simon's hand had moved to her shoulder and his thumb absently caressed along her collarbone.

The touch made her want to purr like a kitten

and arch in delight. She swallowed and replied, "My mother met her years ago in a modiste's shop, when my parents used to live in France."

"Why would the wife of a peer have an appointment at the same time as a courtesan? Usually discretion would prevent such a meeting."

Lynette wrinkled her nose, thinking.

Without warning, Simon's hand cupped the nape of her neck and his lips were pressed to the tip of her nose. His new proximity brought the scent of his skin to her nostrils, a stirring mixture of leather and horses, musk and tobacco. Her mind became flooded with memories of that scent . . . last night in the library . . . moments ago against the door . . .

Her body responded by aching and she moaned.

He cursed and pushed to his feet in a hurried but graceful movement. "I cannot think when you are near and I need my blasted wits now more than ever."

"Simon—"

"Is there any possibility that your mother had a child that you do not know about?"

Lynette lowered the hand she had held out to him. "No. The birth of my sister and I destroyed her womb."

"Before you, perhaps?"

"No."

"Are you certain?"

"Absolutely. I will ask her directly, if I must."

"And your father?"

"The Vicomte de Grenier. His coloring is very dark. My sister and I take after our mother. Some have thought she was a sister to us."

"De Grenier?" Simon moved to a console against the far wall where various decanters waited. A painting of the countryside hung above it, the blues of a stream and the greens of a forest lending color to the room. "He is unknown to me."

"My parents quit France before I was born. We have lived in Poland these many years."

Holding a thick crystal glass in one hand, he faced her, resting his hip against the furniture and one palm flat atop the surface. There were now several feet of space between them, which left her feeling oddly bereft. "When did your family return to Paris?"

"We have not returned." Her splayed fingers brushed nervously over her skirts. He was watching her like a hawk, focused and predatory. "My mother suggested a holiday in Spain to distract us from our grief. I begged her to stop in Paris, so I could see it."

"Begged?"

"My mother is not fond of the city."

"Why?"

"I do not know." She stood. "When will I be allowed to question you?"

"When I am finished."

Simon lifted his glass and drank, his throat working with every swallow. Lynette found the sight erotic, which deepened her agitation. She was aroused, confused, and piqued by his arrogance all at the same time.

"Was your mother the other woman with you last night?" he asked, his voice gruff from the burn of the liquor.

"Yes."

"I find it extremely odd that a vicomtess would take her unwed daughter to an orgy."

"It was not an orgy."

"It bloody well was!" he snapped, revealing a fury she had not noted before. "And you nearly lost your virginity there."

She bit back a retort even as her face heated. "She was reluctant." Her reply was petulant, her pride bruised by his condemnation.

"That did not stop her."

"No. Do you wish to know why?" she asked crossly. "Or would you rather continue to frighten me with your boorish temper?"

His nostrils flared. "You are far from frightened."

Setting his glass down, Simon stalked toward her with a deliberate, sensual stride. It stole her breath the way he exuded an undeniable carnal invitation. The response of her body altered the fit of her clothes, making her corset and bodice far too tight for comfort.

"If you come any closer," she drawled, "I might seduce you."

Simon paused midstep, eyes wide with shock at her boldness, and she smiled.

"Witch," he hissed.

"Mon chéri." Her hand rose to her heart and her lips made a moue. "You wound me."

The corner of his mouth twitched. "I see similarities between you and Lysette Rousseau."

Her smile faded. "But, you see, aside from the physical traits afforded to us by our birth, Lysette and I were very different."

"You were the quiet one." There was no question in his tone.

"No," she corrected, "I was the mischief maker."

She could see how that shocked him, which in turn created questions for her. "Mademoiselle Rousseau is not timid and studious?"

"Timid?" He snorted. "Not nearly. However, she is somewhat studious, with a fondness for reading historical volumes."

"Is she wed or widowed?"

"Neither." Simon withdrew to the console again, but his steps appeared to be weighted with reluctance to part from her. Or so she fancied. "She told me she does not enjoy men."

"Truly? How odd." Lynette wrinkled her nose again and Simon growled.

"What is it?" she queried, perplexed as to the cause of his aggravation.

"Have you any notion of what that turned-up nose does to a man?"

She blinked. A great many compliments had been paid to her over the course of her life. However, her habit of wrinkling her nose while contemplating had never been the subject of platitudes.

His resentful infatuation was touching, and Lynette's mouth curved upward. "Have you any notion of what your ill-temper does to me?"

"You flirt with danger," he warned.

"I flirt always. It is my nature."

"Not any longer." He turned his back to her and downed his libation.

"Was that possessiveness I heard, *mon chéri?*"

"You assume I meant that you will no longer flirt at all." Simon faced her and crossed his arms. "Perhaps I meant you will no longer flirt with me."

Her head tilted to the side. "How dull that would be, *non?*"

"I doubt life is ever dull around you."

The more she teased him, the more dangerous he became. She could sense the lust in him coiling tighter with each word she spoke, readying for the moment when he would pounce. The alcohol might have eased him somewhat, but not enough to render him harmless.

Simon Quinn could never be harmless.

Lynette directed the conversation back to the mysterious Lysette, knowing she was out of her depth. "She does not like men, you say."

"That is what she said," he rumbled.

"Did she like you?"

"I doubt it."

"She must truly be touched, then."

"Of course." He grinned. "A woman would have to be insane not to want me."

Lynette laughed and felt the pressure between them lessen. Not that the tension was uncomfortable. Far from it.

"You should go," he said, unfolding. "While I can still let you."

"What of Mademoiselle Rousseau? You said you would take me to her."

"No." He shook his head. "I said I should like to see you together. I did not say I would facilitate such a meeting."

Her hands settled on her waist. "Why not?"

"Because she is dangerous and unsettled, as are the individuals she works for. I have no idea what the sight of you will do to her mind. I will not risk you for a whim."

"A whim?" she scoffed. "Would you call it a whim to learn that there is another man in the world, in the *same city*, who is identical to you in appearance? Now compound that with the person bearing the name of your sibling—"

"I have no siblings," he retorted, his jaw clenching. "I have no family, no name of any value, no property."

She stared at him, knowing there was only one reason a man listed his marital value. "You are a mercenary," she murmured, repeating Solange.

"Yes." His squared shoulders dared her to want him after such a revelation.

She still did, of course.

"I will pay you," she said.

"Damned if you will! For what?"

"For taking me to see her. I could be concealed in a carriage—"

Moving with the lightning speed that continued to catch her unawares, he snatched her close and shook her. "What do you intend to pay me with?" he snarled.

Lynette met his livid gaze, unflinching. "You know very well what I have to barter."

His fingers tightened in the delicate flesh of her upper arms, then he pushed her away, causing her to stumble. "Curse you. I am attempting to be honorable."

"Honor is a cold bedmate."

"Is your innocence worth so little that you would concede it to the likes of me?"

"Perhaps my sister is worth so much, I would pay any price for her."

"Is she dead or not? It cannot be both." Simon's hands went to his lean hips, a pose that widened the neck opening of his shirt and revealed a tantalizing glimpse of his tawny skin.

"I saw her buried."

"Did you see her body?"

Lynette shook her head. "I wanted to. I begged

to. But I was told she was too badly burned in the fire." Her eyes stung and she blinked rapidly to hold back tears. "My mother saw her."

"Do you trust your mother?" His tone had softened, as did his handsome features.

"In a fashion." Despite her efforts, a tear fell. She swiped at it with the back of her hand. "But there is much I do not know. Much she will not tell me. Such as why she fears Paris."

"Fears?" He was alert now, intensely so.

"We are staying with Solange. No one knows we are here. I am to tell no one my name—"

"Lynette," he murmured, enfolding her in a warm, powerful embrace. "You knew I was an English spy, yet you revealed yourself to me, regardless. I cannot decide whether I should kiss you or shake some sense into you."

She sniffled. "I prefer the kissing."

Simon laughed and set his cheek to her temple. She clung to him, taking comfort in his sympathy and caring.

"Last night," she whispered, hugging his waist, "Solange commented on our interest in one another. My mother protested."

"Wise woman."

"To which Solange replied, 'Seems to me the daughter has the same taste in men as her mother.' "

Lynette knew he was frowning, even though she did not see his face.

"Do you know what that means?" he asked.

"No. And I am equally ignorant about many other statements made within my earshot." She pulled back to beseech him. "What if this woman is my sister? Or worse, what if the connection is malicious? What if she met my sister at some point, noted the resemblance, and has taken advantage of her memory?"

"Lynette—"

"I cannot explain it," she blurted, before she lost her courage, "but the bond I always felt with her is still here." Her hand fisted over her heart. "It has yet to be severed. W-why would it still be there i-if she is g-gone?"

He exhaled wearily and smoothed her brow with callused fingertips, then followed with the press of his lips to her fevered skin. "I fear your grief has invented hope where there is none."

"Then lay it to rest," she pleaded.

Simon's head went back and he gazed at the ceiling, as if looking for divine guidance. Beneath her palm, she felt his heart beating steady and strong. For the first time since Lysette passed, Lynette felt as if she had a purpose and Simon gave her the support she needed to pursue it.

"How did you find me?" he asked finally, returning his gaze to her face.

"Eavesdropping." She smiled. "I think Solange champions you. She was describing your home in detail to my mother this afternoon. She was quite flattering in regards to your taste and wealth."

A change came over him, a steely resolve taking hold with such tenacity it was tangible.

"From now onward," he directed resolutely, "I want you to follow your mother's admonishments to stay hidden. No more parties. No more outings." He cupped her face and reinforced the severity of his words by touch. "Whatever reasons your family may have for their discretion, you must add the risk of being seen by Lysette Rousseau or someone she works with or for. That cannot happen, Lynette. You trusted me when you came here. I need you to trust me when you leave, as well."

"What is she?"

"She is an assassin. And I am not certain murder is the gravest of her crimes."

"*Mon Dieu . . .*" Lynette shook violently, the chill starting from the inside and spreading outward to coat her skin with gooseflesh. Her hand rose to his face, her quivering fingertips brushing over his sinner's mouth. "I am grateful to have your guidance."

She drew strength from him and comfort. For the first time in two years she felt like herself. It was a precious gift and meeting Simon had given it to her.

"*A thiasce,*" he whispered, his eyes darkening. "I wish we had never met. No good can come of it. The only path on which I can guide you is one that leads you straight to hell."

Chapter 10

It was nearly midnight before Simon found Richard Becking in a tavern in an undesirable part of town. The Englishman was occupying a far corner of the room with a buxom serving wench on his lap and a singing Frenchman to his right. Richard himself was grinning from ear to ear and he lifted a hand in a wave when he spotted Simon approaching.

"Richard," Simon greeted him, pulling out the only vacant chair at the table. He glanced at the seat, arched a brow, then laid his kerchief atop it before sitting.

"Putting on airs, Quinn?" Richard laughed, as did the maid and the drunk, although Simon doubted they'd understood a word.

"I have recently come into financial difficulty," Simon said, his mouth curving on one side. "I ruined one set of garments last night. I cannot afford to ruin another."

"Fighting again?"

"In a fashion."

Simon studied Becking closely, searching for any lasting ill-effects from his stay with Desjardins. Fortunately, there did not appear to be any. He was fit and trim, and maintained the understated genial appeal that enabled him to blend in anywhere. His brown hair and eyes were nondescript, his height and build unremarkable, his voice lacking any distinguishing qualities. In short, Richard did not attract undue attention and people found him both innocuous and pleasant to associate with.

Richard kissed the maid on the cheek before shooing her off to refill his ale, then he tossed a coin at the Frenchman and waved him away, too. "How is it that you are suddenly lacking coin?" he asked when they were alone.

"Eddington has seized my accounts." Simon's fingertips drummed into the tabletop. "Stupidity on my part. I had no plans to return to England anytime soon. I should have cleared all my assets before departing."

"Bloody hell."

"Let that be a lesson to you, eh?"

"I cannot believe he had the audacity to aggravate you in that manner." Richard whistled and leaned into his spindle-backed chair. "He must be desperate. Quite frankly, I enjoy picturing Eddington in that light."

Simon's chuckle turned into a cough, the result of the tobacco smoke in the tavern aggravating lungs irritated by the smoke inhalation of the night before. "When I returned to France with Mademoiselle Rousseau, I thought I would proceed with my life unencumbered. Now, I am beset on all sides.

Eddington has proven that my interests are of little concern to him, which leaves me with no one to turn to but you, my friend."

"I knew it was not happenstance that you would seek me out." Richard's face beamed with a broad smile. "But I admit to having had a faint hope that you joined me simply for a night of tupping and drinking."

"Some other time," Simon said, thinking of Lynette as he glanced around the large room. She was the only woman he was interested in tupping. He was interested to such an extreme that his ballocks ached, a discomfort he had not felt in so long he could scarcely remember it.

"So tell me," Richard yelled, as a makeshift orchestra began playing a raucous tune, "what can I do for you?"

There had been a time when Simon deliberately sought out such noisy, boisterous venues. The revelry of others masked his personal discontent, as well as shielded the secrets passed between agents. Now, he found the din irritating.

"What task did Eddington set for you?" he asked, bending low over the table to be heard.

"He would like me to investigate Mademoiselle Rousseau and also Mr. James."

"I ask the same, with an added request for you to learn whatever you can about the Vicomte de Grenier and his family."

Richard's brows rose, then he smiled. The man loved a challenge.

"Exercise more caution than usual," Simon said, straightening slightly as two sloshing tankards were thumped down on the table between them. "There is something amiss. They hide secrets, something or someone they fear enough to flee France."

"I will take care, and I will give you a day's notice."

"Day's notice?" Simon shouted, just as the music fell from its crescendo and faded into silence.

Richard laughed at Simon's scowl. "I will send whatever information I uncover regarding James and Mademoiselle Rousseau to you, then to Eddington the following day. I will keep any news about the vicomte separate, of course, as he did not ask for it." Richard shrugged, then drank deeply. "I wish I could do more."

"It is more than enough." Simon lifted his own ale in a toast. "I am tremendously grateful."

Eddington was paying for his request. Simon was begging a favor. Lacking any family of his own, Simon treasured every gift that came from loyalty and friendship.

"I am in your debt for ensuring our release," Richard dismissed.

"It is what anyone would have done."

"No, it is not, and well you know it."

Simon's lips had barely touched the rim of his stein when he was bumped from behind, causing his ale and its frothy head to spill over his chin, down his chest, and into his lap. He glanced at the subsequent mess and growled. Pushing back from the table, he confronted the man.

"Beg my pardon," he demanded, damning the fate of another set of garments.

The offender, a man of equal height to Simon but twice the weight, looked at the stain running down Simon's clothes and made a monumental error.

He laughed.

"Poor chap," Richard muttered. "Has no idea what's about to hit him."

Simon drew back his fist and swung.

"I deeply regret returning to Paris. This place has only ever brought me misery."

Lynette flinched at the pain in her mother's voice and moved to sit beside her on the edge of a pink velvet chaise.

Late morning sunlight spilled in through the sheer-covered windows and bathed the upper parlor in soft, welcoming light. Despite having dreamt of Simon in ways that made her blush upon rising, Lynette had slept well. Refreshed and determined, she had approached her mother to share some of what she had learned yesterday and to ask her the questions that had waited too long for answers.

"*Maman . . .*"

"I told you to stay away from him!" Marguerite cried, her shoulders shaking. "Why could you not obey me?"

"Because I have to know who this woman is!"

"Lysette is dead!" Her mother pushed to her feet, her robe and night rail swirling around her feet. "I saw her with my own eyes."

"You said her f-face was . . . too badly burned."

"I saw her hair. Her dress. Her s-shoes—"

Covering her mouth to stifle a sob, Marguerite turned away.

"You may have made peace with her passing," Lynette said flatly, her gaze turning to Solange for a moment, then dropping to the floor when tears threatened. "But I have not. I feel as if a part of me is missing."

"This man is taking advantage of your grief!" Marguerite's hands fisted at her sides.

"To what aim?"

"You are wealthy and beautiful. Marriage to you would be any man's aim."

"He is an English spy!" she argued. "What would he gain from wedding a French woman connected to a family who resides in Poland?"

"Perhaps he wishes to enjoy the rest of his days in comfort."

Lynette snorted.

"There are things you do not know, Lynette."

"Yes, *Maman*. I never forget that. I am reminded every day, when something else is said that everyone else seems to understand except me."

"Events of the past should remain in the past."

"That is ridiculous. I am not a child."

Marguerite pointed an accusing finger. "What is ridiculous is that I have allowed myself to be browbeaten into behavior I knew was ill conceived and it has led to this end. *You* have taken advantage of *my* grief. I missed your smiles and the brightness of your eyes. It affected my judgment and you exploited that."

"The brightness is back," Solange interjected in a murmur.

"Courtesy of a charlatan!"

"He is not a charlatan," Lynette defended in as calm a tone as she could manage.

"Reconsider the facts," Marguerite snapped. "This man—one of little consequence, whose presence in France has been compromised—eyes a lovely and obviously wealthy woman at a licentious gathering. He approaches her, removes her mask, kisses her . . . I *know* he kissed you, Lynette. Do not lie to me!"

Lynette flushed and swallowed her intended rebuttal.

"He whispers her name," her mother continued, "and the girl—naïvely lost in her first seduction—hears what she wants to hear. 'Lynette' becomes 'Lysette.' Later, a well-acted and dashing rescue fuels her misguided infatuation and she follows him. She tells him just enough information for him to effect a brilliant scheme to win her trust and the opportunity to bed her and access her funds."

"Mon Dieu," Lynette muttered, crossing her arms. "That is a fantastical tale."

Marguerite laughed without humor. "As fantastical as the story of a woman who might be your dead sister? A woman you cannot see with your own eyes because she is an assassin? Of all things, Lynette. An *assassin?*"

Said in that light, the whole story did sound remarkably improbable. But then, her mother had never spoken at length with Simon Quinn.

"You do not understand," she said. "If you would only meet him."

"Never," Marguerite spat. "I am done with this excursion into madness. As are you. I forbid you to see him again. If you disobey me, you will deeply regret doing so. I promise you that."

Lynette leaped to her feet, her palms dampening. "Give him time—"

"For what?" Her mother began to pace, occasionally glaring at Solange, who sat meekly at a small table sipping tea. "For him to continue raising doubts in you about your family? Creating a rift between you and those who love you so that only he remains for you to lean upon? Or perhaps we should wait until you are fat with his bastard child, so there can be no doubt that you are ruined?"

"You insult me without cause," Lynette said, hiding her rising panic behind cool dignity. "He asked me to stay away from him. He told me to leave him be, to put as much distance as possible between us."

"A clever tactic to win your trust. Do you not see?" her mother asked, holding both hands out to her. "By making *you* pursue the connection rather than the reverse, he creates the appearance of innocence."

Marguerite moved to Solange. "Help me," she begged.

Solange sighed and set down her cup. "There are men such as your *maman* describes, *chérie.*"

"But you do not think Simon Quinn is one of them," she countered.

"Frankly, I do not know. I have never formally met the man."

"Regardless," Marguerite said, her shoulders squaring. "Your father is due to arrive in a few days and I will turn this matter over to him. In the interim, you will not leave this house for any reason."

"Perhaps *he* will listen to reason!"

Her mother's blue eyes took on a steely cast. "Perhaps he will wed you to a stern man who will manage your waywardness properly."

"Maman!" Lynette's heart stopped, then raced madly. Her *grand-mère* had done the same to her mother. While her parents were cordial, there was no passion between them. No fire. Theirs was a cold

marriage and Lynette violently eschewed such a fate for herself. "You could have threatened anything but that," she said bitterly, "and I might have heeded you."

Marguerite stiffened and her arms crossed. "Enough. Not another word. Go to your room and calm yourself."

"I am not a child! You cannot prevent me from discovering the truth about this woman."

"Do *not* think to gainsay me. I will not tolerate these dramatics."

Lynette's eyes stung, then tears overflowed. Marguerite flinched, but did not relent.

"Go now."

Turning on her heel, Lynette stormed from the room.

"I wish I could have seen his face," Eddington said, laughing with such abandon that he was forced to put his wine goblet back on the dining table. "I so enjoy watching you brawl."

Simon spoke around a bite of veal. "There was nothing to see. One moment, he was standing. The next, he was on the floor."

"Until the rest of the assembly joined in."

"Well," Simon shrugged, "that is the way such things are done."

Eddington gestured for a servant to take his plate. "What were you doing there?"

"Spoiling for a fight, of course," Simon said dryly. He noted the earl's studiously casual deportment across the dining table and was not fooled by it. "Something about extortion puts me in the mood."

The corner of Eddington's mouth twitched.

There was a soft scratching at the door. Simon called out and the butler entered.

"Excuse me, my lord." He glanced at Simon. "Sir, you have a visitor."

Immediately, Simon's gut tightened with a volatile mixture of concern and anticipation. He did not ask who it was due to the earl's presence. He simply nodded and pushed back from the table.

"If you will excuse me, my lord."

"Of course."

Simon felt Eddington's gaze on him until the door shut on his retreating back. He glanced at his butler.

"Blonde and beautiful, sir," the servant said in answer to the unasked question.

Sweat dotted Simon's brow. He breathed shallowly, lamenting the fact that he had only to *think* of Lynette and his body responded with ravenous ferocity. If only he had the means to go away. For her sake.

Inhaling deeply, he crossed the threshold of the lower parlor and paused, noting the vivid blue of Lynette's gown. She stood with her back to him, her fingertips caressing a lovely China vase displayed on a wooden pedestal. But she was not relaxed. Her shoulders were tight and the air around her vibrated with tension.

"Lynette," he said softly, infernally glad to see her, "you should not have come."

She turned and he realized his mistake.

"Mr. Quinn." The voice was low and throaty, yet underlaced with steel.

He bowed. "Vicomtess de Grenier."

Gesturing for her to be seated, he glanced back

out the door and nodded to his butler to bring refreshments. As the servant hurried away to inform the housekeeper, Simon sat opposite the vicomtess and contemplated her openly.

He was in agreement with the sentiment that the mother could pass for a sibling. Their coloring—pale blond hair and blue eyes—was identical. In addition, the vicomtess's beauty remained unmarred by lines and her figure was as svelte and sweetly curved as Lynette's.

"You are very handsome," she said, studying him with narrowed eyes. "I can see the appeal."

Simon's mouth curved on one side. "Thank you. I can see whom your daughter favors. You are both the loveliest women I have ever seen."

"What of the assassin?" she asked coldly. "I assume she is lovely, too?"

"Yes, of course." He settled more comfortably, admiring the vicomtess's fire, which she had passed on to her daughter.

"Of course." Her smile was tight. "What do you want?"

He arched a brow. "Cut straight to the point, I see."

Her bare fingers tangled in her lap, the knuckles adorned with various precious gems of impressive size. Small diamond clips glittered in her hair and a sapphire hatpin secured her chapeau to her head.

The woman had come prepared to dazzle him with her wealth. He was impressed with her, but also deeply insulted. The latter emotion made him laugh. He had survived these many years by selling whatever someone would buy, including his body. It was a fine time to develop scruples.

"I want for nothing," he said.

"You want my daughter," she refuted, "or the money at her disposal."

"I don't want her money."

She snorted. "Do not tell me it's love. I can only stomach so much."

"No," he agreed, "it isn't love. But I do want her and I am cad enough to have her if presented with the opportunity, which is why I have asked her to stay away."

"How honorable of you," she sneered, reminding him briefly of Lysette. Her blue eyes took on a brittle cast and the lush curve of her lips twisted with distaste.

"So pleased you approve," he drawled, laying his arm along the back of the settee, knowing the overt familiarity would prick her already considerable temper. He, too, was growing angrier by the moment. It was all well and good to call him a selfish libertine when the label fit. It did not sit well when he was attempting to be self-sacrificing.

"Why choose my daughter?" she asked. "You could have any woman you want. A wealthy widow, perhaps? Or are they not malleable enough?"

Simon smiled without humor. "I know you find it difficult, if not impossible, to believe, but I am not fortune hunting. I admire your daughter. She displays the same strength of conviction that you show in coming here. She is also lovely and I am a healthy man. I cannot help but notice her physical charms. However, beyond that, I have no ulterior motive. She seeks me out, not the reverse. If she did not come to me, I would not go to her."

Her jaw tightened.

"My lady." Simon straightened. "It would be best

if you leave Paris. I cannot stress that point strongly enough. The woman who so closely resembles your daughter is enmeshed in dangerous affairs. It would be deeply unfortunate if the two women were to be confused for one another."

"This woman you call Lysette," the vicomtess hissed.

"Lysette Rousseau, yes." He shrugged. "I did not give her that name, so if you do not like it, do not upbraid me."

The vicomtess paled and Simon took note.

"Is the name familiar to you?" he queried, setting his forearms on his thighs. "Any information you can share that would shed light on this matter would be greatly appreciated."

"What concerns my family does not concern you!" She stood, a diversionary tactic designed to draw attention away from her distress. "You say my daughter seeks you out. Let us remove you, then. Allow me to send you on holiday."

Simon rose with her. "No."

"Come now, surely there is somewhere you should like to visit. Spain? Perhaps return to England?"

"Poland?" he bit out, linking his hands behind his back to keep from fisting them. His knuckles, sore and bruised from the tavern brawl the night before, protested. The pain focused him and reined in his growing temper.

"How about an extended holiday? One that lasts the duration of your life, hmm?" The vicomtess's shoulders were pulled back, her chin lifted, her smile innocuous. A mixture of charm and determination. So like Lynette.

The woman did not realize it, but the deeper

glimpse into Lynette's life only made him want her more. The vicomte was a fortunate man to have such a wife. Lynette's future spouse would be equally blessed.

The thought deflated him, draining his anger and resentment away and leaving only weary resignation behind.

"Name your price," she urged.

Simon crossed his arms. "You assume I am inexpensive."

Triumph lit her eyes. "To afford this?" She gestured around the room with a wide sweep of her arm. "I am a woman, Mr. Quinn. I am ever aware of price and affordability. Your departure will cost me a fortune, I know."

His stomach churned and a bitter taste coated his tongue. To accept money to part with Lynette made him ill, but there was no denying the plan's merit. If the vicomtess was willing to provide him with even half of what Eddington had confiscated, he could live comfortably for the rest of his days. He would be free of any encumbrance. He could pack his belongings, or leave them behind, and start anew elsewhere.

Lynette would be safe from his desires and the means he provided for her to explore her curiosity about Lysette.

Simon growled low in his throat, hating Eddington for putting him in the position of needing money to begin with. Because of the earl's machinations, he was trapped here, in proximity to a woman he could not resist, yet could not have.

Unless he accepted the vicomtess's offer.

He exhaled harshly, suddenly exhausted by the events of the last few days. "I need time to think."

She seemed prepared to argue, then simply nodded. "I will send a messenger over in the morning. Will that suit you?"

"No, it does not suit me." Simon glared at her, knowing she was only trying to protect her daughter, but detesting the fact that *he* was the hazard. "You believe it is concern for my welfare that goads me to even consider your insulting offer. But it is, in truth, concern for Lynette and the fear that if I do not take myself far away, she will cross paths with Lysette Rousseau."

"And fall victim to ruination by your hands."

"Certainly," he agreed, seeing no need to mince words while having a conversation such as this one.

"Pity you will not use your own funds to travel."

"Yes." His jaw clenched. "A pity."

Marguerite descended the short steps to the street and paused a moment to look at the home behind her, shaken by her meeting with the debonair Simon Quinn.

The man was dangerous.

She had not seen him well enough in the Orlinda garden. The air had been filled with smoke and her concern had been for Lynette and taking her to safety. In the clear view of a well-lit and tastefully decorated parlor, he had been breathtaking, his coloring of ink-black hair and brilliant blue eyes jolting to a woman's equanimity.

Over the years, she had met many men. Rarely had she crossed paths with one possessed of the same voluptuary's appeal as Saint-Martin. They boasted more than mere physical beauty as a lure;

they looked at women with their senses, making her feel as if she were the only thing in the room worth paying attention to. Their favor did not waver nor wander. They focused on her with knowing eyes, making her wonder if such attention to detail would carry into the bedroom.

Some women were immune to such confident sexuality. Marguerite was not one of them and Lynette was so like her.

Sighing, she gave her hand to the footman and climbed into her coach. She had once been certain that Lynette would marry young. Like Marguerite, she adored men and was sensual by nature. But the similarities between them were even more pronounced than Marguerite had first realized.

Just as Marguerite had once postponed the selection of a spouse until her mother had chosen for her, Lynette also did not seem inclined to pick. For years, she had thought her daughter was simply enjoying herself and felt no haste. Now she suspected Lynette had been searching for her own Saint-Martin. A man who would sweep her away and satisfy the cravings no lady should admit to having.

Unsettled, she placed her hand atop her corseted stomach. She knew Lynette well. By rashly threatening an arranged marriage to tame her daughter, she had incited a war of wills. Lynette was too headstrong, passionate, and staunchly independent to accept the will of another without a fight.

If she had been thinking clearly instead of in a panic, Marguerite would never have suggested such a thing. Now Lynette would rebel; she knew that like she knew the dawn followed the night. The only way to keep her daughter safe was to remove temptation. So she had dealt with Quinn immediately before Lynette had a chance to act.

But now that she had set her plan in motion, she required the money. She could not access de Grenier funds in sufficient quantity before morning.

There was only one person she could turn to with such a request, but meeting with him would require stealth, calculation, and more strength than she was certain she possessed.

"My lady?" the footman queried. "The direction?"

Marguerite took a shaky inhalation. "Take us home."

Chapter 11

Lynette impatiently waited two hours after her mother returned from her outing before sneaking out.

It was not uncommon for the vicomtess to take some time away after a row. Lynette had inherited the same wanderlust when aggravated, so she knew the feeling well. Sadly, she was not allowed the freedom tonight. Her only recourse was to pace the length of her room and think endlessly of Simon. No matter how it appeared, she believed him and she needed to see him, needed to warn him that her family may react in disturbing ways. She would not see him harmed in any fashion due to her.

And so it was that when the hour turned sufficiently late and the odds that her mother would attempt to speak with her diminished greatly, Lynette set in motion her plan to leave.

She stuffed pillows under her counterpane and topped the body-shaped form with one of her wigs. The ruse would not bear close inspection, but a quick peek from the doorway would give the impression that she was abed and sleeping.

Shielded by a cloak and hood, she exited to the rear garden, then out to the alley. There a stable-boy waited, a young man named Piotr who had been with her family for years. She had always been kind to him, bringing him sweets and treats when possible, deliberately cultivating a bit of favoritism that had enabled her frequent bouts of mischief at home. Tonight he provided her with a pair of his breeches, a man's cloak, and a tricorn. She changed in an empty stall in the stable, then met him outside.

He handed her the reins of a saddled horse, then mounted another to accompany her, as he always did. He had been trained to use a pistol with precision, as most of the male servants in the de Grenier household were. Simon's admonishment to avoid confusion with Lysette Rousseau was foremost in her mind. To the casual observer, they were two young men riding alone.

The horses' hooves clopped rhythmically along the street, lulling her into a semidreamy state. The night was dark, the moon half hidden by clouds. The breeze was slightly chilly and it slipped through the arm slits in her cloak, cooling her heated skin.

Would Simon be at home? Or would he be out? Perhaps he was not alone . . .

What would she say if he was entertaining someone when she arrived? A woman.

Lynette inhaled slowly and deeply, trying to calm her racing heart. Her posture while riding—head and shoulders bent low to hide her features—only added to her sense of falling off a cliff. She was not a woman to cower in the face of anything, yet she was afraid now.

Afraid to be seen, afraid to find Simon occupied or gone, afraid her parents would never forgive her this transgression.

Yet she did not turn about. Her need to be with him was stronger than her apprehension. He calmed her, at the same time he revived the spirit she'd once had. The spirit suppressed when Lysette died. She felt like herself with him. Free of airs or evasions. Freed from the need to maintain an unfamiliar timid deportment.

Do not upset the balance. Do not give her parents reason to lament the misfortune of losing the good and quiet daughter, instead of the unruly one.

Lynette drew her mount to a halt before Simon's home. She was not certain how she ended up standing before the door or why she was breathing as if she had run the distance traveled. She felt dizzy. Disoriented. More than ever, she wanted to cling to Simon's strength.

She blinked and found the butler standing before her, a stocky man whose wig did little to disguise his youthful features. His only sign of surprise upon seeing her dressed in the garb of a male servant was a slight rise in his brow line, then he stepped out of the way without her saying a word and closed the door behind her.

"Mademoiselle," he said, his voice sounding as if coming from a distance due to the rushing of blood in her ears. "May I take your cloak and hat?"

She gave him the hat, but clutched the thick wool like a shield.

"I should warn you, mademoiselle, Mr. Quinn is in poor humor this evening."

"Is he alone?" she whispered, emboldened by the kindness in his eyes.

"He has a guest in residence, but his lordship is otherwise occupied." The butler gestured ahead with arm extended. "May I show you into the parlor while I inform Mr. Quinn of your arrival?"

"Would you mind terribly if I s-showed myself up?"

She was afraid Simon would make her leave if she stayed downstairs.

But she knew what would happen if she went upstairs.

The butler did as well, if the flushing of his cheekbones was any indication. His head tilted slightly. "Second door on your right," he murmured. "I will see that your servant is shown to the kitchen."

"Thank you."

Gripping the staircase railing with white-knuckled force, Lynette ascended carefully, her steps hesitant due to the shaking of her legs. She gained the landing and paused.

The hallway was barely lit; only two tapers in widely separated sconces shed any illumination. Although the décor was vastly different, she was reminded of the Orlinda manse. Her blood heated in response.

Light peeked out from beneath two doors. One on the left, the other on the right. She was passing the first when voices within arrested her. Her nerves were already strung tight by existing circumstances. She had no notion how she would survive a chance meeting in addition to that.

Fear of discovery froze her in place. Then, mercifully, the conversation grew more animated, ensuring that the participants were too engaged to hear her pass by. She was about to continue on when conversation ceased and the creaking of a bed was plainly heard. Biting her lip, she remained motionless.

A woman's throaty laugh floated through the door, followed by a man's.

The soothing baritone of the man's voice thickened and became coaxing. The woman purred something that incited a masculine groan . . . followed by a rhythmic thumping that permeated the walls, strong and steady and endless.

Sex.

Lynette's lungs seized. Her hand rose to her throat as sweat beaded on her forehead.

Unable to stop listening, she sagged into the wall, her free hand fisting and releasing in the folds of her cloak. She clenched her thighs to ease a growing throbbing, and bit her lower lip as fevered cries of pleasure rose in volume and spilled freely out to the hallway.

She had no idea how long she stood there. She knew only that her senses were overstimulated, her skin too hot, her mouth too dry, her breasts too full and aching unmercifully.

The door on the right wrenched open and golden light flooded the hall. Lynette straightened as Simon strode out with a thunderous scowl. Breeches were his only garment. They were unfastened, revealing a tantalizing triangle of tawny skin and a thin trail of dark hair that disappeared beneath the doeskin . . . just above the long, thick evidence of his arousal. His abdomen was laced tight with muscle, his fisted hands causing his powerful biceps to bulge. His hair was unbound, the silky ebon strands swaying around his powerful shoulders.

She had never seen anything as savagely beautiful.

Or wanted anything more.

Simon paused midstep, staring at her, unblinking. The tempo of the rise and fall of his chest altered, as did the air surrounding him. Fury turned into lust so hot it scorched her.

"Simon," she whispered, raising her hand to him.

Two strides and he had her in his arms, cradled to his chest. Her arms circled his neck, pressing her breasts to his torso and her lips to his throat.

He smelled of tobacco and brandy and musk, and the fragrance soothed something restless inside her. She was where she needed to be, in Simon's arms. Boneless, she held him as he carried her into his bedchamber and kicked the door closed.

I need you. She wanted to say the words, but her throat was too tight.

Simon knew. His features were austere with hunger, his eyes feverishly bright in the light of the many candles. He set her on her feet by his massive bed and unfastened the frog at her throat. The shield of her cloak puddled around her feet, leaving her feeling as if she were naked, despite being fully clothed.

"What in hell are you wearing?" he barked.

"A disguise."

"Christ." His jaw tightened. "Turn around."

Frowning, she did as he asked. She jumped as his hands cupped her buttocks and squeezed.

"Have you any idea what the sight of you hungering to be fucked does to me?" he asked crudely. "Then you compound the problem by displaying every curve of your body."

It aroused her to be spoken to in that manner. She would not have guessed that would be true.

She faced him. "Is it anything like what the sight of this"—her fingertips touched his navel, then followed the trail of dark hair until impeded by his breeches—"does to me?"

He caught her hand and squeezed gently. "Why did you come?"

She smiled. "Would it ruin the moment to say I am here for me?"

"No."

"My mother thinks marriage will rein me in. If that is truly her intent, I will take my pleasure now."

Tension caused his chest to tighten into rock-hard, delineated muscle. She thought him beautiful, not in the elegant refined lines of statuary, but in the unpolished power of a man who survived by his physical strength.

"She came to see me tonight," he murmured, gripping her hips and tugging her closer. "She offered to pay me to go away."

Indignation and deep sadness warred for dominance. "What did you say?"

He met her gaze directly. "I told her I would consider it."

Pain, sharp and searing, pierced through her chest. She inhaled sharply, but did not pull away. Perhaps she was naïve, but she did not believe a man could look at her as he did and not care for her at least a little. "Why?"

"My accounts have been seized. I cannot leave of my own accord, I cannot afford to."

"Do you need to leave?"

"For your sake"—he pressed his cheek to her temple—"I would have."

"Would have?" she whispered, her fingers kneading along his spine, feeling the way he tensed and quivered beneath her touch like a skittish stallion.

"No need to go now. I will have your virginity within the hour."

Tangling his fingers in the tie at her throat, Simon tugged it free. His breath gusted hot and damp across her forehead, the sensation primitively arousing. "By the morning," he purred, "there will be nothing innocent about you, I'm afraid."

He had pounced, caught his prey, and was preparing to devour.

She shivered, more than ready. More than eager. "I am not afraid at all."

He stilled. The energy he radiated was raw, possessive. She could smell the lust on him. Felt it in the shaking of his industrious fingers. Heard it in the laborious rhythm of his breathing.

Lynette offered him her mouth. He took it, his lips slanting across hers, his tongue thrusting deep, making her sex quiver and grow damp.

Simon's hands cupped her breasts, the feeling intensified by the lack of material between them. Only the linen of her shirt and her chemise separated his touch from her skin. Then his right leg hooked behind the back of hers and tugged.

With her feet knocked out from under her, she toppled. Holding her firm to his chest, he cradled her down to the bed.

"Simon?" she gasped, suddenly finding herself beneath him.

"Every time you look at me, you beg me for sex with your eyes." He crouched between her spread legs and began unlacing her boots. "You have driven me half mad. No more, or I will be in you before you are even undressed."

Lacking experience, Lynette still knew that such was not the normal order for going about the business. The thought that she was with a man of uncommon appetite and skill kept her on a knife edge of anticipation, sharp and perilous.

As her feet were bared, gooseflesh spread across her skin. Simon must have taken note because he paused, his hands cupping the backs of her calves and stroking soothingly. He rubbed and massaged, moving down to her stocking-covered feet and pressing his thumbs into her arches. The heat of his sensual touch affected her deeply, arousing her as if it were the flesh between her thighs that he ministered to.

She moaned, her eyes closing in delight.

He pressed a kiss to the pad of her foot and stood, reaching for the placket of her breeches.

Without her vision, the sounds of the crackling fire and the distant sounds of his guests' carnal activities were more pronounced, adding another layer to the sensual cocoon she floated in. The bed smelled of Simon, pure delicious masculinity. She turned her head, pushing her nose into the turned-down linens and breathing him in.

"I want the smell of you on my skin," she confessed, her hands fisting into the bedclothes as his fingers brushed across her stomach.

Simon yanked too hard on the waistband of her breeches and she heard a tearing. She smiled.

"Hold tight," he ordered. His arms were thrust beneath her and she was pulled upright. She gripped his forearms and held on, inhaling sharply at the sudden violence of the movement. She was stood on her feet, then summarily undressed.

Her breeches were pushed to the floor in one fell movement. The shirtsleeves took more effort, but not much. Her chemise was pulled up and over, leaving only her stockings as the last garments on her body.

Oddly, she felt overdressed.

Simon caught her up, lifting her feet from the floor.

Lynette's head went back and she gazed up at him with wide eyes, her brain attempting to process the heretofore unknown sensory input—the feel of coarse hair and damp skin against her breasts, the kiss of air against her bare buttocks, the feel of a man's arms against her naked back.

His features remained taut and strained by desire. Perhaps she should have been afraid of the lack of softness, but she could not fear anything about him. Lynette knew, as only a woman could, that the only thing that mattered to him in this moment was her.

Taking the necessary steps to the bed, Simon laid her down again. He stood over her, his gaze drinking her in. He followed his eyes with his fingers, caressing the marks her confined chemise had left in her skin. The touch warmed her and brought an ache to her chest. It was not a touch given in the act of seduction, but one designed to comfort, to say that he found her beautiful even when marred.

Lynette struggled to keep from closing her eyes, fighting the feeling of surrender and vulnerability. Her body was not her own. It burned and clenched and quivered for him, ignoring any control she might have exerted to bind him to her as tightly as he bound her to him.

"Such beautiful breasts," he murmured, the splayed fingertips of both hands brushing over the upthrust tips. "Such lovely nipples."

Simon caged her to the mattress, his hair coursing over her fevered skin in a curtain of ebony silk. His breath blew hot and moist over the tender peak, in and out. Her nipple hardened and ached, demanding more.

"Simon," she whispered, absorbed in the sight of such a powerful, sensual animal so passionately focused on her. "Please."

The look he gave her was both amused and sharply intent. "Not yet."

"Please!"

The rough pad of his tongue licked across her. She arched upward, crying out.

"Is that what you want?" he crooned.

Lynette shook her head. "It aches, Simon."

He relented then, tenderness sweeping across his features. His mouth opened, straight white teeth gently biting the firm flesh before circling the tip with his lips.

"Yes," she whimpered, straining upward.

Kneading her breast with one hand, his other slid down her side, briefly cupping her hip to hold her steady. "Lie still," he admonished, lifting his head to look at her.

"I need you."

His slow smile caused a painful tightening in her womb. "I know."

As his fingers ruffled the pale curls at the apex of her thighs, Lynette's breath caught and held in her lungs. A single blunt fingertip pushed between the slick folds and stroked across a point of agonizing pleasure. Her legs widened in helpless invitation, beyond shame.

"So hot and wet." Simon licked his lips and she moaned, her head thrashing as he began exploring every curve and crevice of her spasming sex. She felt the tiny entrance pulsing, straining, weeping freely.

The tip of a finger circled the clenching opening, then pushed a scant bit inside. Her body sucked hungrily at it, luring it deeply into the spot where she throbbed for him.

"Dear God," he groaned. "You are so tight and greedy."

"Take me," she begged, tortured by the feelings of emptiness and desperation. She lifted her hand and pushed it into the thick silk of his hair, tugging him toward her.

"Not yet." The lilt of Ireland in his voice was more pronounced now.

She adored it, as she was beginning to adore all of him. Except for those two words.

"I cannot take anymore." She was shaking violently, a creature of desire and longing.

"You will take all of me, *a thiasce.*" A wicked smile preceded the return of his lips to her breast.

"A thiasce." Her eyes stung from the reverence with which he said the words. "What does that mean?"

"My treasure." His mouth surrounded her aching nipple with drenching heat and she writhed, broken by his endearment and the whiplash of pleasure created by his suckling.

This was what she had needed, what she had refused to forfeit for her family and the future she was destined to have. In all of her life, only Simon had inspired these feelings of complete trust and mindless need. If this was all she could have of him, she would accept it without fear of reprisal and treasure the memory as he claimed to treasure her.

His tongue curled around the tight, hard peak and pressed it against the roof of his mouth, his cheeks hollowing with every drawing pull. An invisible thread led straight to her womb and tugged in timed rhythm to his ministrations. The teasing finger between her legs slipped inside her to the first knuckle, causing a burning stretching that scorched her skin and made her perspire.

"Simon!"

He moved, fitting his mouth over hers, his thumb rubbing into the sensitive knot of nerves just above where he entered her. Pleasure swept through her body in a rush, bowing her spine and freeing a relieved moan that poured into his mouth. Her sex clenched like a fist, then rippled in release, moisture flooding her body and easing the sudden thrust of his hand.

The rending of her maidenhead was scarcely more than a pinch of discomfort amid the violence of her first climax. It seemed to affect him more than her, his groan louder than her cry, his powerful frame shuddering brutally. His kisses grew shorter, more fervent. His finger thrust gently, soothingly through the tender tissues of her ravished sex.

"Lynette," he murmured in a broken voice. "Forgive me."

Her arms wrapped around him and pulled him tighter to her, her tearstained cheek pressed tightly to his. "I wanted this, *mon amour*. I wanted all that I can have of you, however much or little that may be. However short or long the duration."

He leaned heavily against her for the space of several heartbeats, his hands leaving her body. Then his voice came rough and needy, "I must move you higher."

She tried to help by holding tight to him, fighting through a penetrating languidness that slackened her muscles. He lifted her, his knee pushing into the mattress, then the other, moving them both in a half-crawl across the bed.

He set her down amid a profusion of pillows of various sizes, textures, and colors. Resting back on his haunches, his hands on his thighs, he watched her. Lynette held her arms out to him, giving him the invitation he seemed to be looking for.

Simon rose to his knees and reached for his waistband, drawing her gaze to that tantalizing triangle of skin.

Her mouth dried.

The thick crown and top few inches of his erection were visible there, peeking out defiantly in a straight line toward his navel.

For the rest of her life she knew she would remember this image of him vividly—his knees spread wide, his dark hair loose about tawny shoulders, his abdomen ridged with muscle and glistening with sweat, his cock hard and thick and thrusting hungrily upward. She moistened dry lips and a dangerous growl rumbled up from his chest.

A moment later, his breeches were around his knees. Simon rolled to his back and kicked them the rest of the way off. Gloriously naked and impressively aroused, he climbed over her in a dazzling display of rippling strength and golden skin.

There was nothing languid about her any longer. She was as hot for him now as she had been in the gallery earlier. And as always, he knew it. A slight smile softened the harshness of his taut jaw. It shattered her, that gentle curving of his voluptuary's mouth and the adjacent tenderness in his eyes.

His thighs pressed her legs open wider. One arm rested in the mattress by her shoulder, the biceps bulging with the strength required to support his torso above her. The other reached between them, taking his weighty cock in hand and tucking the thick crest into the slick entrance of her body.

The heat of him made her whimper and writhe. He set his other hand into the mattress. The only parts of his body touching hers were his outer thighs and the broad head of his cock. Silky smooth and burning hot.

Lynette's fingernails dug into his forearms as he rolled his hips and pushed into her. Her head fell back, her eyes closing. Panting, she clawed at him, certain she would lose her sanity in the maelstrom of sensations flooding her senses.

The scent of his skin was stronger now, surrounding her, filling her mind with every breath. The feel of the coarse hair on his chest and legs was unbearably arousing, emphasizing the differences between them—his hardness to her softness, his strength to her litheness, his size to hers.

"Sweet." He groaned. "Dear God, you are so sweet and tight."

"Please . . . Simon . . ." She struggled to arch her hips and take him deeper, faster. His weight held her down, forcing her to accept his pace and the short, fierce digs of his cock inside her. Advancing and retreating in tiny increments, allowing her body time to adjust to its first claiming by a man. But she did not have time to spare. At any moment she would go mad, she was sure of it.

"Beautiful," he praised hoarsely as she tightened around him. His hips circled expertly, pushing the length and width of him ever deeper into the heart of her. Simon cupped her face in his large hands. "Look at me."

Lynette forced her heavy lids to lift. He was devastating to gaze upon, his eyes brilliantly blue and glittering, his cheekbones flushed, his hair swaying with his movements.

She whimpered and clung to him. "Deeper."

"Soon," he rasped.

"Simon . . . I beg you . . ."

But he refused to be goaded, maintaining his slow relentless drive until finally he was seated to the hilt, impossibly thick and throbbing. She felt every beat of his heart, every ropelike vein, every straining inch. It was the basest, most primitive of dominations. She was crammed full of him, stretched too tight to move.

"I am finally where I have longed to be since the moment I first saw you." His hands left her face and captured hers, his fingers linking with hers and pinning her down. He moved then, withdrawing until the veriest tip of him remained, then gliding deep and slow.

The friction curled her toes, the wide flared head of his massive cock stroking across nerve endings she had never known she possessed. She could not believe she fit him, or that he fit her, but they were tailor-made for each other, despite the snugness of her untried flesh.

His hips rose and fell again, still leisurely and sure, his expertise evident in his ability to make every plunge an exercise in unalloyed bliss. He watched her like a hawk, noting every gasp and sob of delight so that he could continue to rub those tender spots. Lost in the rapture he imparted so skillfully, she still noted his intense perusal. It was why she had wanted him, why she had come to him at such great cost. She had wanted to be pleasured like this, to be the sole focus of an expert lover's attentions, to be cherished by a man whom she adored.

Simon was deliberately and methodically imprinting himself deep into her, making absolutely certain she would remember his touch, his scent, the minutiae of how he felt inside her. Forever. The sense of the end approaching, of the fleetingness of this night, incited a potent desperation. Sweat soaked her skin, causing her hair to cling to her forehead and cheeks in damp tendrils. She twisted and slid beneath him, her head thrashing as he rode her with studious leisure. In and out. Driving deep. Retreating to the tip. Building her arousal moment by moment, making the climb to climax a lengthy, unhurried, unforgettable affair.

Her legs wrapped around his pumping hips,

pulling him into her, trying to increase his pace to the pounding tempo his guests had used, but unable to match his strength. Nothing could sway or move him. He simply laughed softly and teased her aching nipples with the hot lash of his tongue.

When the orgasm finally hit, it was devastating, the slow stoking of her arousal releasing in a violent jolt through her body, her sex sucking hard on the swelling cock inside her, her womb spasming in grateful relief. She cried out, over and over, shivering violently and sobbing his name.

"Yes," Simon purred, his mouth to her ear. "Melt for me, *a thiasce.* Mold to me."

And she was, she could feel her body softening to hold him more perfectly. He extended her pleasure until she thought she might die of it, the drugging thrusts of his cock prolonging her tremors until she could hardly breathe for the joy of it.

Only when her legs fell wide in exhaustion did he take his own pleasure, shafting her quivering sex in fierce strokes that were nearly too much after the ravaging intensity of her climax. He gasped lewd praise in her ear, remarking on the feel of her, the scent of her, the totality of her submission.

"For you," she whispered, her fingers tightening on his. "Only for you."

He wrenched out of her with an agonized groan, kneeling above her and fisting his cock, spurting his seed across her stomach in long, silky skeins. Guttural cries tore from his throat as he came with such force, it awed her to see it.

She had done this to him, led him to this end. But even in the extremity of his orgasm, he thought of her and protected her.

When he had finished, his head hung low, his face shielded by his hair, his chest heaving with the need for air. A stallion winded from a long, hard ride.

Lynette would have spoken, if her mouth were not so dry and her body so weary. When he left the bed, she held her hand out to him and he kissed her fingertips, his eyes dark with emotion.

He moved behind the screen in the corner. She heard water poured and a cloth wrung out. When he reappeared, his face and locks were damp, his chest glistening, his stride sultry and relaxed. Unabashedly naked and half-erect. He sat on the edge of the bed and smiled, setting a chilly wet towel on her stomach.

"Oh!" she gasped, jerking in surprise. "Wicked man."

The sensation of cold on her fevered skin revived her slightly, although she felt even better after drinking the glass of water he poured for her.

"Thank you," she murmured, handing it back.

Simon retrieved the cloth and stroked it over her sticky skin, cleaning off his semen and soothing the flesh between her thighs. His touch was reverent, his gaze warm with something akin to gratitude.

"You are very quiet," she said when he had set the towel aside. "Have you nothing to say?"

He paused, breathing deeply. His throat worked on a swallow and tension weighted his shoulders. The more time that passed, the more she adored him. There were no practiced platitudes, no teasing gambits, nothing to take the moment from the extraordinary to the mundane.

"Could it be," she wondered, tapping her chin with her fingertip, "that Simon Quinn, lauded lover, has been rendered speechless by a virgin?"

Rich, masculine laughter filled the air and stilled the beating of her heart. He leaned over and kissed the end of her nose. "Witch."

She smiled, and lured him back to bed.

Chapter 12

Marguerite paced the length of Solange's upstairs parlor and wrung her hands. She was nervous as she had never been, her palms damp and pulse erratic.

She had returned from Quinn's and fought with herself for hours, wanting to apologize and right things with her daughter, but knowing it was her responsibility as a mother to take extreme steps when necessary. She hated these machinations, hated threatening Lynette with marriage when she knew well how it felt since her own mother had done the same to her. They were too alike, she and Lynette, and now their lives were even more paralleled than ever before. Considering the end she had come to, Marguerite did not consider that to be an acceptable state of affairs.

Solange was out at the theater with a paramour. Lynette was sleeping, as were most of the servants. The house was quiet, the night still. The serenity of her surroundings only emphasized her roiling disquiet.

How did one face her missing heart, knowing she would have to lose it again?

But as time passed, she feared he might not come at all. Did he believe she had betrayed him? Did he not understand that she had left him to protect him?

A soft scratching came to the door, the sound so obtrusive in the silence that it felt as if they had scratched directly across her high-strung nerves. She jumped, tried to call out, and found her throat too dry. She caught up the glass of sherry on the table, drank it down, then tried again.

"Come in."

Her voice was low and throaty from the alcohol, but she was heard and the portal opened. The maid dipped a quick curtsy and stepped out of the way. A moment later, Philippe filled the doorway.

Marguerite's hand rose to cover her heart, her senses wracked by the barrage of emotions that assailed her at once.

Mon Dieu, he was still impossibly perfect, his body still lean, his countenance made more distinguished by the lines of time. Even the silver hair at his temples blended beautifully with the gold—an enhancement, not a detriment.

He glanced at the maid and sent her away with a flick of his wrist. She withdrew, closing the door behind her.

He stood unmoving for several moments, studying Marguerite with the same ravenous hunger, the same need to catalog every outward change. His enduring love struck her like a blow to the chest, stealing her breath and making her heart throb in her chest.

"Mon coeur," he said, bowing. "Forgive my delay.

I took great pains to ensure that I was not seen or followed."

Philippe was exquisitely dressed for riding in tan-colored breeches that hugged powerful thighs and a dark blue coat with tails. He held his hat in both hands, carried low on his middle, like a shield.

"You look well," she managed, gesturing toward a slipper chair with a shaking hand.

"A façade, I'm afraid." He sat only when she did, choosing a position directly opposite her. "You, on the other hand, are beyond ravishing. More beautiful now than when you were mine."

"I am still yours," she whispered.

"Are you happy?"

"I am not unhappy."

He nodded, understanding.

"And you?" she queried.

"I survive."

He did not live. That broke her heart and a tear fell unbidden. "Do you wish we had never met?"

"Never would I wish such a thing," he said vehemently. "You have been the one light in my life."

She felt the same and told him so with her eyes.

"How ironic," he said softly, "that I joined the *secret du roi* in order to give my life meaning and instead it is the thing that took away my lone joy. If only I had waited for you. How different our lives would be now."

"Your wife . . ."

"She died." A tinge of regret weighted his tone.

"I heard." A fall from a horse while riding. Too much tragedy in their lives. A punishment, perhaps, for their indiscretion. "You have my sincere condolences."

"You have always been sincere," he said with a fond smile curving his mouth. "She was away with a lover at the time. I like to think she was happy in the end."

"I hope she was." *I wish you were.* But she did not say the words. There was no help for it, and wishing for things that could not be only added to the misery.

"You have two daughters."

"Now only one. One was lost to me two years ago." Marguerite breathed deeply. "They are the reason I asked you here tonight."

Sadness shadowed his features and she knew he'd hoped she might have sent for him for a different reason. He was a wise man, he would know that such a liaison would be agonizing for both of them, and yet he could not help but want it. She understood. Part of her wished he would seduce her, as they both knew he could. Make her mindless with lust so that her conscience could not intercede.

"Whatever you need, if it is in my power to give it to you, I shall."

"My eldest daughter met a man here in Paris. Simon Quinn. Have you heard of him?"

Philippe frowned. "Not that I can recall."

"He has somehow convinced her that there is a woman here in Paris who is identical to her, as her sister was, and that she goes by the same name. Lysette."

"To what aim?"

"Money, I believe." Her fingers smoothed nervously over the muslin of her gown. "I went to him earlier and offered him whatever he required to leave and not return. He did not decline."

"I sometimes think I should be grateful to have only sons. I am not certain I would tolerate fortune hunters well."

Marguerite's stomach clenched into a knot. "This has been my only experience in regard to my daughters. I am at a loss for how to manage the business. I must protect Lynette without alienating her."

"I admire your courage in facing this man. What can I do?"

"Can you tell me more about him? What would goad him to approach my daughter? He is a wealthy man by all appearances. He also confessed to Lynette that he was once an English spy. De Grenier assists the king only on the periphery and not in any covert capacity. We reside in Poland. What would he gain by an association with my daughter?"

"Is there any possibility that he truly cares for her? If she is even half as beautiful as her mother, any man would find her irresistible."

Marguerite gifted him with a sad smile. "Thank you. But if that were the case, why concoct the tale of this woman?"

"I do not know." Philippe bent forward. "Do you know who she is? Do you have a surname?"

She hesitated a moment, her fingers twisting in her lap. "Rousseau."

He drew back as if struck. "*Mon Dieu* . . . You believe this woman is a relation of mine?"

Edward lay for a moment in the darkness, attempting to discern what had woken him. When a sob rent the still night, he leaped to his feet, abandoning the chaise he slept upon to cross the short distance to Corinne's bed.

He lit the single taper on the nightstand and sat upon the edge of the mattress, his hand reaching out to touch her burning forehead. Tears coursed from the corners of her eyes and wet the hair at her temples, and her chest heaved with gasping cries.

Another nightmare. In the past two nights, she'd had several, all resulting in quiet sobbing and pleas for mercy.

Was every night of her life like this? Were these fever dreams, or the torment of the damned?

His chest tight with sympathy for her plight, Edward dipped a clean cloth in the bowl of water by the taper and wringed out the excess liquid. With soothing strokes, he wiped at her forehead and cheeks, unable to stop the river of tears or ease her distress.

Standing, he caught up the end of the counterpane and tossed it back, baring her night rail–covered body to the chill of the evening air. She whimpered and curled into a ball.

He cursed, hating the sight of her cowering, filled with fury by the violent quivering of her lips and the fist she pressed against them in a vain attempt to stem the sounds of pain spilling from her.

His hands fisted, the water from the cloth showering to the rug by his bare feet.

Why was he not running far, far away? Corinne was so damaged he wondered if she would ever be right again. He had not slept a single hour's length of time in four days, which diminished his capability to do his job, the one thing in his life that held any meaning to him.

"No cunt, however tempting, is worth this trouble," he growled.

Her shoulders jerked in time to each of his harshly stated words and remorse filled him. Sighing, Edward returned to her. He set the cloth in the bowl, then climbed into the bed beside her. He sat up, his back to the gilded headboard, his long legs stretched out before him.

Settled comfortably, he reached for her, warding off her blows and vicious curses, confining her wrists in one of his hands and hauling her against his side.

Corinne struggled with stunning force for so slender a woman, her fear giving her unnatural strength. But Edward held fast, his jaw clenched against the occasional painful strike of kicking feet, his limbs kept carefully away from snapping teeth.

Weakened by fever, lack of breath, and sufficient sustenance, she tired quickly and soon collapsed against him, coughing and shivering.

He began to sing then, a simple song remembered from his childhood. The sound of his voice seemed to calm her. He pondered that even as he continued.

Eventually, she clung to him. Her small hands fisting in his shirt, her cheek atop his chest. She still smelled like a drunkard, but he did not care. She was a slight, sweet weight against him, her curves molding perfectly to his hardness.

This was why he was here, why he had lied to Corinne's staff and intimated that they were lovers so they would cease trying to turn him away.

It was the way she felt in his arms, the rightness of it. He owned a favored knife that had a similar appeal to him. The hilt fit into his palm as if it were made for him alone. Yes, the edges were sharp and he had injured himself occasionally in the caring of it, but it was worth the effort to own such a unique and valuable piece.

And then there was the way Corinne responded to him, even in slumber. The way his touch and voice penetrated through the shell around her. As if some part of her knew that he would fit her just as well.

Edward felt her heartbeat slow against his chest and his own followed suit. Soon, they were breathing in unison, their hearts beating as one.

His eyes closed and he slept.

Simon smiled as Lynette's fingers drifted through the pelt on his chest. She was tucked against his side, her leg tossed over his thigh, dangerously near his cock. The feel of her silken limbs tangled so intimately with his kept his prick hard and aching. If tonight had not been her first for sex, he would have been at her again by now. As it was, he was biding his time. His end goal was too important to ruin for mere impatience.

He had been staring into the grate, one arm tucked behind his head, the other draped around her bare shoulders. Now, he looked down at her and felt a familiar knotting of his gut. Her hair was in glorious disarray, part of it restrained by pins, other parts sticking out wildly owing to the fervency of her desire.

How devastating she was in the heights of passion, unabashed and shameless, begging for his cock as if she would die without it. Not as a separate and interchangeable device of pleasure, but because of him alone. Out of all the women whose beds he had shared, he was positive only Lynette wanted Simon Quinn and not merely any available lover of sufficient skill and attractiveness.

Having met the vicomtess, he knew some of the censure Lynette would face, he understood the future she could have and the value of her maidenhead to her future husband. She had forsaken a lifetime of breeding and training for one night with him. It humbled him that she thought he was worth such a price.

"Why were your accounts seized?" she asked, glancing up at him.

"Extortion," he said dryly, his hand caressing the downy softness of her shoulder. "I resigned and they did not want to take 'no' for an answer."

"So you are a slave then," she said, anger lacing her tone.

"In a fashion, but only temporarily."

"What do they want you to do?" Lynette sat up and tucked the sheet modestly beneath her arms. Her lithe legs were curled beneath her and visible, creating a seductive montage for his eyes.

"Our friend, Lysette Rousseau, is up to mischief again. She is consorting with a Revolutionist and there is a need to know why."

"They could find no one else?"

"Apparently not." He thought a moment, then asked, "Does that surname sound familiar to you?"

"Rousseau? Not in an extraordinary fashion. Why?"

"Nothing. Just exploring a suspicion."

Her fingers rubbed along the ribbon-edged hem of the linen. "Are you expected to seduce her?"

"It was suggested," he murmured, watching her carefully.

Her pretty mouth thinned. "You won't, of course."

Simon grinned. "Of course."

"Are you being serious?" she asked crossly, eyeing his humor with an adorable scowl.

"Are you being jealous?"

She looked piqued for a moment, then chagrined. "Will you tell me how you know her?"

He patted his chest with his hand. "If you come lie against me again, I might be persuaded."

Lynette did as he asked. He tugged the sheet away so that nothing came between his skin and hers. Her breasts were a soft pillow against his chest, the curls between her legs a teasing tickle against his thigh. He had never truly absorbed such delights before, not to this degree. Every cell in his body was acutely attuned to every facet of her.

"Recently," he began, wrapping his arms around her, "Mademoiselle Rousseau accompanied me on a journey to England. She claimed to be searching for the perpetrator of a crime and the main suspect was an associate of mine whom I knew to be innocent."

"Did you find him?"

"Yes, and all ended well, but it was revealed that Lysette's purpose was not the hunt for my friend at all. It was another search entirely. She failed, but it was a lesson learned for me. I watched the woman stab a man to death and callously betray a comrade in an effort to save her own skin."

"Oh . . ." Her head rested more heavily against him.

"What is it, *a thiasce*?" he murmured, feeling her mood alter.

"She does not sound anything at all like my sister. She sounds like a monster."

Simon clutched her closer to him, giving her what little comfort he could. "In her defense, at times she seems to loathe herself and the man she killed was not a good one. The venom with which she attacked him also suggested that he had harmed her in some way in the past. There was no glee in her when she acted, only fury such as I have rarely seen in a woman."

Lynette shuddered. "I cannot imagine killing anyone."

"I hope you never have to. Regardless of the reasons for doing so, the taking of a life is not something one forgets."

Her head tilted back, revealing wide China-blue eyes. "Have you ever taken a life?"

"Regrettably, yes." He flinched when she did, fearing that her adoration of him would change and doubting he could bear it.

"A large number?"

"More than a few."

She was silent for so long, he wondered if she was thinking of a way to extricate herself and depart. Instead she said, "Thank you for your honesty."

"Thank you for not running away."

An ivory shoulder rose in an elegant shrug. "I can see they haunt you."

"Can you?" he asked hoarsely, riveted by a sense of vulnerability, of being naked in far more than body.

"Yes, it is in your eyes." She touched his brow

with a cool hand. "I know you would not have done what you did if not forced to by necessity."

Catching her hand, he pressed his lips to her palm. "I am laid low by your faith."

He treasured her generosity, treasured her. Her steadfast belief in the goodness of his character—based only on his treatment of her—altered everything. She knew his hands had blood on them, yet she trusted that he would act so decisively only by necessity. She did not judge or disparage, his already negligible assets were not further diminished. She did not color his future with the sins of his past.

"I am not the only open book in this bed," she said, smiling. "I can read you as well."

"Oh?" His brows rose. "What are you reading now?"

"You are mad for me," she pronounced, without a drop of humility.

Simon laughed. "You are incorrigible."

"You should have known that when I allowed you to kiss me."

"Allowed?" His grin widened. "Darling, you hadn't the wherewithal to stop me. You were clay in my hands."

"I suppose you are just irresistible?" She snorted.

He rolled and pinned her beneath him, enjoying the view of her pale hair and skin against the burgundy and dark woods of his bed. "Resist me, then," he challenged.

"That would be a bit difficult with you mashing me into the mattress."

"Mashing?" He lifted hastily.

"Well, you are a big man."

"The better to please you with," he purred, punctuating his claim with a nudging of his bone-hard prick into her thigh. He nuzzled his nose against hers. "You would not want a smaller man, *a thiasce.*"

"Are you talking about your cock?"

He laughed at her obvious astonishment.

Lynette pushed on his shoulder. "I am serious, Simon! Does size vary greatly in that area?"

"Yes, of course. As varied as height and weight."

Her eyes were wide as saucers. "So a smaller man might have had less work to push inside me?"

He growled at the thought. "The size of a man's frame is not an accurate indicator of the size of his prick."

"Oh. Interesting."

"Not too interesting, I pray."

"Are you being jealous?" she tossed back at him, smiling coyly.

With a wiggle of his hips, Simon settled more firmly between Lynette's spread legs. He stroked the length of his cock through the petal-soft lips of her sex, groaning at the feel of her quickening response.

Her hands gripped his shoulders, her curved nails digging into his flesh in a way he found highly arousing instead of annoying, as he had in the past. He usually eschewed marks on his skin that would pique another woman's pride, but here, now, forever, he wanted Lynette's mark on him. He wanted it to be visible by one and all that she had given herself to him and taken him in return.

He reached between them and positioned the broad head of his cock at the tiny slit that led to heaven. She began to pant, her eyelids growing heavy as the spark between them kindled to burning.

"See?" she whispered. "I think you might be a size too large for me."

Lowered his head, Simon kissed her, slanting his lips across hers in needy hunger. Everything about her mouth set him on fire, from the words it spoke to the pleasure it bestowed. Her lips were soft and moist, delicious. And the way they trembled beneath his and parted so willingly ripped his heart right out of his chest.

"God, the feel of you," he groaned, sinking his cock slowly into the snug depths of her burning hot cunt.

"See?" he mimicked gently, sliding his arms beneath her shoulders to hold her in perfect position. "I can touch you at your deepest point"—he plunged—"and stretch you to your widest . . ." He circled his hips in an oft-practiced motion to make her insensate with delight. "I am perfectly proportioned to service you in every possible way."

She sighed. "I see . . ."

He lingered at certain depths, stroking over discovered pleasure points, reveling in the feel of her slick, succulent tissues. He had never been as enraptured with the sexual act before, never known it was possible to feel a woman's pleasure as if it were his own. Not in a proprietary way, but in truth.

As before, he took his time, pumping deep and slow. The sun would rise, she would leave, her family would intercede, and their time together would be over. He felt the ticking of the clock keenly, even in the midst of mind-numbing delight. But his goal was not to fuck her as many times as possible. He did not strive to curb his craving for her or make her remember him by sheer number of orgasms bestowed. Any man worth his salt could make a woman climax.

Not every man could make love to her.

It was quality he wanted, orgasms that shattered her soul, burrowed deep inside her, became a part of her.

Simon buried his face in the mass of her fragrant hair and held her tightly, absorbing the feel of the tight tips of her nipples against his chest and the pillowy cushion of her lovely breasts. Lynette was soft, sweetly curved perfection, so damn beautiful it made him ache to look at her.

She writhed beneath him, her head tossing, her lips whispering his name in a breathless litany. She was so generous in her passion, restraining nothing, giving him everything she was. No other woman in his life had ever come to his bed without reservation. His common breeding, his Irish heritage, his lack of social stature, his lack of property and family . . . He had nothing to recommend him beyond a few hours of pleasurable bedsport.

Lynette's innocence and purity destroyed him. Not simply her virginity, which he prized, but her pristine heart and mind. Even a whore was pure of heart the first time she fell in love. No wariness to hold her back, no past hurts to fear, no shattered dreams to mend.

Lynette had never loved a man before, in any fashion. He was the first.

He would sell his soul to be her last.

In all of his life he had never had a home, never had a place he belonged or had anything that belonged solely to him. He had never owned any-thing irreplaceable and precious.

Except for Lynette.

Tonight, she belonged solely to him. The enor-mity of her gift made him tremble.

"Mon coeur," she breathed, encircling him with slender arms, anchoring him to her.

Simon continued to ride her slow and deep, de-termined to make the joining last as long as possi-ble. His cock throbbed and ached, his ballocks were hard and drawn tight to his body. If he were less than completely mad for her, he would not have endured. She was so greedy, rippling along his length, tightening deliciously.

"Christ," he gasped, arching as white-hot sensa-tion wrapped around the base of his spine and fisted tight. "It's so good," he groaned. "So damn good . . ."

"Please," she begged, her voice throaty and se-ductive.

"Tell me what you need," he purred, licking the shell of her ear. "Tell me, and I will give it to you."

"Do it again," she breathed. "Again . . ."

Hitting the end of her, he rolled his hips, grind-ing into her, giving her clitoris the final stimula-tion she required.

She stiffened, then keened, climaxing hard. Scratching his back and sobbing his name, she fell apart in his arms, her cunt clinging to his tor-mented cock with a viselike grip that clenched and released in a powerful massage.

He growled, grinding his teeth and fisting the pillows as she quivered around and beneath him, luring his seed into the spasming depths of her. He resisted by dint of will alone, waiting until her explosive tremors had faded to yank free and spill on the linens. Spurt after furious spurt shook his frame, the orgasm violent in its release, decimating everything he thought he knew about sex.

As liquid warmth bathed his straining cock, he railed at the injustice of it. His seed would never find purchase in her womb, his future would never have her in it.

He was finally home, but he would not be allowed to stay.

Chapter 13

"Rousseau is not an uncommon surname, Philippe," Marguerite said wearily. "I would have asked for your help, regardless."

She stood and picked up her empty glass. Moving to the console, she refilled her drink, then poured brandy into a goblet and warmed it expertly over a taper. She carried it to him.

He had pushed to his feet when she rose and now stood, watching her with the loving eyes she still dreamed of. His fingers wrapped around hers when he accepted the libation, burning her skin and inciting potent remembrances of those fingers touching other, more intimate parts of her body.

"Why not ask your husband for assistance?" he queried softly.

"I have my reasons."

"Tell me what they are."

Marguerite's lower lip quivered and his head bent, his tongue slipping out to follow the trembling curve. He groaned and his fingers tightened on hers.

At the taste of him, heat swept across her skin, her dormant body reawakening at the proximity of its long-mourned lover.

"I have been faithless in my heart all of these years," she whispered, shaking so forcefully that sherry sloshed over the rim of her glass and soaked her fingers. "The only dignity I have is that I have not been faithless in truth."

She felt the effort he exerted to release her and step back. His chest heaved from the labor of it and his nostrils flared as if scenting his mate.

"Then give me the truth," he growled, taking the drink she had prepared for him and downing the entirety of the contents. "If you will not give me anything else, give me that much, at least."

Although she knew he had reason to be angry, the sound of his pain was too much for her to bear. "I gave you everything!"

"I wish you would have trusted me to protect you."

Her mouth fell open. "You think I left for *me?* I parted from my family and friends, left every item I treasured behind, and went to you with only the clothes on my back, and you think I left you for *my* benefit?"

Philippe's grip tightened dangerously on his goblet.

"You were half dead!" she cried, feeling echoes of the remembered pain. "They beat you so viciously I was told you would not live out the week. But I had hope." She set her glass on the table and turned away. "I believed you would survive because I could not imagine life without you in it."

"Marguerite . . ."

She heard his glass join hers on the table and sensed him approach. Facing him, she lifted her hand to keep him at bay. "Please. You are my weakness. If you touch me, I will crumble and then hate myself. I do not love de Grenier. I cannot, because I love you. But he has been good to me, even though he knows how I feel. Even though I cannot give him the son he desires."

He stopped, his jaw tightening. "If he is such an exemplary spouse, why not turn to him?"

"Will you not help me?"

"You know I will. I would cut out my heart and give it to you, if you wanted it."

She flinched, her eyes watering. "He has been good to me, but less so to my daughters. He is not cruel; he simply is . . . indifferent." Her breath left her in a shaky rush and she looked away. "After the birth of the girls, I was unable to conceive again. I fear he resents them for that, perhaps unknowingly."

"He is a fool." Philippe exhaled harshly, his frame losing its combative posture in favor of one of weary resignation. "So, you would like me to delve into the history of both Simon Quinn and Lysette Rousseau. Is there anything else you need?"

"Money. Mr. Quinn has not yet accepted my offer, but if he does, I should like to settle with him immediately. De Grenier was set to leave Vienna for Paris a sennight behind us. If he departed on schedule, he will not arrive for another few days. Not long to some, but for my daughter, an hour can be long enough to land into trouble. She has already ventured out to see Quinn once."

"She is like her mother, then," he said, with a fondness in his voice that made it difficult to breathe.

"Too much so."

"Allow me to ease your burdens, *mon coeur*. If you need funds, you have only to ask."

"Thank you, Philippe. I will reimburse the expense as soon as possible."

"I ask for only one thing in return." His gaze darkened. "When I have information to share, I want to do so in the flesh. I want to admire you from afar, since I cannot have you."

Her mouth dried. "It is too dangerous."

"Yes," he agreed. "Very much so, but I cannot resist. You will not return to Paris, will you, when you leave again?"

Marguerite shook her head. "No."

He crossed his arms, his coat stretching over the beautifully defined musculature she remembered so well. The years had been kind to him. She found him just as devastatingly handsome now as she had when first laying eyes on him.

"I will protect you from discovery," he promised. "You will have to protect you from yourself; you know I will never turn you away."

"Philippe . . ."

"You do not trust yourself as you should. You are decided against sharing my bed again, therefore, you will not change your mind. You are too honorable, too loyal, too stubborn." The smile he gifted her with was so despondent, she sobbed for being the cause of it. "I cannot resent those traits in you, since they are why I love you as I do."

She tried to hold her tongue, but could not. It was unfair that their love was like a flower destined to grow in the dark, stunted by lack of warmth and sunshine, struggling to survive in the barren soil of their hearts, watered only by tears and the mist of memories.

"*Je t'aime,*" she whispered.

"I know."

Lynette awakened to the feel of something tickling the tip of her nose. Exhausted, she swiped at the offending sensation with her hand. Her eyes remained squeezed shut in the hope that she could drift back to sleep again.

"Time to rise, *a thiasce.*"

The sound of Simon's deep burr woke more than just her brain. Every nerve ending in her body tingled at the sound.

"Simon." She smiled, but did not open her eyes.

He leaned over her, his skin smelling of bergamot soap. His lips brushed featherlight over her brow. "A bath awaits you."

"What time is it?"

"A quarter past three."

She groaned. "Your servants must hate you."

He laughed and straightened. "Perhaps it is a usual request."

A low growl rumbled in her chest.

"Thoughts of you have led to a recently acquired need for chilly submersion," he drawled, soothing her ruffled feathers.

Opening one eye, she peeked up at him and marveled that he could look so wonderful with no sleep and hours of sweat-inducing exertion. His hair was tied back now, but he was still shirtless and clad only in breeches.

A black brow arched. "Again? You are insatiable."

"Hmm . . ." She rolled to her back and stretched, gasping as his hands cupped both breasts and squeezed. "Who is insatiable?"

"I am not a man to miss an opportunity."

She exhaled harshly, tired and loath to leave these hours behind. "Is that what this was? An opportunity?"

He gave her a chastising look, then stood and held out his hand. "I think you should parade around naked for a few moments, by way of an apology for that question."

Wrinkling her nose, she took his hand. He tugged her up, caught her close, and grabbed her buttocks with a firm smack, making her gasp in surprise. He kissed her nose. "Lack of sleep does not suit your temperament, I see."

Lynette wrapped her arms around his lean waist, her fingers sliding beneath the waistband of his breeches. "Leaving you does not suit me, *mon amour.*"

"*Shh.*" He pressed a finger to her lips, while lacing his other hand with hers. He tugged her toward the adjacent sitting room.

A lovely and quite large copper tub waited there, luring her to sink deep into the steaming water and melt away the unfamiliar aches and pains that plagued her every step. The thoughtfulness Simon displayed moved her deeply, showing her that he valued her for more than mere sexual gratification.

There were no servants about and the tension created by walking around unclothed faded away. She smiled.

"What thoughts inspired that siren's smile?" he asked, his arm providing her support as she stepped into the tub.

"I was thinking that I have become a wanton woman to cross a room naked with a man and not feel painfully awkward."

"Let me assure you, there is nothing even slightly awkward about you."

Lynette settled into the oversized tub with a blissful sigh. She was sore in places she had not known could feel discomfort and her limbs were weighted by exhaustion. However, for the most part, she felt better than she ever had in her entire life. There was a certain unique contentment that came with having one's carnal needs sated so thoroughly. Solange always had an air of indulgence about her that was very alluring. Now, Lynette understood why.

Simon kneeled beside her and began to bathe her himself, covering a cloth in fragrant soap and washing her gently limb by limb. Eyes half-closed, she watched him, admiring the glorious rippling of powerful muscles beneath his skin. What a potently virile animal he was, yet he touched her with such gentleness.

His hands slipped between her legs and she winced.

"Are you overly sore?" he asked gruffly, his movements stilling.

"No more so than should be usual, I imagine." She winked. "Especially considering your size."

But his frown did not fade. With steady, yet tentative fingers, he felt along the swollen lips of her sex. She spread her legs as much as possible within the confines of the tub, showing him that she was not afraid or wounded unduly.

His breath hitched at the gesture and his eyes,

so softly affectionate a moment ago, heated with something more profound. His touch became less examining, more arousing, his callused fingertips parting her and slipping over the tiny knot of nerves that brought her so much pleasure.

Her hands wrapped around the hot lip of the tub, clenching as he touched her there, his caress featherlight and teasing.

"Simon?"

"Let me watch you," he whispered, stroking rhythmically. "Keep your eyes on me."

She whimpered as her womb tightened again, her muscles tensing, her cheeks flushing from the heat of the water and the added heat of the fire he sparked within her.

He purred. "You feel like the softest silk, *a thiasce.*"

She was completely exposed, pinned by his gaze, her lips parted on desperate pants as her body grew taut as a bow, tightening in anticipation of climax.

The water began to slosh in measured waves, spurred by the movements of his hand at the most private part of her. Over and over, circling around and across the source of her torment. Her head fell back against the tub rim, her hips rising, her body instinctively working toward that blinding release of pressure.

"I wish you were in me," she gasped, feeling her sex grasping for him, reaching for him.

"Come for me," he crooned, pushing a finger gently inside her and thrusting shallowly. "Let me feel how much you need me here."

Arching, she climaxed silently while he watched her, the moment so intimate she felt as if there were no secrets between them.

She turned her head, offering her mouth to him with a breathless plea. "Kiss me."

He accepted with a groan, his head angled to create the perfect fit between them. This time, she took all that he had taught her about kissing and gave it back to him, her tongue stroking into his mouth until he wrenched away with a curse, breathing heavily.

Pushing to his feet, Simon held his hand out to her. "We must dress you and return you before the hour grows any later."

His groin was eye level and she could not fail to see how much her passion inspired his. If he cared for his own pleasure, he could have her again now. Whether she returned home or not did not affect him at all. Aside from de Grenier's wrath, he would incur no penalty. Her father would not insist Simon wed her, because he was unsuitable.

Therefore, the desire to see her home swiftly was for her benefit. Another display of his concern for her well-being.

Lynette dressed swiftly, as did Simon. Her hands shook slightly when she saw the tear in the placket of the borrowed breeches. That she inspired such a primitive response in him awed her, but not nearly as much as the thought that he tempered such fervency. For her.

Heavy-hearted, she followed him down to the front door and exited out to the chilly night air. The sky was dark; the streets mostly quiet, aside from a few eager vendors preparing for the soon-to-dawn morning. Piotr waited by the curb, the reins of their horses held in his hands. Simon's mount was there, too, the one she had espied him upon the night she arrived in Paris.

He assisted her up, then mounted, sitting tall in the saddle, his hand loosely resting atop the hilt of a small sword. His gaze was sharp, though his posture was relaxed. A hunter in disguise. She stared at him, finding it nearly impossible to believe that so formidable a man had been quivering in her arms.

They rode in silence back to Solange's home, Piotr falling deliberately behind them, while they traveled side by side. Although she had been overly hot during the ride to Simon's, she was now shivering on the journey home, the chill starting from the inside and working its way out.

When they reached the alley and dismounted, Piotr hurried to the stables with the two horses. Simon stood with her, eyes bright and frame stiff with tension.

"I will send word to you and the vicomtess," he said, "if I learn anything of note. I trust that you will heed my warning and leave Paris as soon as possible. Until then, stay out of view, I beg you."

Lynette bit her lower lip and nodded, her chest tight with an emotion akin to grief.

Simon cupped her face with both hands and pressed a far-too-swift kiss to her trembling mouth. "Thank you." His hands shook as he held her, then he backed away. "Go inside now."

With dragging steps, she headed toward the stables, where her clothes waited. She glanced back at him once and found him staring after her, hands behind his back. Her vision blurred with tears and she looked away, departing the alley with silent sobs.

* * *

It was a painful crick in his neck that pulled Edward from the depths of dreamless sleep into waking. He groaned and straightened, discovering that he had slept for hours sitting up in Corinne's bed. He straightened away from the headboard, rolling his shoulders, glancing to the side to see where she had gone to.

She lay curled atop a pillow on the far side of the bed, watching him with eyes so ravaged by illness they looked bruised.

He stilled, wary. "Good morning."

"Are you drunk?" she whispered.

A smile threatened, but he restrained it. "I am afraid that smell is you. You were feverish and we needed to cool you."

"Why are you here?"

"I have been asking myself that question for three days."

"Three days?" she gasped, clearly horrified.

Leaving the bed, Edward stretched his arms wide and glanced at the clock. He would have to leave for work shortly and, perhaps, not be allowed to return.

He reached for the pitcher and glass on the nightstand, and poured a small ration. Rounding the bed to the other side, he deliberately moved without haste so as not to aggravate the high tension he sensed in her. She rolled with him, facing him.

"Can you sit up?" he asked.

Corinne blinked slowly, wearily. "I think so."

"If you require assistance, you have only to ask."

She struggled to a seated position on her own. "Where are the Fouches?"

"Most likely preparing for the day. They are old," he pointed out.

"Thierry is not."

"Madame Fouche was disinclined to have him tend to you."

Holding out her hand, she accepted the glass. She looked like a child in the big bed, so small and delicate. "But she had no objection to you?"

"Her age gave her little choice, and in the end, she felt a lover would be more acceptable to you than her son."

Corinne choked on her first swallow and he thumped her carefully on the back.

"A lie, of course," he pointed out, in case she thought more had happened to her while ill than she knew.

"You are impossibly arrogant," she gasped.

"Yes, that is true." He straightened. "I must prepare for work now. Would you allow me to visit you tomorrow in the evening?"

She stared at him.

He waited, knowing that he would think of her all night.

However, tonight would best be spent in study of Quinn, a mystery that niggled at him relentlessly over the last two nights. Tomorrow he was free of any duty and he could catch up on missed sleep, enabling him to return to Corinne refreshed and perhaps armed with more information. It also gave her time to rebuild her strength. He knew she felt vulnerable now, which would only make her ill at ease and defensive. One wrong move could ruin everything.

A knock came to the door, and shortly after, Madame Fouche bustled in, huffing from the journey up the narrow servants' staircase. She paused upon seeing Corinne awake and curtsied. "Good morning, Madame Marchant."

Corinne frowned. "Good morning."

She still did not respond to Edward's question and he reluctantly took that as an answer in the negative.

"She will need plenty of fluids," he said to the housekeeper. "Beef tea and vegetable stock, both salted lightly. Lots of water."

"Yes, sir."

Edward held out his hand to Corinne and she placed hers within it. The skin was paper-thin and lined with thin blue veins. So fragile, yet she was so strong in other ways. He kissed the back and withdrew.

He would pursue her anew when she was fully recovered. This would not be the end.

"Where are your spectacles?" she asked.

"They were crushed the night of the fire."

Her fingers tightened on his. "You saved me."

"Actually, you were well on your way to saving yourself. I simply caught you."

"And tended me for three days. Thank you."

He bowed, released her hand, and turned away.

"I anticipate your visit tomorrow," she said in barely a whisper.

Edward's steps faltered slightly, but he gave no other outward sign of his relief. He could not appear eager, not with a woman so frightened of overt male interest.

"Until then," was all he said, but he was smiling as he departed.

* * *

Desjardins was whistling as he entered his study shortly after breaking the fast. It was unfortunate that James had chosen to search the wrong side of the Orlinda manse first, which had led to Lysette being exposed to danger longer than he would have liked. However, the physician assured him she would survive without long-term damage and James was so smitten already that he had spent the last three nights tending to her himself.

But then such fortuitous events were the usual for him. His life had always been a charmed one. Take, for instance, the Fouches. While he regretted providing Lysette with such elderly and subsequently dubious help, he could afford no better without arousing undue suspicion in his wife. Comtess Desjardins was a beautiful woman, far too lovely for a man of his unremarkable appearance, but regardless, she loved him, as he loved her, and she would not allow him mistresses or even temporary dalliances. Keeping Lysette was one of his marriage's enduring secrets, as were his less savory deeds performed with the goal of increasing their social stature.

Now it appeared the age of the Fouches was a blessing in disguise, providing James the excuse to act heroically once again.

The comte had just taken his seat behind his desk when a knock came to the open door. He smiled at the waiting butler and said, "Send him in."

He knew the man's identity already, as his arrival was scheduled and perfectly timed.

A moment later Thierry entered, smiling. "Good morning, my lord."

"Yes, it is."

His returning smile was sincere, his affection for

the man bolstered by over two decades of loyal service. Thierry had filled many roles over the years, from courier to footman. His present guise as the Fouches' son allowed him to stay apprised of the developing relationship between Lysette and James. Despite their years, the Fouches had no difficulty in assimilating new roles quickly, even becoming the parents of a grown man overnight.

"How is Lysette?" the comte asked.

"She woke this morning."

"Lovely news."

"She is tired and weak, of course," Thierry said, "but seems well enough."

Desjardins leaned back, his legs stretched out before him. "Any word on what she and James intend from this point?"

"James will return tomorrow."

"Not tonight?"

"No, not that I blame the man. Mademoiselle Rousseau is not an easy woman to care for while unconscious, courtesy of Depardue and his men."

"Damn the man."

He would never forget his first sight of her, cowering and abused, ruthlessly shared among a coarse lot of men until little of her spirit remained. But again, it was another fortunate event for him, because acquiring Lysette had given him a valuable tool he would not have had otherwise, both in her loyalty and her identity. Only time would tell if he would ever have to use the latter, but it was there, if he should need it.

"I will see her this evening, then," the comte said. "Tell her to expect me."

"Yes, my lord." Thierry straightened and leaned forward, setting a missive on the edge of the desk with a now familiar and much hated black seal on the reverse. "I was handed this on the way here."

Thierry had become nearly the only bearer of the *L'Esprit* orders of late, but then Thierry was one of few whom Desjardins saw on a regular basis.

Clenching his jaw, Desjardins dropped the missive into a drawer and withdrew a nicely weighted purse.

"You may have the night to yourself. However, I should like to know why Quinn came to see her. I will need you in residence when he responds to her summons, hopefully tomorrow."

"Of course." Thierry stood and caught the purse when tossed to him. "I am at your service, as always."

Desjardins responded to a few posts waiting his attention, and when the clock on the wall chimed the noon hour, he stood, straightening the lines of his coat with a practiced tug. A moment later his lovely wife filled the doorway, pulling on her gloves.

"Are you ready, Desjardins?" she asked, her dark hair expertly, elaborately coiffed, and her wrists and ears sparkling with emeralds that matched the exact color of her eyes.

"Yes, of course." He rounded the desk. "I am as eager to offer my condolences to the Baroness Orlinda as you are."

His wife had wanted to see the baroness immediately, but he had delayed the visit, explaining that the number of curious and sympathetic visitors to her sister's residence where she was staying would be prohibitive.

The comtess shuddered. "I feel for the woman," she said, "as I would anyone who suffered similarly, but truly, this is the sort of thing that happens when one engages in such immoral behavior."

"Certainly," he agreed.

He had no fear that his presence at the ball would become known. The baroness never discussed her guest list with anyone, and those who attended never spoke of whom they saw there, since that would be admitting their own involvement.

"Shall we?" he asked, extending his arm to the comtess.

This would be no mere social visit for him; if so, he would have allowed his wife to speak for both of them. He had more interest in this excursion than a need to offer his sympathy. Before he left the baroness's home, he would know if Quinn's presence at the ball had been happenstance or not. With the additional visit to Lysette shortly after, he had begun to doubt that as being the case. Lysette said Quinn had ceased to work for the English, so why was he still in Paris?

Of course, perhaps it would just be simpler to kill the man and be done with it. There would be no reprisal for the death of a man no longer in service.

The idea held merit and Desjardins tucked it away to consider in greater depth later.

Chapter 14

It was barely noon when the first missive arrived on Simon's desk. Written in a beautiful, flowing feminine hand, it asked if he had reached a decision regarding his discussion with the Vicomtess de Grenier the day before. He thought of burning it, but thrust it into a drawer instead.

Later, another arrived, this one containing only the address of a tailor's shop and nothing more. Unlike the vicomtess's, it was a message Simon was relieved to see.

Donning his coat, he left his house posthaste. His residence was now a torment, occupied as it was with both Eddington and memories of Lynette. It was the last place he wanted to be and yet the only place to both wait for news and bide his time until the hour was sufficiently late to allow him to visit Lysette.

He rode swiftly, goaded by the feeling of being trapped, forced to act against his will and in ways that went against the grain. He could not move forward or back, and lack of information was what hampered him.

Familiar with the direction sent to him, Simon was still forced to travel in ever-minimizing circles, searching for anyone who might be following him before finally reaching his destination.

The ringing of bells on the shop door heralded his arrival, but no one he knew was inside.

Simon removed his hat, his gaze sweeping over the various bolts of cloth and the customer speaking to the red-haired woman at the counter before discovering the waving hand peeking out from behind a curtain. Moving to the rear, he slipped behind the thick wool and found himself in the back of the store. He also found Richard.

"Took you long enough, Quinn," the man said, laughing.

Richard was seated at a table covered in multiple scraps of cloth and spools of thread. As always, he looked relaxed and carefree. Simon was not fooled, though the less observant would be.

Taking the seat Richard gestured to, Simon set his hat on the table and said, "Interesting choice of venue."

"Courtesy of Amie"—Richard gestured to a rather plain-faced girl who sat in the corner tugging needle through thread—"and her mother, Natalie."

The redhead rounded Simon's back, set a chipped and mismatched tea service atop the mess on the table, and began to pour.

"Natalie's husband is the tailor," Richard explained. "But he is home ill this week."

"Merci beaucoup," Simon said to Natalie, then he

pressed a kiss to his fingertips and tossed it at the girl. Amie blushed and lowered her eyes.

"Women come too easy to you," Richard complained. "It took me two hours before she would even look at me."

"But your efforts paid off."

"I would rather expend no effort, like you."

Simon accepted the cup and saucer offered to him, and settled as comfortably as possible into his wobbly seat. "Tell me you have something valuable."

"I am not certain how valuable it is, but it's damned interesting." Declining tea, Richard crossed his arms on the table and leaned closer. "The Vicomte de Grenier is most likely one of my easiest assignments."

"Oh?"

"Yes. He was embroiled in a scandal of such note, that it is still remembered to this day."

"Always lovely when that happens."

"Yes, it is. Apparently the vicomte was betrothed to Marguerite Piccard, who was a diamond of the first water, I understand."

"Still is," Simon said, setting his cup down without drinking from it. He wanted liquor, not tepid tea.

"However, before they could wed, she hared off with the Marquis de Saint-Martin, a noted libertine who happened to be married at the time. I heard some diverting tales about women crying in the streets over the man, but his reputation was obviously not a deterrent to Mademoiselle Piccard."

Simon remembered the haughty and icy woman he had met in his parlor, and his brows rose. Then he thought of Lynette and the heat of her passion.

It seemed both women were determined to have what they wanted.

"She was his mistress for over a year," Richard continued, "then she returned to de Grenier, who married her anyway. He is some sort of diplomat to the Polish and she has been living in Poland ever since. De Grenier returns quite often, always alone. They had two daughters, but one is deceased."

"Was the parting with Saint-Martin amicable?"

"It is said the libidinous marquis suffered a great decline after they separated. He was not seen for months after she wed, and afterwards, was never the same."

Frowning, Simon considered the news carefully. "What year did this transpire?"

"In '57. Also, I am not certain if they are connected in any way, but Saint-Martin's surname is Rousseau."

"It cannot be coincidence. There are too many of those as it is."

"What does it mean? Do you know?"

"I might." Suddenly wishing he'd had more sleep, Simon growled and damned his brain for being sluggish. "Say nothing of this to Eddington."

"Of course not," Richard muttered. "You know me better than that."

Simon pushed to his feet.

"Well? Are you going to tell me what in bloody hell is going on?" Richard demanded.

"No, not yet."

"Damn it, Quinn . . . Do not go yet! I haven't finished."

Pausing midturn, Simon waited.

"I will tell you mine," Richard offered, "if you tell me yours."

"Becking . . ." Simon rumbled.

"Oh, very well. Since I felt rather successful after last night, I stopped by Mademoiselle Rousseau's residence this afternoon. Just before I came here, actually. One of her servants was leaving at the time and I followed him. He went directly to Desjardins's residence and was shown in like a guest, not a servant."

"A bit odd perhaps," Simon murmured, "but not surprising. I am certain Desjardins supports her and pays her staff. He would expect reports of her activities and visitors."

Which was why Simon would not be announcing his next visit to her.

"That is not the best part." Richard sat back and grinned. "That James chap was following him, as well. Damned good at the business, too. I had no notion he was in pursuit until after I mounted to meet you. I was turning a corner when he caught my eye."

"So . . . the mouse senses the trap." Simon nodded. "Excellent work as always, Becking. You can share that part with Eddington. It should keep him happy for a time."

"Eh. It was a lucky day."

Simon patted him on the shoulder. "See what news you can find regarding the marquis."

"Already working on it," Richard assured. "As much for my benefit as for yours. Been a while since I had anything this interesting to chew on."

Smiling, Simon departed the shop and rode toward Lysette's.

* * *

Desjardins fingered the missive in his pocket as he climbed the stairs to Lysette's room. Another *L'Esprit* query, this time in regards to Simon Quinn. The man was coming far too close to Lysette for the comte's comfort. If he was not careful, he would lose her.

He reached the door and knocked once, then entered without waiting for permission. It was his house, after all.

"Ma petite," he said, striding toward the bed.

Lysette was reclining, though more upright than on her back. Dressed in a night rail and covered to the breasts in the counterpane, she seemed so small and fragile. He was reminded of his daughter Anne and his throat tightened.

"My lord," she murmured, her voice still tight and raspy.

"How are you feeling?" He grabbed a nearby chair and pulled it closer to the bed before sitting.

"Tired. Confused."

"I cannot help you with the former, but perhaps the latter is in my power to soothe."

She sighed, which led to a brief fit of coughing. She caught up the large handkerchief resting in her lap and held it to her lips.

"Has the physician returned?"

"Not that I have been aware."

"I will send for him when I leave."

"Thank you."

Desjardins smiled. "I would do anything for you."

She nodded, her features grave.

"I hope you feel the same charity toward me," he said.

"Have I not proven that over the last two years?"

"Yes, of course." He placed one ankle over the opposite knee. "But the world is changing, wars are raging. Friends become enemies and enemies become friends. Such is the way of things."

Lysette blinked at him, a slight frown marring the space between her brows. "What has happened?"

The comte glanced around the room, noting a pale pink chaise set in an awkward location. He gestured toward it with a jerk of his chin. "Is that where James slept?"

"I assume so."

There was an odd note to her voice and he looked back at her. "Is that where your confusion stems?"

"Yes." Her slender fingers twisted the handkerchief into a tangled rope. "I do not understand why he would go to such trouble, unless he is not as innocuous as he appears. Could he have some returning interest in you?"

"Doubtful. Is it so difficult to believe that he tended to you because he cares for you?"

"How? He does not know me."

Desjardins shrugged. "What is there to know? Your favorite foods, favorite places? Such tidbits are interesting and can lead to conversation, but truly, does that change the feeling one has about a person upon the first meeting? You know instantly, within a few moments, whether you wish to know a person better or not. Obviously, James felt that way about you."

Her lips pursed.

"I think you are a puzzle to him," he said, "and he is the sort of man who enjoys such challenges."

"A puzzle," she repeated.

"I think so."

"Hmm . . ." Her gaze sharpened on him. "So tell me why you are here."

"To make sure you are well."

"Thierry would have told you that."

The comte grinned. "Yes, but I prefer to see some things with my own eyes."

"Think I might run away?" she drawled softly.

"You might. Quinn seems disinclined to forget about you. Perhaps there is more to your association than you want me to know."

"You say that simply because he came by?"

"I say that because he has a man watching your home."

Lysette stiffened, eyeing Desjardins carefully. There was something odd about him today, a moody tension that was far removed from his usual ease of deportment. It set her nerves on edge and made her wary. Restless predators were always dangerous.

"I must say," he murmured, "it does ease my mind to see that you are not pleased to hear that."

"Of course not," she scoffed. "I do not like anyone prying into my life. It is hard enough knowing that nothing escapes your notice."

"I wish that were true."

Dropping the kerchief, she crossed her arms. "Tell me what ails you." She presently lacked the patience to continue with meaningless discourse when something important was afoot.

He removed a missive from his pocket and tossed it in her direction. It spun gracefully on its side and landed near her thigh. She picked it up and examined it, noting the broken black wax that bore no seal. The front was blank, not addressed to anyone.

She looked up at him and asked, "Should I read it?"

"Please do."

Using more care than usual, she opened the letter and read.

"Who is this from?" she breathed, horrified by the curt and heartless way it demanded information about Simon, at the cost of Desjardins's daughter if the request was not met.

"A man known only as *L'Esprit*," the comte said, his voice dripping venom. "A thorn in my side for over two decades."

Her hands fell to the bed. She was so startled by the thought of Desjardins being as helpless as she often felt. "Has he been using your family against you all of this time?"

"From the beginning. I would never assist him otherwise." The comte stood and began to pace angrily. "*L'Esprit* is the reason for your work with James. He is highly interested in Benjamin Franklin and I had hoped that you might learn something of such great import that it would lure *L'Esprit* out of the shadows."

"I will do what I can, of course."

"It is beyond that now. You read his latest demands. Quinn's man was seen following Thierry to my home. It will not be long before *L'Esprit* follows Thierry or Quinn to you."

Suddenly cold, Lysette burrowed deeper under the covers. "That upsets you a great deal."

"It should upset you as well," Desjardins said. "Depardue was his spy within the *Illuminés*. If *L'Esprit* learns that you killed his most trustworthy lieutenant, he will take you from me. If he kills you, that would be kind. I have seen him destroy men."

"Destroy?" she whispered, more frightened by Desjardins's obvious disquiet than by the tale itself. After all they had been through, she had never once seen him anything less than completely self-assured.

"He once bore a grievance against the Marquis de Saint-Martin. He robbed Saint-Martin of everything he held dear. Nothing was sacred."

"What can we do?"

"Use your illness as a way to ingratiate yourself into James's life. Allow him to do what he can to make you comfortable. Allow the bond between you to grow. That should not be too difficult, he saved your life."

"And what about Quinn? He will return."

"I will manage Quinn."

Menace laced the comte's words and Lysette felt her stomach roil. Desjardins's urgency goaded hers. "I will do what I can with James, I promise."

"Thank you." The comte approached and kissed the back of her hand, then he retrieved the note from *L'Esprit* and returned it to his pocket. "I will look into moving you. I no longer feel this residence is a safe haven."

With that, he left, closing the door behind him. Lysette lay with her cheek to her pillow and wept silently, fearful that she would not be allowed to learn of her past before her future became the death of her.

"Your life is a mess."

She jumped, her heart racing at the sound of the low voice behind her. Rolling, she faced the sitting room door and found Simon lounging there, his gaze trained on the exit Desjardins had just made his egress through.

"How did you get in here?" she asked, struggling to sit up while swiping furiously at her wet cheeks.

"Come now," he chided, straightening. "We all have our ways."

Lysette watched him enter her bedchamber as if he owned it. He caught up the chair the comte had just vacated, spun it about, and sat with his arms crossed atop the back.

He was so blatantly male and dominant in the overtly feminine surroundings of her rose-hued bedroom, making no effort to meld or be less incongruous. Simon contrasted so completely with Edward that she could not fail to note it. Edward was every inch a male and a strikingly intense one at that, yet he had tempered that for her this morning. Her chest grew tight and she pushed the memory away. She could not think of him now. It was simply too much for her beleaguered and weary soul to manage.

"Tell me about yourself, Lysette," he drawled, his gaze narrowed and examining.

"I should kill you for trespassing," she hissed, hiding her tumult under aggression, as she had learned to do to stay alive.

"I should like to see you make the attempt. You are as weak as a kitten."

"If I scream, help will come."

"The servants Desjardins provided?" Simon laughed.

Her jaw clenched. He was right, she was weak, something she had promised herself she would never be again.

"I am not here to injure you," he said softly, the levity leaving his features. "I simply want to know who you are."

"Why?"

"I believe I have met a relation of yours, and I want to see if I am correct."

Lysette paled, her palms dampening with distress.

"What did your parents do to make you resort to this elaborate ruse?" he asked quietly. "Threaten to marry you off? Cut your allowance?"

"What do you want?" she bit out.

His brow rose. "This does not have anything to do with me."

"My family is dead."

He made a chastising noise with his tongue. "Lying is a sin. Though I suppose it is probably the least of yours."

"You are so smug," Lysette snapped. "As if you know everything. As if you are so superior."

"At the moment, I feel as if I know nothing at all. I do hope you will enlighten me."

Having survived due in large part to her ability to accurately judge others, Lysette labored under the feeling that Simon was being sincere. Her mind told her it was a trick of some sort, her heart told her otherwise. "I have no idea what you are talking about."

"Your sister loves you a great deal and mourns deeply over your loss. Do you care nothing for her? Is your heart so cold that you can excise her from your life without a qualm?"

"My s-sister?" Lysette's hand went to her throat as the room began to spin. Her stomach roiled and she reached blindly for the basin on the nightstand.

Simon moved so quickly, he was at her side the same moment the chair he had occupied toppled to the floor. He held the basin beneath her mouth as she retched violently, her body so weakened it was unable to tolerate the stresses of the day.

When she had finished, and had fallen back listlessly into the pillows, he moved to the door and locked it. A moment later a knock came and then the knob was tried, rattling briefly in an attempt to turn it.

A feminine voice came muffled through the portal, "Madame Marchant? Are you well?"

Arching a brow, Simon dared her to reveal his presence.

Lysette gasped for a deep breath, then answered. "I knocked a chair over on the way to the chamberpot. There is nothing to worry yourself over."

"I will fetch the key and help you," Madame Fouche offered.

"No! Please. I want sleep, nothing more."

There was a long pause, then, "Very well. Ring the bell on the table if you need me."

Simon stood with his ear to the door. Eventually, he nodded and returned to her, righting the chair and sitting in it properly. He waited patiently for her to speak.

"What do you want me to say?" she asked, her head throbbing unmercifully. Spots danced before her eyes and sweat dotted her brow.

"I am attempting to understand how you relate to Lynette."

"Lynette?"

A shadow passed over his handsome features. "You do not know the name, do you?"

She shook her head, feeling a spark of hope that made her nigh as dizzy as casting up her accounts.

"Where is your family, Lysette? Who are they?"

"I do not know," she whispered, feeling as vulnerable as if she were naked in a crowd.

"How can you not know where you come from? I am a bastard, yet I know I was born in Dublin and my mother was a seamstress."

Swallowing hard, she reached for the damp cloth on the plate beside her and laid it around the back of her feverish neck. "I do not remember anything of my life prior to two years ago."

He stilled, staring at her unblinkingly. "How is that possible?"

"I wish I knew!" she cried, sobbing quietly. "I wish it every day."

"Bloody hell." Simon stood and paced, just as Desjardins had. "Two years ago, a young woman with your name was killed in an accident and buried by her family. She is survived by a twin sister, Lynette, and her parents."

"A twin?"

Could it be true? Would fate be kind to her at last, giving her a sibling whose identity could not be questioned?

"Yes." He stilled and exhaled harshly, running a hand through his hair and setting his queue in disarray. He did not appear to notice, nor care. "How did you come by your name?"

"Depardue called me Lysette. It felt . . . right. So I kept it."

"Depardue?"

"Yes. Regrettably, he is my earliest memory." She shuddered and felt ill again. She might have retched anew, if there had been anything remaining in her stomach.

"And Rousseau? Or is it Marchant?"

"Desjardins gave me the surname *Rousseau*, said it suited me. I use Marchant as a rule, as added protection against Depardue. He was angry to lose me, and while he could not keep me permanently after Desjardins interceded, he would have come to me at his leisure, if he knew where to find me."

"You did not use it with me."

"My journey to England was to have been my last assignment for Desjardins. He promised me that if I was able to bring back the name of your superior, I would be free. I saw no reason to hide who I was, most especially since I was not even certain the name was true."

"I think Desjardins knows very well who you are," Simon said, standing with arms akimbo. "I think he has kept you close as leverage, a hidden asset to withdraw when necessary."

"No . . ." Her lip trembled and she bit it to hide the display of weakness.

"Do you truly think he cares for you? Sending you to kill those who impede his plans?"

Lysette said nothing, heartbroken at the feeling of having no one at all to turn to. No, she did not believe Desjardins loved her in any fashion, but she did hope that he might have some kindness for her, if only a little.

Simon came to the bed and sat next to her, taking one of her hands in his. He searched her face, his own starkly austere. "Your family loves you. They miss you. Despite all you have done, they would welcome you home with great joy, I am sure of it."

She swallowed hard. "I am not worthy. Not any longer."

"That is not for you to decide," he said gruffly, his callused fingertips rubbing soothingly across the back of her hand. "However, someone wants you dead. And someone went to great lengths to make it appear as if you were. There is a body buried in Poland with your name on the crypt. For now, you should stay buried."

"Do they know about me?" she asked, disengaging her hand from his to wipe at her tears.

"In a fashion, but only your sister holds out hope. Your mother saw a body, as did her spouse. She finds it harder to reconcile."

"I see."

"One look at you and there will be no doubt." He growled low in his throat.

"You have never liked me," she whispered. "Why are you telling me this? Why not leave me for dead?"

"I wish I could." Simon shook his head. "I cannot see how you could bring them anything but pain."

Lysette considered what he had told her, how angry he had been on behalf of her sister. Her eyes widened. "It is for Lynette, is it not? You do this for her."

His jaw tensed.

She laughed softly and he pushed up from the bed with a curse.

"Poor Simon," she crooned, "how taxing it must be for you to have a tendré for a woman who looks like me."

"Witch." His glare was chilling, but it did not alarm her. All bark, he was. He only bit when necessary.

"What do we do now?"

"You will continue on as you are," he said. "Tell no one what I have told you. Give me time. There is still a great deal we do not yet know."

"There is a man hunting you."

"So I heard. Leave him to me."

Lysette held her breath a moment, attempting to think of something suitable to say, some way to help and show her gratitude. "I wish I could do something."

"You can. Whatever you learn from James, pass it along to me first."

"James?" Her heart stopped beating for a moment. "Why must you involve him?"

"He is the reason why I am still here in Paris, tangled in the web of your past." Simon moved back toward the sitting room, clearly distracted by his thoughts. "Get well," he muttered. "In the days ahead I may need you."

As quickly as he had come, he was gone.

Lysette lay alone in her bed, sick in mind and body, torn between elation and deep regret.

"Edward," she murmured, curling into her pillow.

Fate was so unfair to her, giving with one hand while taking away with the other. Would she forever be a torment to those who were kind to her?

She buried her head in her pillow and cried herself to sleep.

Chapter 15

Simon left Lysette's home possessing more than he had arrived with—namely, a set of garments that belonged to the footman, Thierry. They were of the same size and height, and it would not be notable for Thierry to visit Desjardins, which was Simon's destination.

He hid his own clothes within a yew hedge lining the stone walls of the rear garden and exited out through the alley. Tugging Thierry's tricorn low over his brow, Simon thrust his hands into his pockets and began the journey to Desjardins on foot.

The distance was neither short nor long. It was perfectly timed to allow him to think carefully about what pieces of information he had and which pieces he lacked. He glanced around furtively as he went, but found nothing amiss. Because he was so prepared, he was startled by the gloved hand that was thrust out of an unmarked and somewhat dilapidated carriage sitting just around the corner from the Desjardins residence.

He paused midstep, then quickly recovered, accepting the missive with his head tilted away to prevent recognition. The curtains were closed, the hand and arm completely covered.

"Tell him I am growing impatient," growled a raspy, grating voice from the interior.

There was a rap on the roof and the carriage rolled away.

Simon kept walking, tucking the letter in his pocket and maintaining the appearance that nothing of note had transpired. Inside, however, he was plagued with a growing disquiet.

L'Esprit was apparently not a creative ploy by Desjardins, as Simon had originally assumed. He was real, which made him another threat to manage.

He reached Desjardins's front steps within moments and rapped on the knocker with obvious impatience. The door swung open and the butler appeared prepared to allow him entry, then he noted the caller was not Thierry.

"*Monsieur* Quinn."

Withdrawing his calling card, Simon extended it, then he shouldered his way into the foyer before he could be denied.

The servant opened his mouth to protest, but a narrowing of Simon's eyes seemed to alter his mind. Instead, Simon was led to the study, and he made himself comfortable by pouring a ration of brandy before sitting on a settee.

"Quinn," Desjardins greeted, as he entered shortly after. "What a pleasure."

But the comte's gaze rested on Thierry's clothes overlong and revealed a wariness that Simon took advantage of.

"I have something for you," he said, setting his goblet on the table and reaching into his pocket for the missive from *L'Esprit*. He examined it with theatrical interest. "Interesting seal. Or lack thereof."

"Give that to me," Desjardins said crossly, snapping his fingers.

"No." Simon broke the seal and withdrew the contents.

The comte lunged and ripped the note from his hands.

Simon smiled. "What does *L'Esprit* want now?"

Desjardins paled. "What do you know of *L'Esprit?*"

"Not enough, but you are about to tell me more."

"Get out." The comte shoved the torn letter into the pocket of his coat with shaking hands. "Before I have you thrown out."

"You would have me leave without investigating further? That is not your nature." Simon hummed and mimicked confusion. "I wonder what would make you act out of character. Terror perhaps?"

"Ridiculous!" the comte scoffed. "You are nothing. Nothing to me, nothing to the English. If you were to be misplaced, there is no one to miss or worry over you."

"Is that a threat?" Grinning, Simon leaned forward. "You must have thought the same about Lysette Baillon. Or is it Rousseau? I admit, I am confused. Regardless, you were wrong. She is missed and now she has been found."

Desjardins's fists clenched. "Explain yourself."

"No, no. The only explanations we shall be hearing are yours."

"You would be better served by forgetting whatever it is you believe you know and leaving the country. The matters into which you pry will lead you to hell."

"You have been bound to *L'Esprit*'s whims for twenty years. Obviously, you are unable to extricate yourself on your own. I can help you," Simon said, "if it suits me."

Desjardins sat, betraying his interest. "To what aim?"

"I will have Lysette and you will leave her life as if you were never in it."

The grin that split the comte's face was so triumphant, Simon laughed softly.

"I knew you fancied her!" Desjardins said smugly.

"Never mind what you believe you know. Tell me about *L'Esprit*."

Desjardins's lips pursed and he sat back, crossing his arms. There was a long, measured pause. Then he began to speak and Simon listened with great interest.

When the tale was finished, Simon asked, "How long was the gap between the ruination of Saint-Martin and the time you received the next correspondence?"

"Ten years, more or less."

"And when next you heard from him, he did not come to you in the cellar?"

"No."

"You did not find that strange?"

"I find the entire association to be strange," the comte snapped.

"The original notes bore no traceable handwriting and *L'Esprit* met with you in the cellar. The later notes came handwritten and *L'Esprit* does not approach you at all. The first notes bore jewels; the later notes do not."

"One did," the comte corrected. "It was only when I refused it and him that he began to pay me with threats against my family."

"And you never wondered if the origins were different?"

Desjardins stilled. "Why would I?"

Simon shrugged.

"He is unique, Quinn. Even you must see that."

The insult was not lost on Simon, but he ignored it. "Anything can be replicated, if one is clever enough."

The comte considered that thought carefully. "How do you intend to help me?"

"I think we proved today that the man can be fooled."

"You think we can lure him with Thierry?"

"No." Simon drummed his fingers atop his knee. "I think Thierry might know *L'Esprit* better than you realize. There was something in the man's voice when he spoke to me. It was not entirely an order. More of an admonishment. Such as one given to someone not completely an underling."

"*Absurde.* Thierry has been with me for years."

"The loyalty men such as you and I inspire can be purchased, and you fail to see that perhaps *L'Esprit* has also known Thierry for years."

"I fail to see nothing, aside from how you can help me," the comte said. "If Thierry worked for *L'Esprit*, he would have betrayed Lysette by now."

"Why? Did *L'Esprit* arrange her abduction?"

The comte said nothing, which told Simon a great deal.

"Arrange a meeting with Saint-Martin," Simon said, standing. "Then apprise me of when and where it will be held."

"You act as if I trust you," Desjardins retorted, standing.

"Who else do you have?"

The comte's already thin lips thinned further. "What do you have in mind?"

"A trap."

"For whom?"

Simon grinned and walked toward the door, exiting to the right in the hallway and moving toward the rear of the house. "You will have to do as I say, if you hope to find out."

He moved through the kitchen, then down the stairs to the cellar. Desjardins was fast on his heels, nearly running to keep up with Simon's much longer stride. Opening the door to the catacombs, he looked down.

"I need a torch," he said.

"As if there are any simply lying about," the comte scoffed.

Glancing aside at him, Simon raised one brow. A long moment passed, then the comte cursed and exited to the kitchen. He returned within moments with a blazing torch.

"There is nothing of note down there, Quinn."

"Of course not." Simon stepped into the rock-lined hallway and closed the door behind him.

As he suspected, a half hour later Simon found himself emerging in the cemetery where he had been led to see his men. The paths below the city were winding and miles long, but the trail of charred torches and smoke trails on the walls betrayed the path most often traversed.

The home where Lynette was staying was not too great a distance away. Simon discarded his torch and set off in that direction, determined that Lynette and her mother should know about Lysette as soon as possible.

The following hours and days would grow more hazardous—digging up buried secrets always was—and if something untoward were to happen to him, Lysette did not know enough about her family to find them and Lynette might never know that her sister was alive, if not quite well.

He approached the courtesan's house through the alley and knocked on the delivery door. To say the young maid who answered was shocked to see a guest there would be an understatement. However, in short order, she recovered her aplomb. She allowed him entry and left him in the lower receiving parlor while she announced his arrival to the butler.

As he was left cooling his heels, Simon strolled about the tastefully decorated room and discovered hidden amusements which made him smile. While the palette of cream and pale gold was fit for a king, hints of the sensuality of the owner were evident if one looked close enough at the details. Half-dressed nymphs and satyrs danced across the moldings and frolicked on the bases of lamps, and miniature Grecian statues had modifications to their designs that would make many a lady blush.

"Mr. Quinn. So good of you to dress for the occasion."

He pivoted to find the lovely vicomtess sweeping regally into the room. Her attire was more informal than it had been on her visit to him. Wearing a floral gown of thin muslin, she appeared no older than her two daughters. On her heels was a lovely brunette who flashed him a smile so warm and genuine he could see why she was in such demand. He sketched a courtly bow to them both.

The vicomtess made quick and curt introductions, then gestured for him to sit.

"A note would have sufficed," she said coldly.

"To inform you that Lysette is alive and well?" he drawled. "Even I, with my admitted lack of breeding, have more tact than that."

Stiffening, she shot a glance at Solange seated beside her. The brunette reached over and linked hands.

"What do you want, Mr. Quinn?" the vicomtess asked. "I am not in the mood to play these games with you."

He ignored her curtness, believing it understandable in light of the circumstances. "She claims not to remember her life prior to two years ago, which is why she has not sought you out before now."

"How convenient," she said cloyingly. "No possibility of remembering the details incorrectly if you do not remember anything at all. When will you be bringing her by? I am certain she will wish to rejoin us and our wealth."

"I will not bring you together until I am certain it is safe to do so."

"Oh, I see. How much will it cost me to make it safe for you?"

Simon smiled, thinking he should like to speak with the vicomtess one day when she was in charity with him. "Were you aware of a man named *L'Esprit* when you were with the Marquis de Saint-Martin?"

She paled.

"I see," he murmured. "Have you heard from him in recent years?"

"What business is it of yours?"

"I find it odd," he murmured, "that both you and Comte Desjardins are so defensive about a man who plagues you."

"Some things are private and painful. They are not easy to share with strangers and those you distrust."

"I trust him."

Lynette's voice flowed over his skin like sunshine and brought an ache to his chest that was painful in its intensity. He stood and steeled himself to look at her. When he did, he inhaled sharply, noting the bruising around her eyes and her kiss-swollen mouth that betrayed his mark on her.

She had never been more beautiful.

He bowed. "Mademoiselle Baillon, you are a vision."

"Mr. Quinn." Her voice was low and throaty, reminding him vividly of her passionate cries in his bed. "How dashing you look in disguise."

"Lynette . . ." the vicomtess chastised. "Please return to your room."

"No." Lynette crossed the room and sat on a gilded armchair with her slender hands curled around the carved claw ends. "I believe I will stay. Mr. Quinn would only be here in regard to me."

Simon smiled and sat.

"I do not—"

Solange squeezed her friend's hand and the vicomtess fell into silence.

"Desjardins has been receiving demands from *L'Esprit* for the past ten years," Simon continued.

"I cannot think of a better man to torment," the vicomtess said.

"I believe he may have something to do with Lysette's ailment, although I wonder if he is the same man you knew as *L'Esprit* twenty years ago."

Solange leaned forward. "Why do you say that, Mr. Quinn?"

He explained the differences between the two communication styles.

"But I do not understand why someone would effect such a ruse," the vicomtess said, "or why they would want anything to do with Lysette."

"Is it her?" Lynette asked with hopeful eyes.

"Yes," Simon said softly. "I believe so. But she is not the sister you once knew. Her memory is lacking beyond two years past and the woman she has become during that time is not the one you remember."

"I do not care," Lynette said stubbornly.

"You might when you meet her," he warned, but his gaze promised support to her. She nodded and looked at him with such adoration he wondered how he remained seated.

"I think," he said, turning his attention back to the vicomtess, "that the *L'Esprit* who once demanded vengeance *from* Saint-Martin has become one who demands vengeance *for* him."

The vicomtess frowned. "I still do not understand."

"Who would have a grievance against you and your children? Who would resent your happiness and wish to destroy it?"

She pushed to her feet. "Are you speaking of Saint-Martin?"

Simon stood. "Desjardins told me that *L'Esprit*'s goal was to ruin Saint-Martin, yet the new *L'Esprit*— the one who handwrites his notes and does not visit him in the cellar—makes demands that have nothing to do with the marquis. Their purpose is to bedevil Desjardins."

"Saint-Martin would never hurt me," she refuted. "Never."

"Who is Saint-Martin?" Lynette asked.

"By all accounts he fell into a rapid decline when you left him," Simon continued. "Yet you married, had children, lived life."

"How would he know about *L'Esprit*?" the vicomtess challenged. "I received the one and only missive from him the night I left France and I took it with me. Saint-Martin never saw it."

"If *L'Esprit* was so determined to take every happiness away from the marquis, would he not gloat when he succeeded? Would he not have sent something to Saint-Martin advising him that his misfortune was not an aberration but a well-planned attack? What satisfaction would there be in defeating your enemy if they did not know they were defeated?"

"*Mon Dieu,*" Solange whispered.

"He isn't capable of such viciousness," the vicomtess insisted.

Simon glanced at Lynette, but spoke to the vicomtess. "A man can be driven mad with wanting, my lady."

"What do *you* believe has transpired, Mr. Quinn?" Lynette met his gaze directly.

"I believe your sister was taken," Simon advised. "I believe another body was dressed in her clothing and burned in the carriage. I believe these acts were committed by a man named Depardue, who was working on behalf of Saint-Martin. Somehow, Lysette's brain was damaged and her memory lost. Desjardins learned of Lysette and took her in, knowing full well who she was. He created an identity for her and has used her for his own purposes these two years, hoping that one day her existence would prove useful in freeing him from *L'Esprit.* I do not believe Saint-Martin knows she is alive."

"I do not believe any of that," the vicomtess said, but her white face and wringing hands said something else entirely.

"All this because my mother broke off their affair?" Lynette guessed.

"It is a possibility."

"No, it is not." The vicomtess straightened her shoulders. "You do not know him, Mr. Quinn, to make such aspersions on his character."

"Or perhaps you contribute feelings to him regarding your children that he cannot feel. You know more than he, after all."

"You are very clever, Mr. Quinn," Solange said softly.

"What are you talking about?" Lynette asked.

Simon looked at the vicomtess, hoping she would speak up and explain. She said nothing, merely looked away.

Lynette sighed. "*Maman*, you will have to be less secretive, if we have any hope of success."

"We will have to lure *L'Esprit* out into the open," Simon said, "in order to free Lysette completely. She and Lynette will both be at risk as long as his involvement is unaddressed."

Lynette stood. "I will help you however I can."

"You will not become involved in this morass!" her mother said crossly.

"I am sorry, *Maman*." Lynette's voice was sure and unwavering. "It is not my wish to disobey you, but I cannot allow Mr. Quinn to risk himself alone for us and I cannot allow Lysette to continue to live as she has been if I can spare her. She would do no less for me."

"You do not know if this woman is your sister."

"I do," Lynette said. "I know it without a doubt."

Solange exhaled audibly. "What can we do, Mr. Quinn?"

"Speak with de Grenier when he arrives a few days hence. Share my suspicions. We will need every able-bodied man we can find."

"De Grenier . . . Yes, you are correct." The vicomtess's relief was palpable. "He will assist you."

"In the interim," Simon said, "I will do what I can to keep Lysette safe from harm." He looked at Lynette. "Please remain indoors, mademoiselle. I would be much aggrieved if something untoward were to befall you."

"Of course." She offered him a reassuring smile. "I will not jeopardize myself in any manner."

Simon bowed. "I am in your service if you should need me, but please, do not venture to my home during this time. It is not safe for any of you."

"Thank you, Mr. Quinn." Lynette came to him and offered her hand. The smell of her skin as he kissed the back filled his mind with memories he cherished. He released her with the greatest reluctance, fighting his most basic instincts to squire her away and protect her from all harm.

Solange also reached out to him. "Be careful, Mr. Quinn."

"Thank you, mademoiselle. You, as well."

The vicomtess tilted her head. "If what you say about Lysette is true, I will owe you a great deal."

"You owe me nothing. I am not here with any expectation." He looked at Lynette one last time, wishing they were alone so that he could share with her all his concerns. In all of his life, he'd had no one to share his burdens.

"Godspeed."

Simon left the way he had come, leaving behind turmoil he hoped he had the power to help mend.

Simon realized he was being followed within two streets' length from the Tremblay home. His tracker was quite good.

Simon was better.

Slipping through two carts, Simon rounded the opposite side and came up behind him. Tucked in the sleeve of Thierry's coat was Simon's sheathed dagger. With a quick flick of his arm, the hilt slid down into his palm.

"Can I help you?" he drawled from a few feet behind the man.

Maintaining his air of insouciance, the individual slowed his steps gradually, then turned about in an elegant spin and touched the brim of his hat.

"Perhaps I can help you," the man returned.

"Marquis de Saint-Martin, I take it?"

Although he asked, Simon knew it was he.

Saint-Martin tilted his head slightly. "Mr. Quinn."

They eyed each other carefully.

"Shall we find a more private venue?" Simon asked.

"Certainly."

Together they moved cautiously, selecting a small tavern off the street. The air was redolent of roasted meat and hearty ale, and the patrons as a rule were neatly attired and subdued.

The two men settled into a corner opposite each other, and Simon studied the marquis as he removed his hat.

Tall, blond, and well formed, the marquis and the equally golden Marguerite Baillon would make a striking couple together. They had certainly made striking issue.

"The vicomtess asked me to investigate you, Mr. Quinn."

"Enjoying that task?"

"Immensely." The marquis's mouth curved and his fingertips drummed lightly on the table. "You are an interesting individual."

"As are you."

"Buried secrets are often best left beneath the ground," the marquis said in a low, dark tone.

"What an intriguing turn of phrase," Simon murmured, reclining into his seat. "I have one for you: It is too late to close the stable door once the mare is freed."

Saint-Martin's eyes narrowed ominously.

Simon was not fooled by the man's lithe build and pretty face. There was a sharp intensity about the marquis and a tense desperation. Simon was reminded that the man had nothing of emotional value left to lose, which made him exceedingly dangerous. His hardened mien also brought to mind Simon's future, which would lack Lynette. Perhaps Simon would look similar in the years to come. The thought was sobering and heartbreaking.

"Step lightly, Mr. Quinn. You tread on dangerous ground."

"Yours is the fourth threat I have had presented to me today," Simon said dryly. "I believe that must be a record of some sort."

"You inspire murderous thoughts apparently." The marquis's smile was chilling.

Simon snorted. "So do you. Tell me about *L'Esprit.*"

Saint-Martin tensed visibly. "Beg your pardon?"

"I must confess, I am impressed with your ability to inspire such vehement hatred. Perhaps you might care to explain what you did?"

A slight whitening of the marquis's knuckles was the only sign of disturbance.

"No comment?" Simon murmured. "Regardless, I will not allow this new threat to the vicomtess and her family to continue. As you said, some things that were once buried should remain that way. They should not be revived and utilized again."

"Can you stop it?" Saint-Martin asked softly. "I think not."

"A desperate man will resort to desperate measures. You seem to know that very well."

"You are very clever, Mr. Quinn." Saint-Martin stood and set his hat on his head. "Pray that you are also very prudent. You might live, if you are."

Smiling, Simon called after him, "That makes five threats in a day."

The tavern door closed behind the marquis without a sound.

Chapter 16

Lysette woke to the sound of the lock turning in her bedroom door. Blinking gritty eyes, she lifted her head and watched Madame Fouche peek her head around the corner.

"Madame Marchant?" she queried softly, most likely unable to see well into the dark room. "Are you well?"

"Yes, come in," she rasped, clearing her throat.

The housekeeper bustled in and quickly had the lamps lit and coals heating in the grate. She approached the bed, wiping her hands on her apron. "Mr. James is below and would like to see you."

"Send him up in ten minutes," Lysette said, knowing she should change first and receive him elsewhere but feeling too weary to make the effort. She also felt safe in her room, closed off from the world at large, protected from the prying eyes of Desjardins's staff.

Madame Fouche departed and moments later returned with Edward in tow. Lysette was refreshed, her face washed and a robe tied securely over her night rail. She waited in a chair before the fire, her hands linked primly in her lap, her bearing collected and self-assured.

Or so she thought.

"What is it?" he asked, sinking to his haunches beside her with a concerned frown. He was dressed with care, his gray suit unremarkable yet nicely tailored, his cravat perfectly tied. "You have been weeping."

An emotion on his face goaded her to reach out and touch his cheek with tentative, shaking fingertips. He exhaled harshly the moment they connected and the sound so startled her that she snatched her hand back.

Edward caught her withdrawal with such speed it was nearly too quick to see. He pressed his face into her palm, his eyes dark with something that frightened her . . . and made her tingle.

"Why do you come to me?" she asked hoarsely.

"Because I cannot stay away."

"What do you hope will happen?"

He inhaled deeply and slowly, his eyes never leaving hers. "I hope you will give me enough time to show you how it can be between us, if only you allow me to know you."

"The more you know, the less you will like."

"You know that is not true. You can feel it. I can see it in your eyes." He set one hand over her tightly linked ones and squeezed. "You would not be so afraid otherwise."

"Y-you want me," she whispered. "I-in your b-bed."

Standing, Edward held out both hands to her and helped her to her feet. She stood before him, trembling.

His touch drifted over her brow, his gaze hot and tender. "You feel fear, but not of me. It is the memories that frighten you. I can replace those. I can make them fade."

Lysette watched his mouth lower to hers, the pace set to afford her the opportunity to turn away. Part of her wanted to, knowing what he would want after the kiss. Another part of her was enamored with the shape of his lips, so stern, so somber. There was no frivolity about him.

Edward was an anchor. She was adrift. There was no way to fight the urge to cling to him and find steadiness. She had been alone for so long, unable to rely on anyone but herself. And he was here . . . *again* . . . steadfast . . .

"Yes, I want you," he said gruffly, his lips a hair's breadth away from hers. "But I can wait. I *will* wait. Until you are ready, however long that might be."

Lysette stood frozen, her heart racing in a panicked rhythm.

His mouth touched hers, gently but without hesitation. His tongue touched the seam of her lips, glided along it, caressed the curve. The scent of sandalwood and verbena filled her nostrils, warming her blood and causing her skin to tingle.

Low in her belly, heat spread.

Between her legs, dampness grew. She whimpered and clung to his coat, achingly aware of the cool air at her back and the heated length of hard male to her front.

"Let me in, Corinne."

Trembling, she obliged, gasping when his tongue thrust deep and sure. The similarity to the sexual act could not be ignored and her trembles turned to violent shaking.

Breathing harshly, he pulled back. "See?" he rasped. "I can stop. At any time. You lead, I follow."

"Lysette."

He frowned. "Beg your pardon?"

"My name is Lysette." She wrapped her hands around his wrists. "I lied to you."

Something suspiciously like a laugh escaped him. It was rough and abbreviated, almost a bark. "Lysette suits you better."

"I work for Desjardins," she blurted out. "He needs information about Mr. Franklin, and he was using me to pry it from you."

"Was?" His hands moved—one cupping her nape, the other banding her waist.

Lysette stared up at him, afraid to breathe. "I am not a good person. I have done things—"

"I do not care." Edward studied her, his gaze burning. "What concerns me is how you are with me from this moment onward. You must decide, Lysette: Will you trust me to care for you, as I have since I met you, or will you send me away?"

Lysette swallowed hard. "I want to trust you."

"That is a beginning, I suppose."

His fingers kneaded into the tense muscles of her neck, driving her mad. Her brain fought to stay frightened, urging her to flee. But her body, fickle thing, was melting into his touch. The feel of his hard, sinewy frame against her was not unpleasant.

"I have never trusted anyone," she confessed.

"Ever?"

Her smile was wry. "As long as I can remember. Would you like to hear the tale of my life? It is lamentably short but true."

Edward kissed the tip of her nose. "I should relish the opportunity to listen to whatever truths you have to tell me. I would, however, be grateful if you would return to bed and drink some beef tea."

"As you wish." Her smile wavered, shaken by gratitude at the care he displayed for her well-being.

With his hand at her lower back, he walked her to the bed.

To her surprise, she gave him the lead without reticence or fear for hidden intentions. The half-smile that curved the stern lines of his mouth made the concession worth it.

Marguerite was abed and nearly asleep when a raised masculine voice in the adjoining boudoir of her bedroom alerted her. She sat up, tossed back the covers, and fetched her robe from where it was draped over the foot of the bed. Rushing to the door, she pulled it open and found herself faced with her husband.

De Grenier was travel dusty and obviously weary, yet his handsome face lit when he saw her. Celie, her maid, stood behind him, holding his cane and hat.

"I reached Paris tonight," he said, "and found your note waiting for me. I came straightaway."

"You may go," Marguerite said to the maid, linking her arm with de Grenier's and leading him into the bedroom.

She shut the door behind them, briefly noting the disgruntled frown on the servant's face. Celie always looked displeased when de Grenier was with Marguerite. Since the maid had been with her since her affair with Saint-Martin, she suspected it was simply a case of liking one master more so than the other.

"Why are you here in Paris?" he asked, moving to the grate and holding his hands out to the banked fire.

"There is so much that I have to tell you," she said urgently. "So much has transpired since you and I last spoke."

Their marriage was a distant one, with de Grenier gone from their house more often than he was there. Even when he was home, he was often occupied in his study, working on diplomatic matters between France and Poland. But it was her fault, as well. With her heart engaged elsewhere, she had never given herself to him as she should have.

"Perhaps we should retire to our own home," he suggested.

"That would take hours and I cannot wait that long. As it is, I thought I might go mad before you arrived."

Nodding, de Grenier shrugged out of his coat, baring broad shoulders encased in shirtsleeves and waistcoat. He was younger than Saint-Martin by a decade, his body in its prime and beautifully maintained, his dark hair unmarred by gray. Women admired and coveted him, fawned over him, yet he was most often too distracted to take note of their interest.

He sank into a slipper chair and removed his heels. "You have my undivided attention, madame."

Nodding, Marguerite linked her hands behind her back and began to relate the events of the past sennight. She paced with agitation, but her words were spoken clearly. The entire affair was too important to say anything incorrectly.

"And you believe this man? This Quinn?" he asked when she finished. "You saw Lysette's body with your own eyes, Marguerite. How can this woman be our daughter?"

"I do not know. I confess, I am completely confused."

"What do you want me to do?" He stood and approached her, taking her hands in his. His gaze was clear and direct, capped by a slight frown.

"What do you think of Quinn's tale of *L'Esprit?*" she asked. "Do you think it has merit?"

He exhaled, then shook his head. "Are you asking me if I think Saint-Martin is responsible? I've no notion. There are too many unanswered questions. What happened to the original *L'Esprit?* How involved is Desjardins?"

"I detest that man," she hissed. "It frightens me how deeply I wish him ill."

Pressing his lips to her forehead, he said, "I will visit Quinn tomorrow and judge his sincerity for myself."

"Thank you." Marguerite looked up at him and felt deep gratitude. Through every tragedy of her life, he had been available to her, offering support and commiseration.

One of his hands slipped from her shoulders and cupped her unfettered breast. She inhaled sharply, startled by the abruptness of his advance. His thumb brushed across her nipple, then circled it, expertly bringing it to a hard and aching point.

"It is late," he murmured, watching her reactions with heavy-lidded eyes. "Let us retire here.

On the morrow, I will take you and Lynette home, and resolve this dilemma."

She nodded. As always, Philippe came to mind unbidden and her stomach knotted. Marguerite pushed the inevitable feelings of guilt and betrayal aside with effort and took her husband to her bed.

Lysette kicked snow off her boots before rushing through the front door of her home and racing up the stairs.

Once again, Lynette had grabbed her lighter muff, only to discover that it was cold enough to warrant using the fur-lined one. As often as she complained about how cold the Polish winter was, one would think she would never leave the house without being properly attired.

But that was Lynette, and Lysette loved her. Lynette was so vibrant and carefree, so daring. Men flocked around her and admired her beauty. Although they were twins, men did not do the same to her. And her sister was not one to complain about her lack of forethought. Lynette had acted as if nothing was wrong, but Lysette had noted her shivering and commented on it.

Today, they had gone on an outing with their mother to admire the beauty of the Countess Fedosz's winter garden. It was a small party, made up of local families bored by entrapment caused by the lengthy snowfall. Presently everyone was strolling through the various paths, admiring how the ice and snow clung to bare branches shaped especially to look better in winter than they did with leaves.

Running down the gallery, she entered Lynette's boudoir and retrieved her sister's muff, then she hurried back down the hall.

She was passing her mother's room when she tripped,

and a quick glance down confirmed that the laces on one of her boots had come undone, despite being wet.

Lysette kneeled on the runner, setting the muff down on the floor while she retied her boot. In the silence created by her lack of movement, voices were heard—masculine and feminine—coming from her mother's room, the door of which stood slightly ajar.

Who was talking? And why were they talking in the vicomtess's bedchamber?

Pushing to her feet with the muff in hand, Lysette stepped closer. She peeked through the slender crack between the doorjamb and the door, stilling with shock when her eyes found the couple inside.

His hand was at her throat, his mouth speaking harshly in her ear, his buttocks visibly clenching and releasing through his breeches as he thrust himself into her against the wall.

Celie's eyes were wide beneath her servant's cap, her nostrils flared with fear, her gasps punctuated with pleas for forgiveness.

"I need to see every missive that leaves this house," he growled. "You know this."

"I am sorry," she whimpered. "I have not failed you before now."

"One failure is too much."

The slick sounds of sexual congress blended with panting breaths and Celie's sobbing. The scene so horrified Lysette she thought she might faint. Instead she covered her mouth and backed up slowly, fighting a feeling of nausea so intense she thought she might cast up her accounts in the hallway.

Her back hit something solid. She jumped and cried out behind her hand.

"You should not have seen that," growled a masculine voice in her ear.

Pain—sharp and biting—split her skull. The hallway spun, then tumbled into darkness.

Lysette woke with a cry, her body shuddering with remembered fear and horror.

"Lysette." Edward rose from his seat before the fire, his jacket gone, his reddened eyes telling her he had fallen asleep as well. "Another nightmare?"

"Mon Dieu . . . ." she breathed, lifting a hand to her racing heart. She had never been gladder to see anyone than she was to see Edward. "Bless you for being here."

"I will always be here," he said, sitting beside her on the bed and pouring her a glass of water. "I stayed tonight because I thought you might sleep restlessly after telling me your story."

"It seems I have more to tell," she whispered, accepting the glass with gratitude.

He nodded grimly. "I am listening."

Simon was awake before dawn. Although he had slept only a handful of hours, he did not suffer from fatigue. He was alert and primed, so much so that he went to his study and began to plan in depth, knowing he needed a lure and a worthy trap. He was so occupied by the task that the hours passed swiftly, a circumstance he noted only when his butler announced a caller and presented the visitor's card to Simon.

His brows rose and he glanced at the clock. It was nearly eleven. "Show him in."

Setting his quill aside, Simon waited. When a tall, dark form filled his doorway, he stood and extended his hand. "Good morning, Mr. James."

"Mr. Quinn." Edward James's returning grip was strong and steady, as Simon supposed the man himself was.

"An unexpected visit, although not unwelcome." Simon gestured to the seat across from him, eyeing Edward James carefully. "To what or whom do I owe this honor?"

His visitor was dressed somberly in dark brown, his garments well kept, his cravat neat, his heels polished. Unremarkable, really, aside from the obvious fastidiousness.

"First," James said curtly, "you should know that you will never hear a word about Franklin's business from me. Ever. Neither will Desjardins, so both of you will have to find another woman to torment and bully."

Leaning back, Simon crossed his arms and bit back a smile. "I see."

"No, you do not," James muttered, scowling. "But you will."

"Good God!" Simon grinned. "Another threat. I must be doing something correctly."

"You may find this amusing, Mr. Quinn, however—"

"I have to find some humor in this," Simon interjected, his smile fading. "I have a great deal at risk, more than I believe I could bear to lose."

James's gaze narrowed considerably.

"I hope you are circumspect in your association with Madame Marchant," Simon said.

"Mademoiselle Rousseau," James corrected, "or whatever in hell her surname truly is. And I am always circumspect, Mr. Quinn. I know everything about her, as little as she can share. Every sordid, heartbreaking detail. I cannot condone the many wrongs she has done, but I can collect the necessity of some of it and the feelings of helplessness and melancholy that inspired the rest."

James lifted his chin. "But do not mistake my sympathy for weakness. I am not the sort of man who loses his head over a woman. Regardless of my affection for her, you will not find my emotions altering my ability to react to jeopardy and subterfuge."

"Admirable."

"She claims you hope to extricate her from this morass."

Simon nodded. "I do."

"I am here to assist you."

There was a slight rapping on the open door. Simon glanced up and saw Eddington eyeing James with an assessing glance.

"Good morning, gentlemen," the earl greeted, entering with a decided flourish.

James stood. Simon remained seated, although he did make the necessary introductions.

"Forgive my intrusion. I am off to the tailor's this morn," his lordship drawled, fluffing his jabot with a careless, bejeweled hand. "I saw a waistcoat yesterday that was nothing short of divine and knew I must have it immediately. Would either of you care to join me?"

"No, my lord," Simon said, biting back a smile.

"No, thank you, my lord," James said, scowling.

"Pity that," Eddington said, lifting his quizzing

glass to his eye and studying James from head to toe. "Ah well. Good day, gentlemen."

There was a brief silence after his lordship had departed, then James muttered, "I imagine that foppish guise fools most."

"Most, yes." Simon stared out the empty doorway, thinking.

"Why do you have that look on your face?"

Simon's gaze moved back to James. "What look?"

"As if you have discovered something new."

"I was simply thinking that appearances can be deceiving. It is something we could use to our advantage, considering we have two women who are identical to one another."

"Mademoiselle Rousseau is too ill."

"I know." Simon's fingers drummed atop the papers on his desk. "But very few of us know that. You, me, Desjardins . . . That is all."

"You did not inform her family?"

"No. Someone wanted her dead and has yet to learn that she is alive due to Desjardins's hiding of her. Perhaps it is time to relieve *L'Esprit* of his misconception."

"She had a dream. Last night." James crossed his arms. "We've no notion of whether it is simply a figment of her mind or an actual recollection that is incomplete."

"Anything at all, at this point, would be an improvement over what we have."

"I agree. She witnessed a man abusing a maid for failing to intercept all of the vicomtess's outgoing posts."

"Did she recognize him?"

"No. Unfortunately, she saw him only from be-hind. Tall, dark-haired, broad-shouldered . . . Could be anyone."

"But there is one man we know of who enjoys wounding women," Simon pointed out.

"Depardue." The sharp edge to James's voice betrayed a wealth of ill-will.

"Exactly. And I have suspected that—"

Another rap to the door silenced Simon and he met his butler's gaze.

"Another caller, sir," the servant said.

Simon accepted the card handed to him on a silver salver and read it, then glanced at James. "Prepare yourself, James," he said.

James nodded, his posture altering to one more rigid.

"Inform his lordship that I have a visitor," Simon said, standing, "but he is welcome to join us."

A few moments later, a tall and comely man en-tered the room. Dressed modestly but elegantly in rich green velvet, the dark-haired man who ap-proached Simon's desk unwittingly confirmed a few of Simon's suspicions. Curious as to whether the astute James would also latch on, Simon looked forward to the coming introductions.

"Good afternoon, my lord," Simon said.

"Mr. Quinn."

"My lord, may I present Mr. Edward James to you? He is acquainted with your daughter, Lysette. Mr. James, this is the Vicomte de Grenier."

Simon watched James's face closely but furtively, wondering if the man had been aware of the vast difference between his station and the one Lysette occupied. To his credit, James showed no outward sign of any of his thoughts as he greeted de Grenier.

The two men sat, filling the two seats that faced Simon's desk.

"You may speak freely in front of Mr. James, my lord," Simon said.

"As you can imagine, the vicomtess is deeply disturbed by your visit yesterday," the vicomte said grimly. "I am here to arrange a meeting with this woman you claim is our daughter and to discuss your thoughts on this matter of *L'Esprit*."

"Perhaps you will share what you know, my lord?" Simon asked. "Have you had any correspondence from *L'Esprit*?"

"No. However, I was with the vicomtess when she received a missive bearing that name. It arrived the afternoon Saint-Martin was attacked and left for dead, so I comprehend the danger."

"Apparently, some of Lysette's memory may be returning."

"Oh?" The vicomte appeared to weigh the news a moment. "I am relieved to hear that, as memories of events known only to Lysette will strengthen your argument regarding her identity."

"Did you see the body identified as Lysette's?" Simon asked.

"No. Sadly. I wish I could have taken that gruesome burden from the shoulders of my wife, but I was in Paris. I returned a sennight after the event had occurred."

"Were there any other women in the area who went missing during that time?" James asked.

"I have no idea, Mr. James," the vicomte replied. "In truth, I did not pay any attention to surrounding activities for months following. My wife was nearly destroyed by our loss, my remaining daughter was deeply grieving and altered by guilt. Apparently, Lysette was running an errand for her when the accident happened."

"Fetching a muff, perhaps?" James asked with narrowed gaze.

"Yes." De Grenier's frame tensed and he glanced with wide eyes at Simon. "It *is* Lysette, is it not? How else would you know that?"

"Yes, it is she."

The vicomte sat back, his shoulders rising as if a great weight had been removed. "The return of Lysette would restore my family to the happiness we once knew, at least in part. Does she remember what happened to her?"

"Not entirely." James did not look away from the vicomte, but Simon sensed he was searching for clues on how to proceed.

"She is in grave danger," Simon said, "as long as this man, *L'Esprit*, hunts her."

"And you believe *L'Esprit* is Saint-Martin?" De Grenier looked between the two of them with bright eyes. "In retaliation for the loss of my wife?"

"It seems a logical conclusion, unless you know of someone else who would wish to harm you so gravely?"

"No. There is no one else."

"So how do we force him to reveal his hand?" James asked.

"I think the best way to go about the business is to bring Lysette out into the open," Simon suggested. "However, my lord, Lysette is not well."

"Not well?" De Grenier leaned forward. "What is the matter with her? She should be attended."

"She has been, my lord," James said. "And she is recovering, but she is not yet well enough to venture out and put herself at risk."

"So how do you suggest we manage this?" the vicomte asked.

"If you are willing, my lord," Simon said, "we could switch the two. Lysette would stay with Solange Tremblay and Lynette would move into Lysette's home. We would set the trap there. I am being followed, so I doubt more than a few public sightings would be necessary to ensure that she is seen."

De Grenier gaped a moment, then snapped his mouth shut. "You want me to risk one daughter for the other?"

"I can think of no other way."

"Well, think harder," the vicomte said. "By your own account, Lysette has learned to care for herself. Lynette is still innocent. She would be an easy target."

"I am open to ideas, my lord. You must trust that Lynette's safety is my primary concern and the impetus for my involvement to begin with. Perhaps you should discuss this plan with both your wife and Lynette, then contact me with your thoughts?"

The vicomte looked to James, who shrugged. "I am at a loss, my lord."

De Grenier stood, shaking his head. "I will speak with the vicomtess and send for you when we have reached a decision. In the interim, please consider alternate routes that do not include Lynette's involvement."

"I will endeavor to keep her separate as much as possible," Simon said.

The vicomte studied him with narrowed eyes,

then nodded. "I think I believe you in that regard, Mr. Quinn."

They shook hands and parted, leaving Simon with James.

"In regards to your offer of assistance . . ." Simon began.

James smiled grimly. "Tell me what you need."

Chapter 17

It was nearly impossible for Lynette to sit still. Her heart raced desperately and the palms of her gloves were damp with sweat. As the hackney rolled inexorably toward the location where they would meet Lysette, Lynette found herself shifting nervously on the seat. Her sister was alive and only moments away. The miracle of that was almost too extraordinary to believe.

"Lynette," de Grenier said, his tone a warning. "You will make yourself ill if you continue to fuss in that manner."

"I cannot help myself, my lord."

"I collect how you feel," her mother said softly, offering a shaky smile.

"I have strong reservations about this," her father muttered. "If this is an elaborate ruse, I doubt I can protect both of you."

"I trust him," Lynette said, bristling. "Implicitly."

Her father offering protection? She bit back a snort. If she added up all the days of her life in which they had occupied the same home, they would be few and far between. He was always away. For years she had pined for any sign of affection or concern from him. Then she realized that he would never forgive her for being a daughter and not a son.

"You are obviously smitten," he said, his lip curling.

"Yes." She lifted her chin. "Yes, I am."

Her mother reached over and set her hand atop her father's. He quieted and Lynette shot her a grateful smile.

The carriage drew to a halt. Lynette looked out the window, frowning at the sight of a cemetery.

"Why are we here?" she asked.

"This is the direction Quinn sent earlier," de Grenier replied.

She felt confusion until Simon stepped into view, so tall and powerful and delicious in cinnamon-colored silk, his gait seductive and predatory. His gaze met hers and changed, becoming hotter. Hungrier. Burning with passion and possessiveness. Her breath caught and heat swept across her skin.

My lover.

Her fingers curled desperately around the lip of the carriage window. Emotions flooded her in a deluge difficult to process—relief and joy, lust and longing. Yet even as the torrent of feeling swirled around her, her heart was firmly anchored in the middle, sure in its intent and the purity of her affection.

I am grateful for you.

The unspoken words lodged in her throat, her eyes burning with unshed tears. He was doing this for her. Everything. All of it. And she could not go through the experience without him. It was his strength she looked toward. His returning affection for her gave her the confidence to face her parents and Lysette, a woman who would be a stranger to her.

Her heart swelled in her breast, aching at the sight of him, grateful for the gift of him.

I have missed you.

Her lips mouthed the words which he saw, his jaw tightening. With a brusque wave of his hand, he gestured the driver away from the door and wrenched it open himself, catching her as she fell into his arms, his lips brushing against her cheek before he set her down.

"Mademoiselle Baillon," he greeted her, his voice gruff. "You steal my breath."

"You stole my heart," she whispered.

His sharp exhale was a hiss of sound in the quiet of the cemetery. The look he gave her scorched her, made her cheeks flush with heat and her lips dry.

"Mr. Quinn."

Her father alighted from the carriage and held out a hand to her mother.

Simon looked away from her, his chest rising and falling with rapid breaths. She felt the need in him, smelled it in the air, shivered as it called to her own desire for him. Her breasts swelled in response and the tender flesh between her legs dampened. It was an animalistic response, purely instinctive. That their reactions to one another were goaded by her original emotional response told her all she needed to know.

"This way," Simon said, leading them through the cemetery. Lynette hurried forward, catching his arm with her own.

"Lynette," her father snapped. "Walk with us."

She looked up at Simon, who frowned down at her, and she winked.

"Witch," he said under his breath. But a hint of a smile curved his mouth and made her heart clench.

"Lover," she purred.

His growl rumbled over her skin and soothed the part of her made restless by the upcoming reunion with her sister. The tension she had carried in her shoulders all morning relaxed. His hand came over hers and squeezed, and the look he gave her told her that he understood her anxiety and agitation.

Simon understood everything about her, in a way those who had known her for years did not.

They approached a crypt with an open door and she slowed.

"We must travel the distance through there," he said.

Lynette nodded and lifted the hem of her sapphire skirts in her hand.

"*Mon Dieu,*" her mother said. "Is this really necessary?"

"Desjardins's home is being watched. This is the most convincing way in which to make the switch. I entered the home with Lysette, I will depart with Lynette. Whoever is watching will never know the difference."

Glancing over her shoulder, Lynette met her mother's frown with a shaky smile. "You will leave with Lysette, *Maman.* Surely that makes you happy."

"But I risk you, *ma petite,*" her mother said gravely.

Her father's lips tightened and he gripped the vicomtess's arm more securely.

Lynette looked forward again and clung to Simon's arm as he led her into the bowels of the city. They traversed a maze of winding stone-lined paths, their way lighted by a single burning torch carried aloft by Simon. Eventually he turned off the main corridor and led them up a short flight of stairs to a wooden door.

Thrusting the torch into a sconce on the wall, he then pushed open the portal and stepped into a cellar. Row upon row of wine racks filled the cool space, startling Lynette for a moment. It was such an innocuous sight after the ominous air of the catacombs. The change in scene was jarring and caused her apprehension to return in full force.

Simon's hand squeezed hers again and her shoulders went back.

Her heartbeat increased with every step, her breathing growing shallower until she found herself standing before a small, slender man dressed in gold satin. He looked her over from head to toe.

"Remarkable," he said, his voice loud in the relative stillness of the house.

"Lynette, may I introduce—"

Simon's words were cut off when de Grenier lunged and tackled Desjardins to the floor. A one-sided scuffle ensued, and Simon reached out to the stunned vicomtess and pulled her into the study, where he shut the door.

Lynette was so startled by her father's attack, it took her the length of several heartbeats to sense the heavy weight of tension in the room. It settled on her nape first, raising the tiny hairs there and sending a shiver down her spine.

Inhaling deeply, she turned slowly, her breath

held within seized lungs, her heart hammering against her corset-bound ribs.

She found Lysette by the grate, pale and ethereally lovely in a gown of white with multicolored embroidered flowers, her arm extended to grasp the hand of a somber-looking man in dark gray.

Lynette studied her without blinking, seeing her beloved sister on the exterior but a stranger reflected in her eyes, one both cold and wary. If not for the man beside Lysette—Mr. Edward James, according to her father—she might have remained reserved. But James was precisely the sort of suitor Lynette would have chosen for her sibling.

Without a word, she took a step forward, unaware that she was sobbing until hot tears fell on her breast.

Her sister looked at Mr. James, who nodded his encouragement. He stepped closer, placing his hand at the small of her back and guiding her forward.

A sob rent the highly charged air and her mother rushed past her, embracing Lysette with a cry of agonized joy. Her sister's face crumbled, the stony façade falling away to reveal a vulnerable young woman with deeply rooted pain.

The sight was so intimate Lynette looked away, searching for Simon, who must have felt her need of him. He drew abreast of her and wrapped his arm around her waist.

"*A thiasce,*" he murmured, handing a handkerchief to her. "Even tears of joy pain me when they fall from your eyes."

His large hand cupped her waist with gentle pressure and she leaned against him, taking comfort from his stalwart presence.

The vicomtess pulled back, her shaking hands cupping Lysette's face. Searching, touching, remembering. Lysette was crying softly, her shoulders folded down and inward, her frame so frail and quaking with the force of her emotions.

Then her eyes shifted, moving upward until she met Lynette's returning gaze.

"Lynette," she murmured, extending her hand.

Marguerite composed herself with great effort, stepping back and hugging herself, rocking gently.

Simon pressed a kiss to Lynette's forehead. "I will be here for you," he whispered.

Nodding, she straightened and stepped away from him. She took one step, then another. She watched her sister do the same, searching the beloved features for any sign of condemnation or fury for being the cause of her torment these last few years.

But there was nothing but hope and a joy so wary it broke Lynette's heart. Like her mother, she ran the rest of the way, one hand holding her skirts while the other was extended in grateful welcome.

They collided, the impact jolting through them both, more for the feeling of having two broken halves reunited than from the physical force.

Laughing and crying, they clung to each other, speaking over each other, words and tears mingling together in a scouring wash that wiped the years away. It suddenly felt as if they had never been apart, as if it had all been a horrible nightmare.

Marguerite joined them and together they sank to the floor, a puddle of feminine skirts and golden hair in the stark whiteness of Desjardins's parlor.

They did not hear the men leave or the door shut behind them.

Simon glanced at James in the hallway as the latch clicked into place behind them. "Does Lysette understand the arrangements?"

"Yes. She was not pleased, but she acquiesced."

"Excellent. Pray the rest of this affair runs as smoothly as the first." He gestured toward the study, where angry voices could be heard.

They paused on the threshold, taking in the sight of Desjardins sitting before the cold grate with a bloody lip and nose and de Grenier seated at Desjardins's desk with a pile of missives from *L'Esprit* scattered all across the top.

"Mademoiselle Baillon remembers more this morning than she did yesterday," James said. "I believe the reconciliation with her mother and sister will jar the rest of her memory loose in short order."

De Grenier glanced up from the desktop.

"Excellent," Simon replied, glancing at the comte. "Have you arranged a meeting with Saint-Martin?"

" 'e replied that the next time 'e sees me will be in 'ell," the comte mumbled from behind a crimson-soaked kerchief.

"Very well, then," Simon said, shrugging. "We shall see what we can do about that."

It was nearing two in the afternoon when Simon Quinn's coach pulled away from Desjardins's house. The equipage moved with studious leisure toward

Lysette's home, the pace deliberately set to enable a greater opportunity of being seen.

Simon reclined against the squab, his face set austerely to give no clue to his thoughts. The curtains were tied back to facilitate viewing by anyone searching them out, so there was nothing to do but wait. If his assessment of the situation was correct, he doubted they would be waiting long.

Occasionally, he glanced at the squab across from him, marveling at how much a garment could change the appearance of the wearer. Lynette and Lysette were identical, yet the floral gown of one and the sapphire silk of the other altered that mirroring enough to make them two separate and distinct women. In close proximity, the differences life's toils—or lack thereof—had wrought in them became noticeable, but from a distance, they easily passed for one another.

As the carriage drew to a halt outside Lysette's home, Simon shot a quick glance at the façade and noted the slight rustling of the sheers on the upper-floor window. A chill swept down his nape and curled around his spine. His instincts told him something was amiss and he trusted them implicitly.

And so the prearranged plan was set in motion. For the benefit of anyone watching, the cinnamon-clad man and the floral-garbed woman exited the equipage with insouciance, her hat set at a jaunty angle atop riotous blond curls and his hand set over the top of hers. The hackney was paid and sent on his way, then they climbed the short steps and entered the house.

The silence inside was deafening. And unnatural.

Lysette's household was small, yet there should have been some sounds of movement.

They stepped farther into the foyer, both tense, breaths caught, their heads turning from side to side, searching for entrapment. His fingers banded her wrist and he attempted to tug her behind him, but she resisted.

Slowly, carefully, they moved through the house. Room by room. Working in tandem as if they always had.

Ascending the stairs, they reached the first door, which belonged to the upper parlor. Reaching for the knob, he pushed the portal carefully open, pausing when the door's progress was halted mid-swing by something heavy on the floor. He looked down. Saw an arm, the hand of which was splattered with blood. He stepped back, but not in time.

The muzzle of a pistol appeared, followed immediately by the person brandishing it.

"*Bonjour,*" the masculine voice drawled.

"Thierry," Lynette murmured, her voice cold and devoid of emotion.

Thierry stepped over the body on the floor and came out to the hallway. He scowled. "You are not Quinn," he barked.

Eddington straightened Simon's cinnamon-colored coat and smiled. "You are correct, chap. I am not Quinn."

Marguerite led her daughter into Solange's house with their hands clasped together. De Grenier brought up the rear carrying a satchel filled with letters to Desjardins written by *L'Esprit.* Marguerite shuddered even to think of the name, horrified by the realization that Lysette had been stolen from her for two long years. Years of purgatory where some days she had survived only because of her love for Lynette.

"This way, *ma petite*," she said to Lysette, directing her toward the curving staircase. "After you are settled, I should like to hear more about your Mr. James."

"Of course, *Maman*," Lysette murmured, her eyes wide within her pale face. Her hand quivered within Marguerite's grasp and her obvious fear and apprehension broke Marguerite's heart.

Setting her arm around Lysette's shoulders, she pressed a kiss to her forehead. "Here is the bedchamber Lynette has been using," she said as they reached the first door off the upper landing.

They stepped inside, finding the room still in shambles after Lynette's frantic search for something appropriate to wear.

"Celie?" Marguerite called out, releasing Lysette to search for the maid. She moved into the suite's boudoir and sitting room, but found no sign of her.

"Wait a moment," she said to Lysette, frowning. "Perhaps she is in my room. I confess, I was equally anxious about seeing you again and made as large a mess."

Nodding her acquiescence, Lysette stepped deeper into the space as Marguerite left and crossed the hall to her bedchamber. Her room was also still in disarray, with gowns and undergarments scattered across the bed and every chair.

"Celie?"

It was not in character for Celie to leave such a mess lying about. Marguerite began to worry, her steps quickening as she rushed toward the boudoir. She hurried through the open door and drew to a halt, lifting her hand to her mouth to stifle a scream of terror.

Celie stared sightlessly from the floor, her mouth foamed and lips blue. In one hand, she clutched a sheaf of papers. In the other, a wax seal.

"Celie!" Marguerite sobbed in grief and horror. A chill seeped through her skin to solidify as ice within her gut, prompting a violent shudder to wrack her frame.

Goaded by terror, she ran from the suite, racing across the hallway to Lysette. She shut the door behind her and turned the key, breathing so heavily she thought she might faint.

"Maman!" Lysette rushed forward. "What is it?"

"Celie . . ." she gasped. "Celie is dead."

In the same manner the servants in her household had been killed years ago. Poison. She would know the signs anywhere now.

"No," Lysette whispered, mouth quivering and eyes filling with tears.

Marguerite's stomach knotted as the room tilted precariously. *"Mon Dieu,* what are we going to do?"

The lock turned. Marguerite spun about, shielding her daughter behind her back.

The door opened, and Saint-Martin walked in.

Seeking purchase in the rocking carriage, Simon held tight to the window ledge and stood, redressing as quickly as possible in Eddington's breeches. The journey to Solange Tremblay's home was not long, but a stone's throw would be too far for him now.

He had never enjoyed gambling. With the stakes in this game being the safety of Lynette, he detested it. But if he should win, they would all be free. Yes, the risks were great, but the possible gain was greater.

With the blessing of her parents, he could court his precious Lynette. He could woo and win her, cherish her. Surely they would at least consider his suit, if he delivered them from the enemy who had tormented them for so long.

"Hurry!" he shouted to the driver, hating the necessary delay. He sat and tugged on his boots, his breathing labored by anxiety.

Dear God, keep her safe.

Grimly determined, he reached for his dagger and sheath.

"Are you *L'Esprit*?" Eddington asked, his gaze never leaving the mouth of the pistol pointed at his chest. The man who stood on the other side was tall and broad, about the same size as Quinn, but this man's eyes were cold and dark.

Thierry growled. "Where in hell is Quinn?"

"Not here obviously."

"Damn you." He glared. "If I had known who she was before now, I could have been a rich man."

"Sorry to disappoint," Eddington drawled, his senses alert despite the casualness of his pose. "Perhaps I can be of assistance in lieu of Quinn?"

"I need Quinn to kill *her*!" Thierry growled, gesturing over Eddington's shoulder with a jerk of his gun.

"Hmm . . ." Eddington nodded. "I see. English spy kills French spy. Nothing too odd about that, is there?"

"It might not be wise to goad him," Mademoiselle Baillon said. "He has a weapon."

"I can see that. So what do we do now? If he is not *L'Esprit*, we've little use for him."

"Who are you?" Thierry snapped.

"A friend of Quinn's."

Thierry's frustration was palpable and dangerous. "Go to the bedroom."

Eddington followed Mademoiselle Baillon as she led the way, thinking that perhaps utilizing Quinn in the future might not be so wise. The man had become embroiled in one morass after another over the last few months, making him less and less valuable. After all, what good was a spy whose covert activities were known to all and sundry? *And* . . . what good was a man who dragged his superiors into tangles such as these?

They had barely stepped into the room when a sickening thud, followed by a loud grunt, was heard behind him. Eddington pivoted and crouched, ready to defend both himself and Mademoiselle Baillon. Instead, he faced Mr. James, who was brandishing a weighty silver candlestick.

Thierry crumpled to the floor, his pistol dropping and misfiring, the report deafening in the enclosed space of the bedroom.

"Edward!" Mademoiselle Baillon rushed toward him and the man caught her close, pressing a hard kiss to her forehead.

"Forgive me," he said huskily. "I came as soon as I could."

Eddington frowned. "You are not Mademoiselle Baillon, are you?" he asked.

She smiled. "I am. But I am not Lynette."

Marguerite gasped as Saint-Martin entered the room, followed immediately by de Grenier . . . who held a pistol to his back.

Her lungs seized with unalloyed terror. "Philippe," she whispered, her heart breaking at the pain and regret she saw in his eyes.

Behind her, Lysette gave a strangled cry, backing away and pulling Marguerite with her. Protecting her mother, when it should have been the reverse.

All of these years . . . she had allowed her children to reside with a monster.

"Look who I found lurking about the place," de Grenier drawled. "Could not be more convenient, I must say. I was expecting a few hours at least before I could lure him here."

"Why?" Lysette asked, her voice shaking.

"To kill you, *ma petite,*" he drawled, the words piercing deep.

"No!" Marguerite spread her arms wide, blocking Lysette from harm. "How could you? She is your daughter!"

De Grenier's smile was icy. "No, she is not. You must think I am a fool. She could not look more like Saint-Martin if she wished to."

Marguerite's chin rose, and her gaze moved to Philippe. He stared at Lysette, a look of wonder and joy erasing the lines of sorrow their tragic past had placed upon his countenance. Tears filled her eyes, the long-dreamed-of moment finally here, but marred by tragedy.

She forced her gaze back to her husband, beseeching. "You raised her," she argued. "Watched her grow. You have been the only father she has ever known."

"And what a delight that has been." His eyes shone bright with malice. "Knowing I had everything Saint-Martin coveted—the woman he loved and the daughters he sired. Fucking his wife and killing her were added pleasures, but fleeting. Having you daily was my true joy."

A low growl rumbled up from Philippe's chest, frightening Marguerite with its unadulterated menace.

"You are *L'Esprit*," Lysette said, her hand tightening on Marguerite's.

"Things would have remained perfect," de Grenier said, "if you had remained dead. I will kill Desjardins when this is done. His machinations have ruined everything."

"Simon was correct," Lysette said softly. "I cannot tell you how sorry I am that he was right."

Something about Lysette's tone set the hairs on Marguerite's nape to rising. Tumultuous undercurrents swirled about the room, buffeting her with confusion and uncertainty.

"What in hell are you talking about?" De Grenier kicked Philippe farther into the room.

Philippe stumbled but recovered quickly, pivoting to take a position before Marguerite, shielding her as she shielded Lysette. She was torn between gratitude that he was with her, and panic that something untoward would befall him.

"Simon suspected you were the culprit," Lysette said.

"Oh? Clever fellow."

"Yes, he is," she agreed. "Hence the reason Lysette is far from you with her memories protected, while I am here."

"You lie." De Grenier's eyes narrowed.

"Lynette?" Marguerite queried, dazed by the revelation that no one was who she had thought them to be.

"I am the healthier of the two of us at the moment," Lynette said with an elegant shrug, "far more capable of dealing with you."

De Grenier's lip curled in a sneer, devastating Marguerite with the knowledge that she had given herself to a man who hated her and wished her nothing but harm. "Do not be so smug, *ma chérie*. Quinn is dead now, along with your sister. Soon you will be reunited for eternity. In hell."

Marguerite whimpered, her free hand reaching for Philippe as her heart twisted with fear and grief. It was torment unparalleled to have her family reunited and intact, only to have it ripped asunder again.

"I have risen from the grave," drawled an Irish-inflected voice.

De Grenier bellowed with something akin to agony. Marguerite watched in horror as the end of a small sword appeared straight through his right shoulder, protruding morbidly. As de Grenier dropped to his knees, Saint-Martin kicked, knocking the gun from his hand to clatter a few feet away. Quinn was revealed to be standing in the doorway, a crimson-covered blade in his hand.

Lynette grabbed Marguerite, pulling her out of the way.

Roaring, de Grenier lurched to his feet and tackled Saint-Martin to the floor.

Quinn leaped over the two writhing bodies, rushing toward Lynette and Marguerite.

But Marguerite would have none of it. Inhaling courage, she skirted Quinn and raced toward the discarded pistol. A hand grabbed her ankle, yanking her balance from her and causing her to land with bone-jarring force prone on the floor. Kicking at her attacker, she reached out for the pistol grip, her sweat-soaked fingertips slipping across the polished wood.

No one would harm her children again. Not while there was still breath left in her body.

And then it was there, the grip seated firmly in her palm. She rolled to her back, searching for de Grenier. He rose to his knees, a blade wielded high above a sprawled Saint-Martin.

"No!"

Lynette's cry reverberated through the room and gave Marguerite the strength to do what she must.

Saint-Martin reared up, the heel of his palm shattering the aquiline beauty of de Grenier's nose. The sound of cartilage breaking was like a thunder-crack.

Marguerite aimed and pulled the trigger.

Chapter 18

Four weeks later . . .

Simon alighted from his carriage and ascended the steps to the front door of Marguerite Baillon's home. The day was bright and beautiful, the air cleansed from a brief spate of early morning rain. From the exterior, the home was cheery and welcoming, with red flowers overflowing from urns flanking the entrance.

The door opened before he knocked, revealing the much-loved sight of Lynette standing on the threshold.

"Good afternoon, Mademoiselle Rousseau," he greeted her, removing his hat and sweeping a low bow.

"You are tardy, Mr. Quinn," she chastised him sternly.

"I am not," he protested, withdrawing his pocket watch. "It is precisely one o'clock, the same time I visit you every day."

"It is nearly five after one." She caught his arm

and tugged him into the foyer, shutting the door behind him. She collected his hat and tossed it agilely to the rack, where it caught and swayed into place.

"Excellent shot," he praised, staring down at her lovely, animated features.

"Do not change the subject."

"You are piqued with me." He smiled. "Did you miss me, *a thiasce*?"

"You know I did," she grumbled, leading him toward the lower parlor. "I thought you might not come."

"Nothing could keep me away," he murmured, the fingers of his free hand clenching with the need to touch her. Everywhere.

Weeks of abstinence were taking their toll, but he was determined to woo her properly. She and Lysette had decided to take Saint-Martin's name in an effort to right the wrongs done by de Grenier. Their declaration of bastardy had ruined them, making them unsuitable for an esteemed social marriage. Because of this, Simon was firm in his intent to court Lynette as she might have been if only he were worthy and she were not tainted by scandal.

"I think you might be falling in love with me, Simon," Lynette purred, her smile wicked and filled with feminine satisfaction.

"I might be," he agreed, squeezing her hand where it rested over his forearm.

She was so brave. He admired as well as desired her. She had not wanted to believe that the man she knew as her pater would be so heinous, but she had trusted Simon and displayed great courage by agreeing to his plan. Her fortitude when faced with the darker side of his world had ensnared him.

He was not an easy man to live with. He was coarse, roughened by years spent in the gutter, surviving by his wits and his fists. It would take an exceptional woman to manage him and love him regardless. What a miracle it was to have found Lynette, gently bred yet strong, demure but passionate. She took all that he was and all that he had ever been, and wanted him, regardless.

Over the last four weeks he had shown her both the best and the worst of himself, visiting her daily, good humor or bad. At times his longing for her made him curt, but she tolerated him easily. She, too, had shown the various facets of her temper—sometimes sweetly cajoling, at others pensive or cross. He'd found that he would rather be with a disgruntled Lynette than any other woman in the world.

He was firmly caught and happy for it.

They entered the parlor, and Simon discovered Lysette and Mr. James sitting on the window seat, sharing a book between them. The vicomtess was engaged in needlepoint on the settee, and the Marquis de Saint-Martin was occupied at the small escritoire.

"See?" Lynette murmured. "Saint-Martin and Mr. James have already arrived."

Simon pulled out his timepiece again and scowled down at it. "I may need a new watch," he said.

"Or a ring."

His gaze met hers and she winked.

"Mr. Quinn," the marquis called out. "Come here, if you would, please."

"Will you walk with me in the garden today?" Lynette asked.

"I will walk with you anywhere."

Her smile warmed him from the inside, offering him the home he had searched for all his years. He belonged somewhere, to someone. After a lifetime of loneliness, her presence in his life was an oasis in the desert.

"I will fetch my shawl while you speak with the marquis." She ran from the room in a swirl of dark green and white striped skirts.

Simon moved to the escritoire. "Good afternoon, my lord."

"You, as well." Saint-Martin straightened and gestured to the profusion of papers before him.

"Are those the items found with the maid?"

"Yes. Poor Celie. I cannot imagine what purgatory she suffered all these years. To take her own life . . ." He shook his head. "I wish she had known that we would not fault her."

"Have you found anything that reveals de Grenier's motivations?"

Heaving out his breath, the marquis sat back and nodded. "There was a woman in my past. The affair was brief and forgettable, if not for her reaction to our parting. She went into a decline, weeping on the steps of my home and creating a scene every time we crossed paths."

"I had heard tales of that, I think," Simon said, wincing in sympathy.

"People still speak of it today. It was dreadful, for both of us. At the time, I had yet to meet Marguerite so I could not collect why the woman was so distraught. I had no understanding of love or obsession." He rubbed the back of his neck. "Regrettably, I did not handle the ordeal well and her family sent her away to avoid further embarrassment for us all."

"De Grenier knew her?"

"He loved her, apparently. She was a distant cousin and he had hoped to wed her. She took her own life shortly after her removal from Paris and he set the blame on my doorstep. Perhaps, rightly so."

Simon set his hand atop the marquis's shoulder. "While your affair may have brought her illness to light, I think it likely that she would have succumbed to madness regardless of your involvement. From de Grenier's actions, I suspect mental defect is a trait in their family line."

"If only it were that simple." The marquis reached up and patted Simon's hand, the paternal gesture startling and deeply moving. "Marguerite is still shaken by de Grenier's death and her hand in it. She has nightmares, as does Lysette. I have lost years of my daughters' lives. Their childhood is gone and they are about to be wed." Saint-Martin arched a brow. "They *are* about to be wed, *oui?*"

Laughing, Simon stepped back. "I cannot see to both of them, my lord. Only the one."

"What are you laughing about, Mr. Quinn?" Lynette asked, sweeping into the room with a soft smile. She held her bare hand out to him and he accepted it, lifting it to his lips.

"Nothing," he evaded, wrapping her arm around his. "Shall we walk?"

"I should like that."

They excused themselves and left the parlor, moving down the gallery to the doors leading to the outside. Once they had exited to the garden, Simon drew her closer, breathing deeply of the scents of rain-cleansed air and the seductive scent of Lynette's perfume.

"You know," she murmured, her lips curved sweetly, "when I first saw you, I marveled at your handsomeness and thought to myself that you would never be tamed."

"Tamed?" His brows rose. "I am not certain I like the sound of that."

"Oh?" She glanced up at him from beneath thick, chocolate-colored lashes. "Do you not have honorable intentions toward me, Mr. Quinn?"

"'Mr. Quinn,' is it?" He sidestepped behind a tall hedge and dragged her with him. Cupping her face, he kissed her, releasing only the veriest portion of his insatiable desire for her.

He licked across her lips, nibbling, teasing. Relishing the wordless entreaties she made, soft pleas for more than he could possibly give her here. His tongue stroked deep into her mouth, licking, tasting, drinking her in. "You would not want me tamed, *a thiasce*."

"Let me come to you tonight," she whispered, her head tilted back, her eyes closed.

"Don't tempt me," he growled.

"Simon." She gave an exasperated laugh and opened her eyes. "You will drive me insane. Have you any notion of how I dream of you? How I miss you? Sometimes at night I think of you lewdly. I feel your hands on my skin, your mouth on my breasts, your body covering mine . . ."

"Bloody hell." He tugged her closer, his hips grinding restlessly against the mass of her skirts, his cock hard and throbbing within the confines of his breeches. "You would drive a saint to sin."

"There is a gazebo in the far corner . . ." she suggested, licking her kiss-swollen lips.

"I am attempting to court you properly, curse you."

"Seems rather late, considering the fact that you have already been inside me." She shivered against him. "Sometimes I feel you, pushing deep . . ."

Groaning, Simon kissed her again, grateful for her passion and the freedom with which she gave herself to him. Without shyness or reservation, trusting him implicitly, as she had from the very first.

"What are you waiting for?" she asked breathlessly.

"I want to give you time," he said hoarsely, tucking a golden curl behind her ear. "I want you to be certain I am what you want."

Lynette's brows rose. "And if I find someone else? You would allow me to go?"

His hands tightened involuntarily into her tender flesh and he forced himself to release her. "No."

Her slender arms wrapped around his waist, bridging the gap he had just created. "I thought not. So you torture us both for nothing."

"I have nothing to offer you."

"Give me your heart and your body, those are all I desire from you. The rest—home, family—we will create on our own. Saint-Martin has promised a substantial dowry."

"I've no need of it," Simon said, resuming their walk in an effort to expend the sexual tension she incited in him. "Eddington kept his word, oddly enough."

"Lovely." Her smile told him she was happy for him, but he knew she would have taken him anyway. "My mother and father intend to wed."

Simon smiled, pleased. It was rare to see a couple so attuned to one another. "I wish them well."

"It would be an excellent time for us to honeymoon in Ireland," she murmured. "It would give them the opportunity to enjoy one another and celebrate their reunion without interference."

"Lynette." He laughed and picked her up, spinning her. "You will run roughshod over me for the rest of our days, I can see it already."

Her hands settled on his shoulders and she pressed her lips to the tip of his nose. "Do you fault me for wishing to start those days—and nights—now? If you drag your feet any longer, I will think you are waiting for someone better to come along."

"There is no one better."

"Of course not." Her fingers sifted through his hair, her blues eyes warm and appreciative. "Ask me," she urged.

With a dramatic sigh, he set her down and dropped to one knee on the gravel path. "Lynette Rousseau, would you do me the great honor of becoming my wife?"

Tears filled her eyes and her lips quivered. "Oh, Simon . . ."

He reached into his coat pocket and removed a ring box.

Her eyes widened. "You had that with you the whole time?"

Simon smiled.

"Ooh!" She stomped her foot, then turned on her heel and left him.

Laughing, he chased after her, unwilling ever to let her go.

Don't miss *Ask for It*, the first in Sylvia Day's Georgian series.

London, April 1770

"Are you worried I'll ravish the woman, Eldridge? I admit to a preference for widows in my bed. They are much more agreeable and decidedly less complicated than virgins or other men's wives."

Sharp gray eyes lifted from the mass of papers on the enormous mahogany desk. "*Ravish*, Westfield?" The deep voice was rife with exasperation. "Be serious, man. This assignment is very important to me."

Marcus Ashford, seventh Earl of Westfield, lost the wicked smile that hid the soberness of his thoughts and released a deep breath. "And you must be aware that it is equally important to me."

Nicholas, Lord Eldridge, sat back in his chair, placed his elbows on the armrests, and steepled his long, thin fingers. He was a tall and sinewy man with a weathered face that had seen too many hours on the deck of a ship. Everything about him was practical, nothing superfluous, from his manner of speaking to his physical build. He presented an intimidating presence with a bustling London thoroughfare as a backdrop. The result was deliberate and highly effective.

"As a matter of fact, until this moment, I was not aware. I wanted to exploit your cryptography skills. I never considered you would volunteer to manage the case."

Marcus met the piercing gray stare with grim determination. Eldridge was head of the elite band of agents whose sole purpose was to investigate and hunt down known pirates and smugglers. Working under the auspices of His Majesty's Royal Navy, Eldridge wielded an inordinate amount of power. If Eldridge refused him the assignment, Marcus would have little say.

But he would not be refused. Not in this.

He tightened his jaw. "I will not allow you to assign someone else. If Lady Hawthorne is in danger, I will be the one to ensure her safety."

Eldridge raked him with an all-too-perceptive gaze. "Why such passionate interest? After what transpired between you, I'm surprised you would wish to be in close contact with her. Your motive eludes me."

"I have no ulterior motive." At least not one he would share. "Despite our past, I've no desire to see her harmed."

"Her actions dragged you into a scandal that lasted for months and is still discussed today. You put on a good show, my friend, but you bear scars. And some festering wounds, perhaps?"

Remaining still as a statue, Marcus kept his face impassive and struggled against his gnawing re-

sentment. His pain was his own and deeply personal. He disliked being asked about it. "Do you
think me incapable of separating my personal life
from my professional one?"

Eldridge sighed and shook his head. "Very well.
I won't pry."

"And you won't refuse me?"

"You are the best man I have. It was only your
history that gave me pause, but if you are comfortable with it, I have no objections. However, I will
grant her request for reassignment, if it comes to
that."

Nodding, Marcus hid his relief. Elizabeth would
never ask for another agent; her pride wouldn't
permit it.

Eldridge began to tap his fingertips together.
"The journal Lady Hawthorne received was ad-
dressed to her late husband and is written in code.
If the book was involved in his death . . ." He
paused. "Viscount Hawthorne was investigating
Christopher St. John when he met his reward."

Marcus stilled at the name of the popular
pirate. There was no criminal he longed to ap-
prehend more than St. John, and his enmity was
personal. St. John's attacks against Ashford Ship-
ping were the impetus to his joining the agency. "If
Lord Hawthorne kept a journal of his assignments
and St. John were to acquire the information—
bloody hell!" His gut tightened at the thought of
the pirate anywhere near Elizabeth.

"Exactly," Eldridge agreed. "In fact, Lady Hawthorne has already been contacted about the book
since it was brought to my attention just a sennight
ago. For her safety and ours, it should be removed
from her care immediately, but that's impossible at

the moment. She was instructed to personally deliver the journal, hence the need for our protection."

"Of course."

Eldridge slid a folder across the desk. "Here is the information I've gathered so far. Lady Hawthorne will apprise you of the rest during the Moreland ball."

Collecting the particulars of the assignment, Marcus stood and took his leave. Once in the hallway, he allowed a grim smile of satisfaction to curve his lips.

He'd been only days away from seeking Elizabeth out. The end of her mourning meant his interminable waiting was over. Although the matter of the journal was disturbing, it worked to his advantage, making it impossible for her to avoid him. After the scandalous way she'd jilted him four years ago she would not be pleased with his new appearance in her life. But she wouldn't turn to Eldridge either, of that he was certain.

Soon, very soon, all that she had once promised and then denied him would finally be his.

Sylvia Day's Georgian series continues with
Passion for the Game.

"If all angels of death were as lovely as you, men would line up to die."

Maria, Lady Winter, shut the lid of her enameled patch box with a decisive snap. Her revulsion for the mirrored reflection of the man who sat behind her made her stomach roil. Taking a deep breath, she kept her gaze trained on the stage below, but her attention was riveted by the incomparably handsome man who sat in the shadows of her theater box.

"Your turn will come," she murmured, maintaining her regal façade for the benefit of the many lorgnettes pointed in her direction. She had worn crimson silk tonight, accented by delicate black lace frothing from elbow-length sleeves. It was her most-worn color. Not because it suited her Spanish heritage coloring so well—dark hair, dark eyes, olive skin—but because it was a silent warning. *Bloodshed. Stay away.*

The Wintry Widow, the voyeurs whispered. *Two husbands dead . . . and counting.*

Angel of death. How true that was. Everyone around her died, except for the man she cursed to Hades.

The low chuckle at her shoulder made her skin crawl. "It will take more than you, my dearest daughter, to see me to my reward."

"Your reward will be my blade in your heart," she hissed.

"Ah, but then you will never be reunited with your sister, and she almost of age."

"Do not think to threaten me, Welton. Once Amelia is wed, I will know her location and will have no further need for your life. Consider that before you think to do to her what you have done to me."

"I could sell her into the slave trade," he drawled.

"You assume, incorrectly, that I did not anticipate your threat." Fluffing the lace at her elbow, she managed a slight curve to her lips to hide her terror. "I will know. And then you will die."

She felt him stiffen and her smile turned genuine. Ten and six was her age when Welton had ended her life. Anticipation for the day when she would pay him in kind was all that moved her when despair for her sister threatened paralysis.

"St. John."

The name hung suspended in the air between them.

Maria's breath caught. "Christopher St. John?"

It was rare that anything surprised her anymore. At the age of six and twenty, she believed she had seen and done nearly everything. "He has coin aplenty, but marriage to him will ruin me, making me less effective for your aims."

"Marriage is not necessary this time. I've not yet

depleted Lord Winter's settlement. This is simply a search for information. I believe they are engaging St. John in some business. I want you to discover what it is they want with him, and most importantly, who arranged his release from prison."

Maria smoothed the bloodred material that pooled around her legs. Her two unfortunate husbands had been agents of the Crown whose jobs made them highly useful to her stepfather. They had also been peers of great wealth, much of which they left to her for Welton's disposal upon their untimely demise.

Lifting her head, she looked around the theater, absently noting the curling smoke of candles and gilded scrollwork that shone in firelight. The soprano on the stage struggled for attention, for no one was here to see her. The peerage was here to see each other and be seen, nothing more.

"Interesting," Maria murmured, recalling a sketch of the popular pirate. Uncommon handsome he was, and as deadly as she. His exploits were widely bandied, some tales so outrageous she knew they could not possibly be true. St. John was discussed with intemperate eagerness, and there were wagers aplenty on how long he could escape the noose.

"They must be desperate indeed to spare him. All these years they have searched for the irrefutable proof of his villainy, and now that they have it, they bring him into the fold. I daresay neither side is pleased."

"I do not care how they feel," Welton dismissed curtly. "I simply wish to know who I can extort to keep quiet about it."

"Such faith in my charms," she drawled, hiding how her mouth filled with bile. To think of the deeds she had been forced into to protect and serve a man she detested . . . Her chin lifted. It was not her stepfather she protected and served. She merely needed him alive, for if he were killed, she would never find Amelia.

Welton ignored her jibe. "Have you any notion what that information would be worth?"

She gave a nearly imperceptible nod, aware of the avid scrutiny that followed her every movement. Society knew her husbands had not died natural deaths. But they lacked proof. Despite this morbid certainty of her guilt, she was welcomed into the finest homes eagerly. She was infamous. And nothing livened up a gathering like a touch of infamy.

"How do I find him?"

"You have your ways."

Read on for an excerpt from the third of Sylvia Day's Georgian books, *A Passion for Him.*

London, 1780.

The man in the white mask was following her. Amelia Benbridge was uncertain of how long he had been moving surreptitiously behind her, but he most definitely was.

She strolled carefully around the perimeter of the Langston ballroom, her senses attuned to his movements, her head turning with feigned interest in her surroundings so that she might study him further.

Every covert glance took her breath away.

In such a crush of people, another woman most likely would not have noted the avid interest. It was far too easy to be overwhelmed by the sights, sounds, and smells of a masquerade. The dazzling array of vibrant fabrics and frothy lace . . . the multitude of voices attempting to be heard over an industrious orchestra . . . the mingling scents of various perfumes and burnt wax from the massive chandeliers . . .

But Amelia was not like other women. She had lived the first sixteen years of her life under guard, her every movement watched with precision. It was a unique sensation to be examined so closely. She could not mistake the feeling for anything else.

However, she could say with some certainty that she had never been so closely scrutinized by a man quite so . . . compelling.

For he *was* compelling, despite the distance between them and the concealment of the upper half of his face. His form alone arrested her attention. He stood tall and well proportioned, his garments beautifully tailored to cling to muscular thighs and broad shoulders.

She reached a corner and turned, setting their respective positions at an angle. Amelia paused there, taking the opportunity to raise her mask to surround her eyes, the gaily colored ribbons that adorned the stick falling down her gloved arm. Pretending to watch the dancers, she was in truth watching him and cataloguing his person. It was only fair, in her opinion. If he could enjoy an unhindered view, so could she.

He was drenched in black, the only relief being his snowy white stockings, cravat, and shirt. And the mask. So plain. Unadorned by paint or feathers. Secured to his head with black satin ribbon. While the other gentlemen in attendance were dressed in an endless range of colors to attract attention, this man's stark severity seemed designed to blend into the shadows. To make him unremarkable, which he could never be. Beneath the light of hundreds of candles, his dark hair gleamed with vitality and begged a woman to run her fingers through it.

And then there was his mouth . . .

Amelia inhaled sharply at the sight of it. His mouth was sin incarnate. Sculpted by a master hand, the lips neither full nor thin, but firm. Shamelessly sensual. Framed by a strong chin, chiseled jaw, and swarthy skin. A foreigner, perhaps. She could only imagine how the face would look as a whole. Devastating to a woman's equanimity, she suspected.

But it was more than his physical attributes that intrigued her. It was the way he moved, like a predator, his gait purposeful and yet seductive, his attention sharply focused. He did not mince his steps or affect the veneer of boredom so esteemed by Society. This man knew what he wanted and lacked the patience to pretend otherwise.

At present it appeared that what he wanted was to follow her. He watched Amelia with a gaze so intensely hot, she felt it move across her body, felt it run through the unpowdered strands of her hair and dance across her bared nape. Felt it glide across her bared shoulders and down the length of her spine. *Coveting* . . .